His Mistress, His Muse, and Other Madness

ART OF LOVE
BOOK THREE

CHARLIE LANE

First Edition

Editing by Krista Dapkey, Chris Hall

Cover art by Anna Volkin

✻ Created with Vellum

For Brian, who is always my muse.

Prologue

May 1822

The solicitor had told Lord Theodore Bromley what the woman looked like—orange hair, freckles, young and slender. The woman framed in the window of the house on Drury Lane must be her, both like and unlike her description, with hair more of a deep copper than orange. And beautiful. The solicitor had not mentioned that.

She seemed a perfect picture, a medieval lady of the castle, more goddess than woman. Her thick, curly hair, a medusa's nest of snakes, coiled high, ringlets escaping to frame her face. Her gown—a spring-green muslin affair, high-necked and long-sleeved—encased a straight spine, confident shoulders, and a slim but lush figure. If not a Guinevere, she could, easily, be taken for a proper miss, a barrister's daughter, sought-after and beloved. Or, perhaps, one might mistake her for a newlywed wife, innocent yet beguiling, waiting for her husband's arrival after a long day of separation.

She was none of those things.

She was a thorn in Lord Theodore Bromley's backside. And he'd pluck her out and stomp her under his heel in less time than it had taken him to walk from his sister's home to here. A quarter of an hour, and he'd be done. His part of fulfilling his father's cursed will completed.

Theo ripped his gaze away from the window and the woman framed within it and glared up at the row house. Nice and neat and well-positioned. He'd only just learned of the house's existence at the same time he'd learned about the lady. A nice house, too, and likely stocked with servants when Briarcliff, the family's country seat, was falling down around their heads.

He snorted and strode for the door. His father had taken better care of her, one of the artistic leeches who'd drained his family's coffers over the last decade or more, than he had his own family. But his father was dead, and once Theo found this woman new coffers to rob, he and his family would be rid of her.

"S'cuse me, mister," a voice said from behind.

He didn't turn around. "Yes?"

"You're blocking my way into the house."

Theo did turn, then, narrowing his attention on the slender man standing in the street. "You've come to visit Lady Cordelia?" The slender man with golden hair queued at the back of his neck nodded. "Go away. She's no time for visitors today."

"I was paid to come here!" The man's face flushed a mottled pink.

She paid lovers, then, did she? With what money? He almost growled.

"Leave." He did growl then, a warning that sent the other man scurrying away.

Good. Theo knocked on the door. Lady Cordelia would have no pleasure today. Only pain.

The door flew open, and a woman with a wide mouth, hooked nose, and frizzy gray hair answered. "Good day. May I ask who's calling?"

"I wish to speak with Lady Cordelia Trent." Better to keep his identity a secret lest the woman run for a back door.

The housekeeper, for that's what she must be, dragged her gaze down the length of Theo's body then back up. "Ah, yes. She's expecting you. I'll show you where to go." She pulled Theo into the house and pushed him down the hallway, stealing his hat and gloves and greatcoat before tucking her hands beneath the lapels of his jacket and tugging the garment off from behind.

Theo jerked out of the woman's reach. "What are you about, madam? Give that back!"

The housekeeper chuckled. "Shy? Very well. You may do the rest yourself. Just trying to be helpful."

"You're not my valet!" He'd never even had a valet. No funds for it.

The housekeeper shrugged but did not give Theo's jacket back. She led him deeper into the house, stopping at a door in the shadows at the very end of the hallway. She pushed it open and ushered Theo inside.

Six women, sitting in a circle, easels stationed before them, pencils nestled between fingers, looked up at him. They were of various ages and two wore unrelieved black. They stared at him unabashedly with clear interest in their eyes, which roamed down the length of his body. Then back up. Some of them at least. A few lost their way somewhere round his midsection. A tad lower, actually. Their gazes ... hovered. As if glued there. They'd stripped him to his skin without lifting a finger.

"What the hell is happening here?" he demanded. He tugged at his waistcoat, the cuffs of his shirt sleeves, feeling naked without his jacket to pull over that region where their collective interest paused.

"Very nice," a young woman with mischievous blue eyes said, tugging at her bottom lip with her teeth. "The agency has not sent so burly a specimen as *this* before."

Another woman, gray streaked in her dark hair, jumped to her feet. "Let me help you with your waistcoat, sir." She reached for his abdomen, tickled the buttons lined up there.

He swatted her hands away. "Hands off, woman!" Hell. He'd inadvertently entered a heretofore unknown level of hell where randy women and *helpful* housekeepers stripped you bare and—

"You're not the model I hired." A voice, low and rich and rather like a good wine, snapped out the observation.

Theo looked to the doorway. There she stood. The woman from the window—Lady Cordelia Trent. The thorn in his backside. His prey.

She stood with absolute composure, and her voice hid no trembling fear. "Mrs. Barkley? Who is this?"

"The ... model?" supplied the housekeeper, Mrs. Barkley it appeared, her arms full of Theo's stolen clothing.

"He most assuredly is not. I chose the model myself." She returned her attention to Theo, head tilted to the side. "I apologize for the confusion, sir. But ... who are you?"

Theo moved to snap his jacket tight but found no jacket, so he crossed his arms over his chest instead. Several women sighed. He scowled. "I am Lord Theodore Bromley, your late patron's youngest son. And you are Lady Cordelia Trent."

The tilt of her head righted, revealing a strong column of creamy throat. Her pale-brown eyes softened. "I am. I ... I heard of your father's passing. It was a blow. But howsoever it pained me, it must have distressed you much more. My condolences. He was a good man. My savior."

"He was a fool. Now, will you tell these women to leave, or shall I?" He wouldn't even ask what hijinks occupied them, prompting them to undress strange men upon entering rooms. He would not ask because he could guess well enough. Models. Agencies. Easels and chalk and pencils. Now that he'd had a breath or two to think on it, he knew. He'd spent his childhood in a home where nearly naked human models were common. The better to study and paint anatomy, his father had always said. The body is a beautiful thing, almost divine, his mother had sighed, the perfect subject for the artist.

Lady Cordelia's pink lips parted with a gasp, but she recovered quickly, clapping her hands and facing the riveted women. "I am deeply sorry for this confusion. It appears we'll have to cancel our class for the day. I'll speak with the agency and find out what's become of Trevor."

"The shivering fellow with the slender build?" Theo asked. "I sent him packing."

Lady Cordelia sucked her cheeks in, and for a moment, her heart-shaped face grew gaunt. Then she let out a frustrated breath, short and staccato. "At least I know he's safe." She forced a smile for the women and ushered them toward the door.

As the women gathered their belongings and exchanged parting words with their hostess, Theo walked the edges of the room, studying it. Newish wallpaper, thick rugs. Fine art on the walls. Naturally. In all, a better room than any in his one-room apartment. A better room than any in his family's country estate, Briarcliff Manor.

Better. He'd hoped to find composure through his observations of his surroundings. He'd found rage instead. Nothing new, that. It always bubbled close beneath his skin.

When the room quieted, he whirled on his toes to face her. "You're teaching a class for women to paint nude men?"

She stood calm, hands folded together before her. "I facilitate it. They are all widows in need of diversion, wishing to learn a new skill. I do not have the skill to teach such a thing. Lady Fordham—the woman who attempted to relieve you of your waistcoat—teaches it."

What a farce he had walked in on. But at least it would make an excellent print for the *Ackermann's* next week. He'd give the women in the sketch greedy eyes and draw his own frame as slabs of ham and chicken legs. He'd title it something like "Widows Take Solace in Learning New Skills." He'd make it clear the solace they actually sought had nothing to do with the application of art.

She walked toward him calmly and with the precision of a soldier. "Who are you to come into my home, send my guests away, walk about as if you own the place, and—"

"I *do* own the place." At least his brother did.

Lady Cordelia rocked back a step, her body going rigid. But not for long. She flowed into movement once more until she stood right before him, her chin held high, her hands fisted tight in the green muslin of her skirts. "No. It is *my* home."

"For now. But it was my father's property. And now it is my brother's." And the only thing that kept his brother Raph from selling the house was its current occupant.

"Then why is your brother not here?" she demanded.

"Because he is in the country trying to avoid selling off all our lands and to keep the manor house from falling into complete ruin." And being an alarmingly content newlywed. Though that was not her business. "Attempting, in short, to right our father's many wrongs. Of which *you* are one."

Her gaze dragged over him as the other women's had, from his beaver hat to his muddy boots, stopping for a moment on the practical and simple knot of his cravat before popping up to his face, and she raked that, too, trying, it seemed, to learn or understand every inch of his visage. She stepped back, her hands loosening on her skirts, revealing the wrinkled inroads she'd made in the muslin. "Lord Theodore. I see him in you. Your father. Same nose, if you don't mind me saying. Same eyes."

Theo grinned, and he knew it showed teeth. Sharp teeth. "I'm nothing like the old man. As far from him as you can imagine. To begin, he bought you a house, kept you here like a little doll because he thought your art special—"

She opened her mouth and raised an arm to interrupt him.

He barreled forward. "But I am going to kick you out."

Her hands became fists again. "You can't."

He raised a brow. "Pretty, but no brains. Pity. Look, if you need proof of the situation, you're welcome to visit the family solicitor. I'll give you his name and address."

Her eyes narrowed. She would have hissed, spit poison at him if she could. "You are a devil."

He bowed, a concession. "At your service."

She blinked, shook her head. "You're not joking."

"I never joke."

"I believe that." She groped for a nearby chair and fell into it, her eyes glassing over. She clutched the scrolled arm of the charm with one hand and waved the other hand at him. "Your face is too stony."

"The stony nature of my face is neither here nor there." He sat across from her. "Now, tell me what sort of art you produce so I can find a suitable patron for you, one interested in your talents." Then they could sell the damn house and be partway to solvency.

She squared her shoulders, met him with chin high. "Nothing."

"I'm in no mood for games, Lady Cordelia. Your housekeeper stripped me to my shirtsleeves. Do not play with me. Tell me now what your medium is."

She laughed, falling forward and burying her face in her palms, her shoulders shaking. Had she gone mad? Hell. Should he leave? Call a doctor? The housekeeper at least. Did she need ... tea? Just when he parted his lips to call for some (it was better than nothing, at least), she breathed deep and stood.

"Follow me, Lord Theodore. I will show you my master-pieces." She swept into the hallway, and he followed her up the stairs to a tiny room nestled at the back of the third story of the house. Its walls were lined with paintings and shelves, on which rested various statuary, silhouettes, and pieces of jewelry.

She held an arm out wide, inviting him in. "Take a look, my lord. Behold my many talents."

He studied the paintings first. "You did these?"

She stood beside him. "Oh yes. Delightful, aren't they?"

The watercolors were of a ... street? With horses, no ... dogs? Pulling carriages?

"They look as if a child drew them," he said.

"And by that you mean they have an air of irresistible innocence about them, yes? A polite man would say so."

"I'm not polite, and no I do not mean that. I mean they show no understanding of perspective or anatomy or, even, of how watercolors *work*."

"I'm aware." She strode to the shelves. "Would you like to view my ceramics?"

He joined her. Hell. Worse and worse. "Is that a ..."

"Soldier riding a horse? Yes, of course it is."

"I meant to ask if it was a likeness of a giant pile of horse sh—"

"No."

He tapped the top of the ceramic. "It's remarkably like it."

"I wish I could say it was. Now come see my silhouettes." She nodded to a nearby shelf and stepped to the side to allow him to better see its contents. "Here's one of your dear father. And one of the king."

They looked like pigs, the both of them, with snouts where noses should be and hair turned up at the top like floppy, pointy ears. What odd hell was this?

"What do you think?" She batted her lashes at him, all innocence.

"I think you're playing some elaborate joke. My father would not have taken you on had you no talent. All the artists he supported were geniuses, had already won fame. I assumed the only reason your name is not a household one is because you're a woman."

"You do not mince words, Lord Theodore."

"Why should I?"

She made her way toward the only window in the room, a small one, curtainless. She leaned her body into the frame and stared outside. "He hoped I would develop a talent." She looked at him over her shoulder. "Do you really know nothing of my story? Your mother knew. She visited several times, first to help me settle into the house and then to check on me. Once."

"I knew nothing at all of your existence until our solicitor gave me a list of the artists my father named in his will."

"He named me? To deed me this house?"

"No. To ensure my brother did not stop funds flowing to you until we'd found a suitable patron to replace his support."

She slumped against the window. "He said the house would be mine. Promised me."

"Ha. He made many promises he didn't keep." He surveyed the room, his stomach sinking. "How the hell am I supposed to find you a patron when you can't do a damn thing?" He snapped his teeth together and crossed the room. "Why did he do this?"

She lifted her gaze to him, and he expected to find it watery but found it strong and clear instead. "Do you mean why did he save my life?"

"No. I mean why did he give part of our family's fortune to house and feed and clothe a young lady as if she were a bastard daughter or a mistress when our own pantry remained empty at home? Tell me."

"Such accusations." She paced toward him until their chests almost bumped. Close enough to smell her. Tea and mint. "I'm not his daughter." A snap of passion in her voice. She wagged a finger in his face and marched forward, forcing him to retreat until his back hit the shelves behind him. "Nor his mistress."

"I know that bit. I said *as if you were*."

"My father is—"

"The Earl of Crossly. Dead."

She flinched, her hand wavering up to a small, gold chain necklace at her throat, a tiny golden bird dangling from it, resting between the folds of her fichu. The movement brought his attention to the hidden swell of her bosom, and he refocused on her face before speaking.

"The last of his line but for a daughter. You. No cousins, even, to speak of." A brittle bit of wall around his heart cracked. She appeared so very alone. His father had been a charitable soul, and despite the woman's lack of artistic talent, he could well understand why she'd pluck on his father's heart strings. The woman had no one. Not even her title could help her. "Why aren't you with friends? Do you have none?"

"I did. Your father." Her words were as hard as bricks and easily shut him out. "It is enough for you to know your father found me a home when I most needed it? And he brought the marchioness to meet me and comfort me. And he sent tutor

10

after tutor to me every month, trying to help me find my talent. Only ... I do not have one."

Slowly, recognizing the wild animal in her eyes and not wishing to scare it, he lifted an arm between their close bodies and nudged her hand to the side until that wagging finger in his face went limp and hit her skirts. Her other hand covered her eyes, and she swayed forward as if she might sway into him, lean on him for support as she had done his father four years ago.

But he wasn't his father, so he cupped his hands around her shoulders and set her aside. "Do you expect sympathy from me?"

She peered into his eyes. "No."

"Good. You'll find none." He took a step forward, walking her backward as she had him. "When my father died, he left us with debts and everything in ruins. He left the only thing of value—his art collection—to the Royal Academy of Arts but for six paintings and a will demanding we continue to pay for the lives of three artists until we found patrons to replace him. The man, you see, continues to penury us from the grave. But not for long. I've found two of these artistic hangers-on already, resituated them—one with a duke with more money than sense and the other with a wealthy merchant of equally substandard reasoning skills. You are last on my list, and I thought it would be an easy matter to rid ourselves of you." Two more steps brought her up against the window once more, a barrier of only a few inches of air between them. "This complicates matters. *You* complicate matters."

She threw her head back and laughed. "A complication, yes. I've often been told so. I have been for a long while now, I suppose."

"I can't find you a patron if you've no talent. And I can't stop payments to your account unless you find a new patron." And he couldn't do his part to save the estate, to rebuild the family, if he didn't do those things. And they couldn't sell the house until she left it. Not because of any will stipulation but because he and his brothers, oddly raised as they had been, *were* gentlemen at the very base of everything. "I'll figure something out," he muttered.

She sauntered toward him, her body swaying but her face a brittle mask. "I could always become your mistress, Lord Theodore. Since your father's death, I have contemplated a life in the demimonde if I run out of options. And with no talent and no one to care for me, I'm already low on those." Her fingers traced the buttons of his waistcoat.

Elegant fingers, long, like those of a pianist. Her nails were rounded and smooth. The hands of a pampered woman. As they trailed, her eyes softened, her lips, too, as they parted slightly.

Theo's cock tightened. She was beautiful—delicate and strong, fiery yet soft—and her touch scorched him, stole breath and warped bones. And she touched him, gazed at him with those soft eyes, as if he were wanted, *needed*. So damn beautiful he had to squeeze his fingernails into his palms, cutting, biting, to keep from reaching for her. Those pinpricks of pain reminded him well—beauty lied. Beauty was false, an illusion that entranced, ruined.

He snorted and turned from her, stopping in the doorway. "You may seek a man's bed in exchange for stability, Lady Cordelia, but it won't be mine. I'll be back." He left the house, never pausing to look back. His father hadn't left him an artist to foist off on someone else, he'd left Theo a moral dilemma. They couldn't continue supporting this woman and her house and her servants and her gowns and frippery. But he couldn't toss her out. He'd investigated her connections. She had none, at least none interested in accepting a woman with a murky past into the bosom of their family. What then?

He stopped cold on the street. Hell. He'd left his clothes.

One

July 1822

Theo did not forgive.

He meted out justice through black ink and satire.

Currently, he meted warming cream into cold coffee in his chamber at his sister's house and doodled a very large-nosed man in the corner of his sketchbook. Morning sun flooded through clean windows, and at a perfect slant and dusty light to give the man taking shape on the paper a bit of a jaunty air, a mischievous one. He made the hair a touch too long, made the man's jacket look like the one worn by Lord Lunly sunup to sundown. Then he drew a puff cloud emanating from his backside. The man was as windy below the belt as he was silent above it. Everyone knew that. And he'd recently sold his eighteen-year-old daughter to his eighty-year-old crony. Not everyone knew that. They soon would, though, the man's crimes wafted into public view by his own flatulence.

Theo's lips curled into a rogue grin, a delight he allowed himself rarely, as his hand wandered lower on the page, drawing another man with a cheeky expression, this one entirely a product of his imagination and blown across the English Channel by his own wind. The scratch of the pencil on paper slowed, and the quiet closed around him until only he and the sketch existed in a world gone black. In the rooms he'd rented before moving in with his sister a fortnight earlier, noises had shaken the walls at all hours. Still, he'd felt more alone than he did here, where his infant niece Merry's cries woke him at all hours, and Maggie could knock on the door whenever she liked.

Knock, knock, knock.

Theo sighed, the silence shattered, his isolation soon to be rather crowded. He slammed his notebook closed, his stubby pencil slipping through his fingers and dropping to the floor. "Come in."

"Good morning, Theo," Maggie said, throwing open his bedchamber door. "I am glad you're awake."

"If I'd been sleeping, I no longer would be."

She opened the door wider. "Look who has arrived with the light of day."

Zander stood behind her, his wife Fiona on his arm. "Don't stand to greet us," Zander said.

"I didn't intend to," Theo said, sipping the cold coffee. But he stood and bowed toward Fiona. "Good morning."

"Theo," she said, "a pleasure." And she sounded like she meant it.

Zander gasped. "It's not, darling. Don't lie to him. No one can find pleasure in that man's scowl."

"I prefer it that way," Theo said. "Isn't my room a tad too small for such a gathering?"

14

The three settled around the room. Zander slouched near the window, and his wife sat in a chair near the fireplace while Maggie bounced down on his bed. Theo disappeared inside a copy of *Ackermann's* near to hand, ignoring them all.

"Did Merry keep you up last night, Theo?" Maggie asked.

"No." Yes, but Merry could keep whomever she liked from sleeping, including him. An infant's prerogative. With her tiny fists and pink cheeks, she could do as she pleased, and Theo would gut whoever tried to stop her.

A hand slammed into Theo's paper from the top. Zander peered at him from above, eyebrow raised. "Aren't you glad to see me? Or at least curious as to why we're here?" Zander possessed a much nicer disposition than Theo. The man grinned as if doing so produced diamonds. And he winked as if he shared a joke with every damn soul on earth.

"You're here to visit her parents, no doubt." He tossed a nod at Zander's wife.

Zander folded his arms across his chest. "But also to bring you news. And to help you."

Theo snorted. "Help me with what?"

"Everything but manners, elegance, and wit." Zander smirked. "There, you're doomed."

"Help me with what?" Theo repeated.

"My point exactly."

"Zander, I'll tell him if you don't," Fiona warned, crossing her arms over her chest.

"Very well." Zander returned to his place by the window. "There's a further snag in the Lady Cordelia dilemma. Raph has received an offer on the townhouse where she resides."

Lady Cordelia. A name he pushed out of his brain a thousand times a day, more for each day he could not push her out of the townhouse. He knew beauty to be nothing but lies, but he saw her beauty everywhere—her hair in the sunset, her eyes in the bottom of a cup of a coffee with a splash of cream—and he itched to draw it, paint it, multiply it to make the dirty world brighter.

Destructive impulse, that, one he squashed as many times a day as he pushed away thoughts of her. He didn't paint anymore. Not like that. He preferred the black of ink against a pale page—truth and lies—a clear distinction. No doubt such as existed in the blur of colors across a canvas. Or those ingrained in a woman's body.

Guilt hammered him down. He shouldn't be so eager to see her gone. She'd helped him twice in the short time they'd known each other. Tormented him a hundred times more than that, of course, but he didn't quite hate her. Felt inconvenienced by her every damn day. But impossible to hate a woman who'd been as troubled as he had been by his brother's disappearance over two months ago. She'd helped him stay calm, helped him gather information to find Zander.

He had to get rid of her, so he'd turned to other avenues of occupation when it became clear she would find no artistic patron. But no one wanted a governess or companion who'd lived under another man's hospitality for four years. And while she could likely perform the duties of a companion, he'd seen no evidence she had the educational foundation to support herself as a governess. For months he'd been trying to find her a new situation. And failing. Perhaps he should find her a husband instead, a man who didn't care about her past, her pennilessness. Or ... she might have to turn to that profession she'd mentioned in such a hard jest the first day they'd met.

He'd never let her go to the demimonde. That would be another failure. Whatever solution he found, he'd have to find it quick. Her time was running out.

"How much is the buyer offering?" Theo asked.

"Triple what it's worth. Because the location suits his needs. If we can meet his time frame." Zander quirked a brow, and Theo whistled before his brother continued. "We cannot refuse the offer, you understand that."

"Of course not. She has to go."

Zander produced a strand of frayed and twisted wires from a pocket and twirled them between his fingers, watched them spin as he spoke. "But we cannot kick her out without having a place for her to go."

"Naturally," Theo grumbled. "Could you get to the help bit?"

"The Baroness Balantine," Fiona said. "The woman who bought your father's paintings from Zander."

Hell. "Not her."

"Why not?" Zander demanded. "She loves a lost puppy."

"By that," Fiona said, "he means Lady Balantine has a charitable heart. She'll take in Lady Cordelia even if she can't paint. Is it true? Zander said she's not an artist at all."

Theo nodded. "She can't paint or sculpt or sketch or do anything other than vex me."

Zander shoved the wire back into his pocket with a laugh. "It's a delight to behold. Our angry Theo flustered and felled by Lady Cordelia's few perfectly placed and certainly scandalous remarks."

Zander would never have met the woman if she'd not followed Theo to an art auction shortly after they'd met. He should never have mentioned the cursed event to her. Should never have gone back to see her. Especially once he'd learned how she fired his blood. But her very existence seemed so vulnerable, alone in that house but for a few servants. Her vulnerability must have been what had attracted his father to her aid. He'd always liked puppies too.

Theo didn't like puppies. At least not cuddling them. He preferred righteously defending them from the shadows. And there existed no doubt—Lady Cordelia *was* like a puppy, and she nipped at his protective instincts like an actual dog nipping at his heels.

But then all of that—her privileged little house on Drury Lane, his father's support—made him angry as a bear, too, gave him claws and amplified his roar.

To hell with her. Why had his father given her everything and them nothing?

"Lady Balantine ... Hm." He tapped the table. "What do you think, Maggie?" His sister did not answer. "Maggie?" He looked up and found his sister sleeping, splayed out crosswise on his bed.

"Oh, poor dear." Fiona stood and nudged Maggie awake, wiped away the trickle of drool at the corner of her mouth with Theo's quilt.

"Terribly sorry," Maggie said with a yawn. "Merry kept me up last night. She'd been sleeping so well, then all of a sudden —" Another yawn. "Perhaps I'll go back to bed now." She slunk back toward the mattress.

"No, no. Come along." Fiona helped her rise and escorted her out of the room.

Theo and Zander stared one another down once alone.

"What?" Theo barked.

Zander zipped across the room and sat near Theo. "You are, you realize, the only one of us that can actually draw." Theo grunted. "Yet you've produced no artwork to win your inheritance."

The stipulations of their father's will required all six of his children to produce an original work of art, judged suitably refined by their mother before she released their inheritance— to each offspring, a Rubens painting worth several hundred pounds. At least.

Bollocks that.

Theo would have chucked the will in the Thames at the first opportunity had he the chance. And he'd burn in Hell's fires before he submitted any drawing to his mother for approval. Not that he needed it anymore. His mother had, after his eldest brother had fallen in love, married, and gone soft-hearted, declared they could have their inheritances without artistic endeavor.

Theo had refused the kindness. He'd not take anything he hadn't earned. If he couldn't earn it the way his brothers and sister had, he didn't want it.

"I won't produce any artwork for Mother to scowl over. My art is not the type she is likely to approve of."

"You never know," Zander said. "Try."

"Raph painted some nonsense all up his wife's arm that showed his love." Theo shivered, wrinkled his nose. "And you defeated a villainous fellow with art supplies and in the process produced the impression of a backside on a canvas that Mother fawns over—also a product of love. Maggie created a silk pattern of Father's favorite flower. I'm likely to give her a drawing of"—he flashed a glance at the closed notebook nearby—"a man with flatulence."

Zander coughed a laugh then winced. "You'll have to consider a different subject, to be sure. Perhaps instead of it just being a man, it could be Father. He always did get a bit gassy when he ate asparagus."

"No, Zander. I am incapable of producing the sort of sentimental nonsense Mother wants from me. So I will never win my inheritance."

"Pity." Zander drummed his fingers on the top of his leg. "I have something for you. Raph sent it." He reached into his pocket and pulled out a square of paper with a wine-red wax seal and a name scrawled above it. He slapped it down onto the table between them.

Theo flexed his muscles, so he didn't recoil. It was no snake. Merely an epistle written in his dead father's hand. "I can't have that. You shouldn't have that." Their inheritances had come with letters from their father, to be won at the same time they won their willed paintings. Since he never planned to win his, he'd never read his father's final words to him. Not that it mattered. He didn't want to know.

Zander sighed. "I realize you're angry all the time. It's your entire personality, and frankly I find it charming, even if no one else does. One always wishes for a growly, scowly brute to round out a dinner party. But Father wrote six letters, one for each of us, and—"

"Tell me, how does a letter buy back the lands Raph had to sell to pay off Father's debts?"

"Raph has come to terms with who Father was."

"And who was that?" A rhetorical question. Theo already knew the answer. Their father had been a brainless, thoughtless child, more interested in his own amusement than in anything else.

Hazy memories of a dreamlike youth poked at him, as if they had something to say. They teased him with images of rides on his father's back across a warm parlor and a soft rug, with bedtime stories that lasted for hours, composed of all little boy Theo's favorite things—knights and dragons and lemon tarts. They held up, on a tarnished silver platter, kisses to forehead and hugs when the skin of a knee proved too soft for a fall.

Theo used his bear claws to rip them to shreds, and they retreated to that locked, shadowed corner of his mind he never visited.

"Father was a flawed man," Zander said, "who loved us. A second son who had never been prepared to care for the estate. He acted wrong. In many, many ways. But perhaps he did not deserve your eternal hate."

"The man's dead, Zander. He no longer cares whether I hate him or not."

"Just read the letter. Since I went to all the trouble of

stealing it for you. I know we're not supposed to get the damn things until we earn our paintings, I thought ... perhaps ... you need to read it *before* you can paint, need it to motivate you to try in the first place."

Theo opened a drawer in his writing desk and pulled forth a letter opener. He twirled it in his fingers then stabbed the letter, the knife point piercing the table beneath so that it stood upright when he released it.

"I see." Zander nodded slowly. "Can you be happy with such hate in your heart?"

"Why should I be happy when so many in London are not?"

"Then do what you do best and draw your pictures revealing the vile underbelly of the London elite, etcetera, etcetera, but do not diminish your own joy."

Theo grunted. "Why must men become wise philosophers once they're leg shackled?"

Zander scratched his jaw and studied the ceiling, as if truly considering the answer to Theo's question. "It's not the leg shackling that does it. It's all that comes before that makes us realize the leg shackling won't kill us."

"Ah. Thank you for that warning. I'll stoutly avoid all that comes before."

"You can try, brother. You can try. And with your winning personality, I've no doubt you'll succeed. But I hope you do not."

"I have work to do." Theo slapped his palms onto the table and pushed to stand, grabbing his sketchbook and heading for the door.

Zander waved him out of the room. "Don't sketch anyone who can land you in trouble!"

As he published every one of his drawings anonymously, he didn't have to worry about trouble. Anonymity allowed him to do as he pleased, to publish drawings of pure truth without worry.

Theo waved to Zander without looking as he stepped into the hallway. "Enjoy *my* room."

Whatever Zander replied, Theo didn't hear. He was already stepping into the foggy London sunshine. He should finish the sketch he'd started this morning, sign it with his pseudonym, and send it to one of the printshops on the Strand. Would they compete for a sketch of an octogenarian passing gas as he auctioned off his daughter? Perhaps. Perhaps not. But he needed them to. He needed to make a name for himself, to do good with each stroke of his pen set to paper. But all the prints he'd put into the world so far had been welcomed with only lukewarm popularity. The silly little sketches he gave away for others to sell had proven more successful. And what good did they do? They made people laugh, no doubt, but what good was that?

No, he needed the printshops to want him so he could reveal the rotten bits of society. He'd not been able to stop his father from rotting out their family. He'd been too young, too helpless. He'd wanted to be a great artist, dedicated himself to it, only realizing too late how utterly useless such an occupation was. His family needed money. And it was his turn to help. But the only skill he'd ever cultivated was the very one that had brought his family low to begin with.

He'd had only one option, then as now—to use his art as a sword, to become a mercenary who made pounds and pence from battle and blood. And if he could stop the rot in other places, for other families if not his own, then so much the better.

That, however, required new material. Gossip. Scandal. Those things made up the very heart of his satirical sketches. He'd not had a good sketch, a really scandalous print, in ages. Worried over his father's will, he'd fallen behind on the gossip.

London needed a shock, and he wanted to be the one to give it.

He couldn't do that with his attention split between gathering gossip and finding Lady Cordelia a new situation. A problem that, by day's end, would be remedied.

Two

%%% decorative flourish %%%

The worst was always yet to come. But so was the best, so Lady Cordelia Trent ignored weeks upon weeks of random visits from an infuriating lord and stayed steady on her course. It was difficult to organize and plan the creation of an art school when a man with a scowl as deep as the Thames could waltz through the door whenever he liked, stomp up to her Gallery of Shame, and study it, brooding at its holdings—her pitiful works of art—as long as he liked before stomping away again.

But he had proved more than merely an irritant in the last couple of months. His first visit had made her own precarious predicament blindingly clear. She must fend for herself somehow or find herself once more tossed to the streets, and this time without the angel who was—had been—the Marquess of Waneborough.

Admittedly, Lord Theodore had given her *more* than a crystal-clear realization. He'd also provided untold amusement on several occasions, and that helped matters significantly. His first arrival, for instance, when she'd discovered him as panicked as a woodland creature beneath the curious fingertips of the widowed Lady Fordham. She chuckled even now. During that first meeting, when she'd offered in a pique of panic and indignation to be his mistress, she'd discovered that Lord Theodore flustered was one of her favorite sights. Oddly, his panic had calmed her own. Now, she flirted whenever she could simply to watch him transform from mean old devil to flustered schoolboy. In those moments, he actually appeared his age—likely not much more than her own three and twenty years. He got all pink across those high cheekbones, and his gray eyes clouded, his large shoulders hunched forward, as if he could hide himself. With that bull of a body and that thick mane of dirty-blond hair that devoured his long fingers whenever he brushed his locks backward in moments of high panic? Ha.

The man would be beautiful if he were not always scowling, always thin-lipped and narrow-eyed. If his jaw ever softened to allow a smile, he might startle anyone nearby with his allure. No chance of that ever happening. But it made the teasing all the more fun. Could she make him crack, catch a glimpse of the handsome man beneath the stone? High entertainment, that.

More than amusement, he'd provided—though he did not know it—*connections*. Connections she sorely needed for her scheme. The men and women currently sitting in a circle in her parlor looked to her for guidance. They needed those connections, too.

"Miss Williams," she said to the violin player sitting opposite her across the circle, "have you found an instructor happy to teach children violin?"

Miss Williams sniffed. "I've not as of yet. And I'll not teach them myself."

"I am aware, Miss Williams," Cordelia said.

"They are sticky."

"So you've said. But we do need such a teacher, so please

do continue asking around." She peered at her list then looked at Mr. Spencer. "Do you have an estimate for the yearly cost of paints for the amount of students we wish to take on?"

Mr. Spencer was a poet with a head for numbers who had volunteered, for now, to operate as bookkeeper as well as instructor of verse. Eventually. When they were able to open. They currently offered a few classes, helped a few children learn new skills, but hopefully soon their rooms would be brimming every hour of every day, filling up the silence of an empty house with the bustle and chaos of art and joy.

Mr. Spencer fumbled with some papers scattered on the table beside him and peered over the edge of his drooping spectacles. "Ah, hm, yes, well, you see, it appears that it's quite a lot."

"I am expecting as much. The number please?"

He swallowed hard. "A hundred students, a quarter to a half of those on scholarship and providing no fees to cover art supplies."

She nodded. "A low number at first to make it feasible, but hopefully shall expand our number of students rapidly." The price of supplies would be steep but unavoidable. They were, after all, running an art school.

Mr. Spencer pulled a damp handkerchief from his pocket, wiped the sweat from his forehead, and replaced it haphazardly. Then he leaned across the table to whisper near her ear.

"Just as I suspected." She used a strong voice, but her lips thinned. "Well, we already comfortably provide supplies for ten students using the tuition of twenty-three. We should consider raising what we charge the paying students."

He bobbed his head, the spectacles falling off entirely. "The colorman I spoke to said the good paints are quite dear, and to order as much as we wish to order so frequently ... I think it perhaps better to take on fewer charity students."

"Absolutely not."

"But the children misuse the paint, use much more of it than necessary," Mrs. Aimes the watercolor instructor said.

"But they are the ones who most need us." They were Cordelia's purpose in life, her way of paying back the man who had helped her, a means, as well, of easing her guilt. For years, she'd done nothing but mourn and paint and sculpt and write. She'd been as good at mourning as she'd been bad at the others. But no more. Not ever again would she be a drain on someone's coffers. She would be an independent woman, and she would give others the chance to develop skills that would grant them independence as well. "We will find funds by whatever means necessary. When I started this scheme two years ago, it was with a singular mission, and I will not give up on it." She shook her list of possible financial backers in the air. "Do any of you have new names to add here?"

The eleven assembled teachers of the future Waneborough Charitable School of Art shook their heads.

"Right. Excellent." Not excellent in the least, but best to be positive when leading the others. She tapped her various lists into order on her lap. "Does anyone have any lessons scheduled today?"

Miss Williams raised a hand, as did Mrs. Aimes.

"I hope your students prove more talented than I." Cordelia's grin returned, and the others chuckled.

They had all, at one point or another, been paid by the late marquess to teach her, to hone talents she did not possess. They had watched her journey into artistic discovery and viewed it not as failure, but as the making of her, no matter how nonexistent her skill. Like her, they loved art. Like her, they knew the myriad ways it could save a soul. It could help widows smile again and give children confidence. And the skills learned did not have to be reserved for art galleries alone. Teaching a mud lark how to draw court scenes could save him from a watery grave in the Thames. Teaching a mother of ten to embroider might earn her a few extra pence for fancy work with the dress shops.

She stood. "I believe we're done for the day."

They began to pack up.

She tried not to let her voice waver. Confidence was key. "Please do keep in mind that I cannot remunerate you for your work until we have more paying clientele." The twenty-three paying patrons they had so far covered, barely, the cost of the paints and other supplies they needed for ... everyone.

Her instructors grumbled their assent.

"And also remember that if Lord Theodore should grace us with his unexpected presence, you are to—"

"Hide," eleven voices said at once.

"Precisely."

Mr. Spencer ambled over and cleared his throat. "We should do something about him, my lady."

"We *are* doing something about him. As soon as he realizes I can pay for the house through my own endeavors, he'll leave us be. I'll buy the house. Or rent it." More likely. Though it should have been hers. The old marquess had promised her. The solicitor she'd visited after Lord Theodore had announced intentions to turn her out had said the old marquess had often talked of signing the house over to her but had never actually done it. A shadow rose up before her, but she put her back to it. Nothing to do but move forward.

"He's a brute," Mr. Spencer said. "I do not like to think of him importuning you at any given moment night or day."

"He only shows up during calling hours, Mr. Spencer. Thank you for your worry, but—"

"He's here!" Mrs. Barkley screamed from the hallway in the loudest of tones, transforming the milling group of artists into statues. "The gargoyle's here! Knocking on the door right now!"

What in heaven's ...? She sighed. He never did ask permission. Just dropped by whenever he pleased. And what could she do? Deny entrance to the man whose brother owned her house? Made her want to stomp his foot. While wearing spiked boots.

Mr. Spencer gulped. "See. What did I say? He's not just a nuisance, he's a danger to you."

"Nonsense, Mr. Spencer," Cordelia whispered. "Now out the window with you."

"Pardon me?" he hissed.

"Out the window with all of you!"

They grumbled, but they complied. Not quickly enough, though. She heard Mrs. Barkley and a man arguing in the hall. Blessed Barkley, distracting him so they could escape.

"Hurry, hurry!" Cordelia pushed them toward the window, opened it, and nudged the first instructor, Mrs. Bellfry, over the edge and onto the street. Then Mr. Spencer and eight others.

"Thank goodness we're on the ground floor." Miss Williams sniffed as she sat on the window ledge and swung her legs over it.

"Do hurry," Cordelia begged.

"I think you should just tell Lord Theodore. He may be able to help."

"I'll consider it."

Bootsteps echoed outside the door. Hinges creaked. Cordelia's heart gave up working at a normal pace and ran for its life about her body. He would catch Miss Williams.

Not if Cordelia could help it. She nudged the other woman. Just a *tiny* nudge. And the violin instructor went flying, her legs arching toward the sky, her gown falling toward the ground, her body making a soft *thunk* against the grass, and—*blast*. The violin case still rested on the window. Cordelia chucked it.

And swung around to greet Lord Theodore, scowling in

the doorframe. "Good afternoon, my lord. Have you come to ask me to be your mistress?"

His cheeks turned cherry, and his attention flew skyward. She heard a loud exhalation that almost resembled a whistle through clenched teeth. "Lady Cordelia, why did I just see a woman's legs and a violin case fly past that window?"

She pulled the curtains closed and waltzed toward him. "I've no idea. Perhaps you should speak with a doctor about it. Now, since you've not addressed my question, should I take that as a positive answer?" She winked.

His cherry cheeks burned a deeper rose shade. "No. I'll never ask you to be my mistress. I don't keep one."

Likely not enough funds to keep one, and if she didn't change the subject, he'd tell her so and she'd feel guilty, and he'd have the upper hand and—

"I don't have the funds to satisfy a mistress."

There it was. Also there, however—a way to tease him with the word *satisfy*. But she would have mercy. She sighed. "So pretty but no brains. Such a pity." She flopped into a chair. "Why have you come, Lord Theodore?"

He sat slowly, precisely, in the chair across from her, his face composed of chiseled granite. "Why did I hear your butler calling me a gargoyle?"

"Oh." She laughed, a fake thing she knew he'd never believe. "He wasn't calling *you* a gargoyle, he ..." She searched her brain. Nothing. "He was calling you a gargoyle. Because you have a stony face. Particularly when you scowl. And you always scowl." She grinned, bright as the sun, she hoped. "Why have you come? I'm busy."

"Why was a woman and a violin case jumping out of your window?"

Because Cordelia had pushed her out, to be honest about it. And she'd pushed her because the woman had dared to suggest Cordelia tell Lord Theodore the truth about her plans, about the school.

"You first," Cordelia said.

"My brother has received an offer on this house."

Cold ice ran through her veins. "Will he sell it?"

"Yes. The buyer is offering triple what it's worth, but only for a month's time."

"I have a month?" The words barely made sense on her lips.

"Do not worry, though. I have a patron for you."

She jumped to her feet. "You do not!"

He leaned back in the chair and stretched out his very long and thickly muscled legs, folding his blunt-nailed fingers together across his taut abdomen. "I do. The dowager Baroness Balantine. She's a particular friend to my brother and his new wife. You should remember her. You met her once."

She'd followed Lord Theodore about one day because his brother had gone missing, and she'd wanted to help, needed to, really. The late marquess had loved his children more than anything, had kept small silhouettes of all six of them in various pockets so that he crinkled when he walked. He'd have been heartbroken to find his son in trouble, and she'd needed to feel useful to the man who had helped her so much.

She touched the necklace at her throat, the small, gold-work bird that hung always about her neck, a gift from her father. The only thing that remained of her former life, and sometimes it filled her with sorrow, with memories that seemed almost unreal, of a time when she'd been a pampered earl's daughter with parents who loved her. Many times, she'd shoved it into a dark drawer, but of late, she'd clutched it tight. Birds took flight, after all, winging above gray clouds and rain to find sunnier climes.

She would be that bird. She wanted to live with that hope.

Before her father had died, she'd been a dependent in need

of a husband. After her father's death, she'd been a future wife with no family connections to bring to her marriage. And after her betrothed had abandoned her, Lord Waneborough had taken her in, protected her, given her hope. But under his protection, she'd become an empty canvas to fill up with artistic skill. None of the paint he attempted to apply there took. Slid right off. Leaving her just as dependent on the men in her life as she'd ever been. As all women ever were.

Her school would change all that—give her purpose and independence, a means to care for herself and for others.

But Lord Theodore wanted her to be dead weight once more, an unneeded companion to a charitable woman when she was *trying* to prove herself useful. She *would* prove herself useful, fly above the shadows of his disapproval and make a new life for herself.

She folded her arms with military precision behind her back. Did she have any other choice than to continue being the burden she'd always been?

"Lady Balantine," she said. "The woman who disappeared and forged all the art?"

"She merely paid for the forgeries, and she's no longer in that sort of business."

"You wish to connect me with a woman who has a nefarious past?" Not that it mattered. Everyone believed her own past to be quite nefarious. The old marquess's by-blow or his mistress? The question kept her instructors debating for days, weeks, *months*.

Lord Theodore shrugged. "Doesn't matter what her past is as long as she wishes to support you in the present. And the future."

"Support me doing what, Lord Theodore?" The man truly had nothing in that brainbox. When he moved, if you got close enough, you could likely hear things rattle. "You've seen the extent of my talents. I'm useless. No one wants useless."

His stone face cracked with a fleeting flinch before it set once more into hard lines. "She doesn't care. Lady Balantine has a soft heart. She'll let you play companion if you like."

"I do *not* like." She marched toward him, stood above in what she hoped appeared an intimidating pose, legs wide, hands on hips, wearing her own Thames-wide scowl. She let passion, not prudence, guide her words. Because while she had nothing of value to offer anyone, she knew she did not want to sit by the side, an observer of everyone else's lives. "I have my own plan, my lord, and I do not need your help."

He straightened, bringing his face closer to hers, then he pushed to standing so that he towered over her. "Oh? Your own plan? To join the demimonde?"

"No." She should never have said that when she'd not truly meant it.

"What is your plan?"

I think you should just tell Lord Theodore. He may be able to help, Miss Williams had said.

Cordelia wanted to shove that idea out the window alongside Miss Williams, but she'd run out of options. Someone wanted to buy her house. Only one option remained: tell Lord Theodore her plans and hope he supported them.

"I wish to buy this house," she said, "and open an art school. For everyone. Not just for those who can pay but for those who *need* it." She would not wince at her own revelation. Or hide. She'd stand her ground even though that ground stood so close to that which he occupied, and she'd hold her chin high. "The Waneborough Charitable School of Art."

"Named for my father." No emotion in his deep rumble of a voice.

"Yes. Of course. He saved me, and in his name, I will save others."

Lord Theodore's eyes flashed like lightning, clear and sharp and frightening. "How will you pay for those who cannot?"

"The tuition of those who can. You've met some of them already."

His eyes brightened. "The widows who tried to undress me."

"Yes. And I'll gather donors as well. I've a list of names I've collected of wealthy individuals who might be interested."

"Can I see it?"

She blinked. Had Miss Williams been right? Would he really help her?

"Ye-yes. Here." She retrieved her list from a nearby table and handed it to him. "I've been amassing it for over a year. I added to it after the art auction we attended in May. I've not utilized it yet because I wanted to have a small working of the model in progress, something to show them the scheme works. Proof."

He looked at the list, then at her, then at the list once more. "That's why you insisted on coming?"

"Yes. To make connections." The auction had been a scandalous affair, half masquerade, wholly unsuitable, but she'd seen faces despite dominos once the champagne flowed thick through enough veins. And she'd stored them in her memory, added them to her list, the names of those who threw pence and pounds at art as if it would save their souls from damnation.

"An art school. Here. How the hell d'you come to that conclusion?"

"I may not be good at art, but I loved learning it. *Doing* the art mattered more than the art itself, helped me—" She snapped her lips closed. He didn't care about her healed heart,

34

still scarred over a bit. Art had given her a place to pour her pain, to find joy, to discover life in ways she'd not seen it before. One of her revelations—art should be for everyone. Not just the few who could afford it. Because even if it did not earn you pence and pounds, it made you human.

Another truth he would likely not care to hear. Better to stick to the practicalities. A man like him would appreciate those.

"The woman whose legs you saw flying out the window," she said, "is to be my violin instructor. She's a grump mostly, and when she told me I should tell you everything, I thought she'd gone a bit mad, but now I see she had the right of it, and—"

"The chairs?" He waved a hand about the room. "The ones circled-up? Those are for ...?"

"My other instructors." Hope brimmed in her on a wave of relief. She should have told him long ago.

"How many of them have you?"

"Eleven, but one—Mr. Spencer, the poet—also acts as my bookkeeper for the moment, until we can afford a real book-keeper, you understand."

"I do." His gaze returned to her, and the gargoyle returned to his face. "You let a poet keep your books and toss likely valuable instruments out the window. And worst of all, you have collected a group of eleven individuals under your care and made promises to them you likely cannot keep."

Her heart quickly became acquainted with the floorboards beneath her feet. Damn Miss Williams to perdition! What did she know after all?

He slammed her papers on the table and stalked toward her. "No."

"No ... what?"

"No, you cannot have this house."

"I can if I buy it."

"Can you afford to outbid the current buyer?"

Likely not. She crossed her arms over her chest. "It's not your house to sell, now is it? Belongs to your brother, as you delight in telling me."

He dug a finger into the paper, ripping it slightly.

She flinched. Felt like a tear in her own skin, it did.

He leaned over her like a mountain blocking the sun, finger still digging, ripping. "Paying eleven salaries, how will you save enough money to buy this house? Saving money to buy the house, how will you pay the salaries? And in a single month." He snorted and leaned away, crossing his arms over his chest. "You've relied on others your entire life. You're helpless as a babe."

She breathed deep and slow and smoothed gently the torn paper, controlling just barely the trembling of her fingers. Then she met his gaze. "You're right. I am helpless. But I am trying not to be. I do not wish to be any longer. You would toss me over to another person to take care of me when I would like to take care of myself, to help others as your father helped me, and—"

He snorted and paced away from her. "My father, my father. It's always him with you."

"He was a good man."

"Who ruined his family's finances."

"And who saved me." Lord Theodore rolled his eyes. "You are a beast."

He flashed his bared teeth. "And you are hopelessly naïve."

"Leave," she barked, stabbing a finger toward the door.

He stalked toward the exit. "Gladly. Mrs. Barkley!"

Barkley's head appeared around the doorframe like magic. "Yes?"

"Bring me my coat and hat."

"Yes, my lord." The housekeeper disappeared.

Lord Theodore chased her into the hall. "And my hat and coat and gloves and jacket from the *first time*!"

Even in her black mood, Cordelia almost laughed. He'd never find *those*. Barkley didn't even know where they were.

"No!" She jumped, shrieked at Lord Theodore's hard voice so very near. He'd returned, and he stood in the doorway, glowering at her. "Mrs. Barkley! Bring your mistress her spencer and bonnet. We're going out."

Cordelia planted her feet to the floor. "Absolutely not. Who do you think you are, telling me what to do?"

"The curricle is waiting outside. It is why I came today. Not only to tell you about Lady Balantine, but to bring you to her, so you can meet and see if you suit."

"Absolutely n—" Memories of her last meeting with the Lady Balantine squashed them entirely. The woman loved art and had a heart the size of London itself. Of course. She might very well wish to back Cordelia's school. "Very well." She brushed past him and into the hallway then rushed up the stairs to intercept Barkley. She needed her best spencer and most serious bonnet, clothing to make her look like a respectable and trustworthy woman, the kind who ran a charitable school with much success.

"I'll only be a moment, my lord!" she called down to him.

She should not have told that odious man about her school. He was the worst that always rolled toward her no matter her efforts. But Lady Balantine would likely love the idea. And Lord Theodore would likely blush and sputter and rage when Cordelia presented it to the baroness. Before he could utter a single word.

She hid her mirth beneath the brim-shadows of her bonnet. Certain backing for her art school and watching Lord Theodore sputter. The day would be a good one after all.

Three

𝒞𝓍𝓍𝒪

T heo slammed the door behind him and stood just
before it in a too-hot puddle of sun for several
breaths, trying to calm his anger. And his lust. They
always came on a wave at the same time whenever she stood
near so that he didn't know if he wanted to yell at her or
kiss her.

Yell. *Yell.* That's what he wanted to do most. Had to be
because she remained a thorn his family must pluck, a woman
whose comfort his father had prioritized over that of his
children.

And now a school? In a house she didn't even own?
Already had employees. The woman was mad, but Theo
would not condone her madness. He needn't do so any longer.
Soon, she'd be Lady Balantine's problem. Thankfully she'd
easily complied to visiting the dowager. She had no other
option. In a month's time, she must vacate her current
lodgings.

He took three more steadying breaths and—

"Oi, mister."

Theo popped his eyes open.

A young boy stood before him, clothes ragged and hair a bit ... crusty. But his green eyes were bright. "You're in the way."

"You're going in there?" Theo pointed a thumb over his shoulder at the door.

"I am. You comin' out or goin' in?"

"Out. What business do you have with Lady Cordelia?"

"Not Lady C. Miss Craigswell. The plump one that plays the violin." He threw his shoulders back. "She's teaching me."

"Ah." The school nonsense again. But the boy seemed so proud, so damn happy. "You like it?"

The boy nodded, sending his hat flying.

Theo picked it up and plunked it back onto his head.

"Thank you, mister." The boy's eyes narrowed. "What business *you* got with Lady C?"

"I'm her ..." What was he? Her guardian? Her adversary? Her landlord? The man who inappropriately lusted after her? "Friend." A lame finish and not even true.

"You don't pay her to kiss her?" the boy asked.

"No! What makes you think that?"

The boy shrugged. "She's pretty enough. My ma says she should give up this school business and sell her kisses. Would make a touch more money than she could teaching kids like me to hold a bow."

She could. His eye twitched. "She's a lady."

The boy shrugged again. "You movin'?"

He still stood like a sentinel before the door, but he stepped aside.

"Thanks, mister." The body darted around him, but Theo caught him with a hand to his shoulder before he entered the house. "What?" the boy demanded.

"Here." Theo reached into his greatcoat pocket and pulled out his sketchbook, ripped the doodle of the man flatulating his way across the English Channel from it, and handed it to the boy. "Take this to a printshop on the Strand."

The boy peered at the sketch, brows drawn together, then his face opened like clouds dissipating on a sunny day, and he laughed. "That's right funny. Why d'ya want me to take it there?"

"Any of the print shops there will pay you for it. Tell them Sir George gave it to you." He wouldn't be the first child with dirt on his cheeks and nothing in his belly to sell one of Sir George's sketches to a shop on the Strand. "They'll know what to do with it. And they'll give you a tidy sum."

"For ... me?"

"Feed your family for a month."

The boy's eyes became saucers, and when the door opened, he didn't even look to see who would appear.

Theo knew, though, without looking, who stood behind him. Smelled her fresh lavender scent as well as if he'd used her soap to bathe.

"Put it in your pocket now," Theo urged, pushing the boy around Lady Cordelia and into the house. He lifted a finger to his lips, and the boy gave him a snaggle-tooth grin. He understood how to keep quiet.

Theo straightened, met Lady Cordelia's quizzical gaze for a brief moment, then made for the gig. She followed, and he helped her up, and soon they sat uncomfortably close in the small conveyance. He'd pulled the hood up to give them some anonymity, but it only seemed to draw them closer together, to cut them off from the public world rolling by on either side of them. Her body, a scant five or six inches away from his own, burned like a hot coal on an already sweltering day.

He pulled at his cravat, scooched as far as he could toward the outside of the vehicle.

She, meanwhile, seemed entirely composed. As ever, damn her. A mere wink from her long-lashed eyes could make him want to run. Not that he would. Her beauty called to him, but he'd long ago learned to distrust beautiful things. She, however, never ran from him. He could growl at her, and she'd not even blink.

"What were you speaking to young Tommy about, my lord?" she asked. She faced forward, hands folded primly in her lap over her yellow skirts. A woman with hair the color of flames shouldn't look so well in yellow.

"Nothing of any importance."

"I doubt that. If you do not tell me, I'm sure he will."

Theo focused on the traffic.

"Were you threatening him?"

His grip clenched on the reins.

"Because I'll not have you warning my clientele off. Tommy gets lessons in the art form of his choice for no cost."

Theo's jaw began to ache, and his teeth to beg for mercy, so he loosened it and stretched it side to side. "It's a cost to someone. How is Miss Williams remunerated for her time?"

"I told you—"

"And I told *you*. Reckless, thoughtless, harebrained." He spit each word, flicking the reins without realizing it until the horses whinnied, danced. He took a steadying breath and calmed them, calmed himself, so both he and the horses rode smoothly once more.

Silence hung between them, as tight and awkward as a pair of ill-fitting pants on a dandy.

"We must disagree," she said, her words barely a whisper. Her bonnet hid most of her face, her expression, but he could still see her lips, pressed into a thin line, her cheeks stained pink.

Ah. So she could be ruffled. Excellent to know.

They did not speak the rest of the way, and when he circled the vehicle to hand her down, he found her already on the ground, looking up at the townhouse before them.

Still, they did not speak as he knocked on Lady Balantine's door and waited for it to open.

When it did, a butler narrowed his eyes at them. "You look familiar."

"Do you greet all the lady's visitors like that?" Lady Cordelia asked. Amusement shaped her words.

"Never mind that," Theo said. "Is Lady Balantine in? She's not expecting us, but if she's in, tell her Lord Theodore Bromley and Lady Cordelia Trent are here."

The butler's eyes widened. "Ah, yes. I remember now. You were here that one unfortunate day. Your brother went missing, yes?"

"Yes. We found him."

"I'm aware. Come along, then." The butler granted them entrance. "She'll no doubt wish to speak with you." He led them to a small parlor on the first floor. Every surface, vertical and horizontal, had been covered with art of some sort. The baroness jumped to her feet at their entrance and bustled toward them.

"Oh, my dears, my dears, my *darlings*. Welcome, welcome. Do sit. I'll ring for tea." The woman was short but bought several inches of height from a turban wrapped around her head and festooned with feathers taller than the turban. Her gray-blue eyes twinkled, and a rather athletic form carted them across the room with surprising strength. She settled them on chairs near the one she'd vacated, pulled a bell in the corner of the room, then took her seat once more, a grin stretching from ear to ear. "What a lovely surprise to see the two of you here. I would never have expected. But here we are, and *what* a delight. Do you have news for me? Or perhaps a request or—"

"A request." Theo threw the words into the half a breath she'd given them for reply.

"An opportunity." Lady Cordelia's words fell at the same

time as his own, and they snapped their heads around to glare at one another.

Lady Balantine watched them. "Fascinating. Do go on."

But which one should go on? Him or her, and—

"Lady Balantine," she said, the words like a rush of roaring water, "I am opening an art school and looking for financial backers."

A keening sort of noise wheeled up and out of Lady Balantine's throat, and it soon morphed into a cry of glee as she clapped hard enough to bring her butler back into the room.

"Yes, my lady?" he queried.

She waved him away. "I am in need of nothing more than something quite large to contain my joy. Oh."

Lady Cordelia beamed, smirked. Preened, even.

Was that ... admiration poking at Theo's ribs? Because the woman had bested him, had thrown herself into the fray and come out the victor? Certainly not.

Lady Balantine produced a fan out of nowhere, snapped it open, and fluttered it about her face. "Oh. What an absolutely perfect project. And that you've asked me to be part of it. I shall expire."

"Do not expire"—Theo raised his voice a bit more than polite—"until you've heard my request." Theo could compete as well.

The fluttering stopped. The dowager's head tilted to the side. "A ... different request than the one Lady Cordelia has placed before me like a rare treat?"

"Lady Cordelia needs a patron. Not a financial backer."

"Lady Cordelia does *not*," the lady in question huffed, and her hands, long and sinewy, wrapped around the cushioned arm of her chair, fingernails almost disappearing into the pale-blue upholstery. Pale-blue chair, pale-yellow gown, pale-green spencer, and fiery auburn hair. The woman could be spring itself, her rage even, an approximation of an angry sun, heating her cheeks into bright-pink flowers.

Lady Balantine snapped her fan shut and tossed it into her lap. "I admit to confusion. I thought you meant to teach art, Lady Cordelia, not make it."

"You've the right of it, my lady. But I will not teach. I'm no good for that. I have teachers already promised to help and a space—"

"Owned by my family, soon to be sold," Theo said.

"Which I intend to purchase as soon as possible, sooner with your donations." Lady Cordelia smiled brightly for the dowager.

"It's a fool's scheme," Theo insisted. "Lady Cordelia has no natural artistic talent of her own. She has been under my family's protection for four years, my father's protection, but we can no longer support her and are soon to accept an offer on the Drury Lane house. She must find some other arrangement. My brother, Lord Lysander—"

"Oh, my darling Zander." The Lady Balantine cupped her cheeks. "How is he and his talented wife? I do hope they visit soon."

"Lord Lysander suggested you might be able to help Lady Cordelia. She can act as your companion or—"

"I do not wish to be a companion, Lord Theodore." Lady Cordelia's voice rose high and firm as she stood to tower over him. "I will care for myself if you would give me time to see my vision a success."

He could tower, too, so he stood, slowly, not stepping away from her to put more space between their bodies. But he seemed to have scared himself instead of her. She stood so close he could smell her, hear her breath, feel its susurrations against his waistcoat, see the tip of her chin as she lifted it to meet him sharp stare for sharp stare. And all her offers, jest though he knew them to be, as well as young Tommy's question about paying for kisses, held knife points to his throat and demanded—look at her, *see* her. Kiss her?

He slammed his eyes closed, whipped around, and stormed across the room, breathing slowly to wipe away those thoughts. Why in hell would he *ever* think of kissing her? She damn well sparkled, and he hated glitter. He turned around to tell her ... to tell her ... What had he been about to say?

She must have taken his march across the room, his silence, as concession, as victory for herself. She sat taller than before; her shoulders squared with confidence. "I have it all planned, Lady Balantine. And I've a list of other possible donors. It is to be a school for *everyone*. We have ten students on scholarship learning everything from writing to painting to violin. To support their endeavors, we also have over twenty paying students. One class is currently entirely full. It's for widows. They learn to sketch anatomy."

Theo snorted.

"And most of the women who attend are wealthy. They pay well for a time to meet with like-minded ladies and delight in a bit of diversion. Learning something new distracts them, you see. From their loss. Helps them move through it." Lady Cordelia sank back into her chair, her hands coming to her belly like armor. "Our young violin student is quite good. He learned fiddle from his father at a young age, and my violin instructor, Miss Williams, ensures me he will in time be able to play with quartets or perhaps for the theater, and bring more money to his family than he could working in a dangerous factory. And my instructors. I am not taking advantage of them. They know they are currently volunteering their time, but they are committed nonetheless. It is not simply my project. It is all of ours. After all, they have what I do not— talent, the ability to teach. I am merely organizing them all."

Lady Balantine had found her fan once more, and with each of Lady Cordelia's sentences, she fluttered faster, leaned closer, and by the time Lady Cordelia had stopped, the dowager fell back into her seat, elation shining in her eyes.

"My, my. What a perfect scheme. Absolutely perfect."

Lady Cordelia's speech hung over Theo like a persistent cloud. Were the instructors truly part of the scheme, willing to give of their time to help others? That changed things a bit, didn't it? Not enough to have him interfere with Raph's intentions to sell the house, but his anger ebbed away, replaced by a glimmer of ... respect.

He had no idea how she'd come to be under his father's care, but she had something of his father's large heart about her, and he couldn't help but admire that, misguided as it often was. She had purpose, the kind of purpose that sought to elevate the world and improve lives. Similar, in an odd way, to his own. But where he sought to reveal the hypocrisy of those who abused and mistreated the less fortunate, she sought to lift up those who needed help. They worked, it seemed, on the same problem but at different ends of it.

His end, clearly, was the superior one. There would be other ways she could do good, but this way, the school, would never work. It was too big a project, too beyond her abilities, and he couldn't figure out how to fight her, to get her to see sense.

All he had to make his point was the truth.

He returned to his seat and licked his lips, then he held his hands out to the women, palms up. "I admit your scheme is admirable, Lady Cordelia. But you do not have the luxury of time. My father settled two hundred pounds a year on you, a sum my brother is required to continue paying until you find another position, another patron. And with the house to be sold so soon, you must find one quickly." He looked away from the worn palms of his gloves to Lady Cordelia's face, soft with listening, lips slightly parted. "I know we are asking you to give up your independence, the house that has been your home for the last four years, but there is no other way. Even my father knew it, or he would not have made it possible for us to stop the payments to the artists he supported, to you. But he did."

Lady Cordelia's lips parted. For a moment she appeared vulnerable, lost, but the illusion quickly dropped, revealing the strong, determined woman he knew well once more. She exhaled, a heavy thing, before she faced the dowager. "How much can you donate?"

What gumption. Not will you donate, but *how much*.

The dowager watched them warily as if they might become birds and fly at her turban. "I can't say off the top of my head. My son has lately found himself in financial trouble, and I've been draining my coffers to fix it. I'll have to speak with my agent."

Lady Cordelia clutched her fists into her skirt, then uncurled them and pressed the heels of her hands into her eyes. When they dropped, her eyes were clear and something like a small smile curled her lips. "I see I have much to think on. And much to do." She stood. "Lady Balantine, would you please contact me when you know how much you can donate? And if you have like-minded acquaintances."

Lady Balantine nodded. "Of course. But please do not leave so soon."

"I have many more potential donors to contact. I'm afraid we must."

"But—look! The tea has arrived." The dowager swept an arm toward the door as it creaked open and a cart pushed through. "Sit, sit, my darling, you cannot leave yet. I've so much to speak of, and no one to speak it to."

Theo stood as well. "Apologies, my lady, but Lady Cordelia is correct. We must take our leave."

"I'm sure I have some gossip to keep you entertained. Such as"—she lifted a finger—"Lord Mason's affair with an opera singer or"—another finger joined the first—"the rumor that Lady Greystone's new twins do not belong to her husband. Or, oh!" Both hands appeared in the air, all fingers flown wide. "The new artists house party that's arose to replace the one your parents used to host, Lord Theodore."

Theo stopped, and Lady Cordelia, who'd been trailing him out of the room, bumped into him, frowned, and rubbed her nose as she rocked onto her heels.

The dowager grinned. "Interested in that, are you?" She folded her hands over her now folded fan. "Have a seat, have a seat."

The maid with the tea cart poured three cups, and the steam rose from each gold-rimmed cup, taunting, inviting.

"Who's hosting it?" Theo asked.

"The Earl of Pentshire. It's to be held at his home near Manchester in three days' time. And oh, but it's delicious."

Delicious. Code for *scandalous*. And Theo needed scandal. Scandal fed him, gave him air and inspiration.

And frankly, he felt a bit like a villain standing so close to a woman attempting to do such good and threatening to evict her as soon as could be. But scandal meant there roamed the world a real villain, one he could uncover and bring to justice, and in so doing, right his own wrongs.

He returned to the chairs, took a cup of steaming tea, and sat in the blue one Lady Cordelia had so recently occupied. "Why is it ... delicious?"

"Well"—the baroness leaned close, dropped her voice— "unlike your parents' house party, it's for couples only. Artists and their ... *muses*." She hissed the last word.

Not muses then. Or not *just* muses. Their mistresses.

Well damn. Gossip, common knowledge, painted Pentshire clean as new-fallen snow, innocent as a babe, sweet as a lamb. He'd only just inherited his father's title in the last year and most considered him a shining new star of parliament with principles as old fashioned as his waistcoats, which he appeared to have pilfered from his grandfather's wardrobe.

Theo whistled. "Do you know who has been invited?"

Lady Cordelia dropped into the chair beside him. "Are we truly gossiping at a time like this? Aren't we in the middle of a row? No, a battle. For my future no less."

He waved away her concerns. "Shh. Lady Balantine, continue."

The baroness popped her fan open and fluttered it before her mouth as she spoke. "The guest list is ... fascinating. An earl who considers himself a genius, a few viscounts, a baron, and wealthy merchants without titles. An actress or two if I've heard right. All influential, all wealthy, all painters. Most married. And *not* to the women attending the party."

Exactly what Theo needed. If he could attend the party, he could gain material for the most successful print of his career. A series of them perhaps. Entitled "The Truth and Beauty of Art." The truth was those who dabbled in it were not beautiful at all.

And he could reveal their ugliness.

The dowager and Lady Cordelia continued their gossip, and he leaned into the back of the chair, sipping his tea slowly, plotting.

He must visit with Pentshire and secure an invitation.

Four

Cordelia traveled the length of her parlor and back, hands on hips, fleeting feet over the carpet, mind racing. So little time. So few options. The clock ticked in the buzz of loneliness surrounding her—a reminder. The only other sound was the soft slap of her feet against the floor. How many hours, days, months, had she paced alone like this, waiting for another instructor to arrive and keep her company, waiting—always in vain—for the marquess to visit. Above her, a violin quivered into unsteady life.

Miss Williams was here!

Cordelia ran up the stairs and threw open the door at the end of the hall where Miss Williams always held her lessons. She and her student—a graying woman wearing a blue muslin day dress—looked up as the violin screeched into silence.

"Miss Williams," Cordelia said, breathless, "may I speak with you? It's rather urgent."

The instructor frowned, pursed her lips, then said, "Mrs. Brown, please do practice your scales. I'll return shortly."

Cordelia grabbed Miss Williams's wrist and dragged her

into the room across the hall. "I am so sorry to interrupt your lessons. Only, it's an emergency."

"Make it quick," Miss Williams grumbled, tilting her ear toward the closed door, through which the muffled sound of shaky violin notes wavered.

"The gargoyle arrived today with unhappy news."

"Oh? Nothing worth tossing me out the window for, then?"

"I do apologize for that. Badly done of me, I know. Forgive me?"

"*Humph.* What is this news?"

"We must be out by the end of the month. Or have triple what the townhouse is worth in order to buy it ourselves."

Miss Williams's mouth dropped open. "Triple? By month's end?"

Cordelia nodded her head so quickly, she rather felt like her neck might snap.

Miss Williams groped about for a chair, and once she found the back of one, she dropped into it.

Cordelia joined her in a facing chair. "Lord Theodore thinks I should serve as a companion to the Lady Balantine. Seeing as how I'm good for nothing else."

Miss Williams tilted her head, a concession. "Hm. The name is familiar. Balantine ..."

"She's a patron of the arts. I've met her a few times, including today. Lord Theodore took me to her home to, I don't know ... I suppose he thought to drop me off like a parcel of packages for her disposal."

"You didn't let him."

"Certainly not. I worked to gain Lady Balantine's patronage for our school. But she's a bit strapped at the moment. The desire is there, but the funds ..."

"A familiar dilemma. What shall you do next? What shall *we* do next?"

Cordelia shook her head, rubbing her thumb across the arch of one eyebrow. "I was hoping you'd have an idea."

Miss Williams bounced to her feet and scratched her chin, pulled at her nose, her earlobe, her eyes narrowed. "It was a good idea to seek the baroness's patronage. We need more like her."

"Your other employers perhaps. The other instructors' employers. I have my list of names you gave me." To which she'd added her own names from the masquerade months ago.

"Yes. We must move up our timeline. You must visit as many as you can as quickly as possible."

"We do not yet have a perfect product to show them, to *sell* them."

Miss Williams sliced her narrowed gaze onto Cordelia. "We do not have time for that now."

"You may be right. I had hoped, also, to procure at least one respectable donor before I began to solicit further donations. I am not ... the kind of person others readily invite into their homes. I am well aware of how my situation appears to outsiders. It would be better if my association to the entire project remains secret. I'm quite content to remain behind the scenes."

"True. Perhaps you can ask Lady Balantine to speak for you, on behalf of the school. Even if she does not donate yet."

"An excellent idea." Money often spoke louder than words, but words were all they could afford at the moment. "I'll pay her another visit tomorrow, give her my list. She does seem terribly knowledgeable about the goings-on of the art world. Have you heard of a house party to be hosted near Manchester? At the Earl of Pentshire's estate?"

"No. I've not. But I'm not the sort to be invited to those things."

"You were never invited to the Marquess of Waneborough's house party?"

"I was," Miss Williams said. "But I did not wish to go. Seemed a waste of time when I could be earning my rent teaching lessons in London."

"You could have, perhaps, gained a patron, someone to pay for you to work only on your art."

"And to dispose of me when they ran out of money or got bored with me. Whichever came first. I do not like to live at the whims of others. I'd rather work for my own keep."

"Very smart of you, Miss Williams." Cordelia's voice echoed a bit hollow, and it coursed their conversation toward a tight silence until Cordelia cleared her throat and found her smile. Her entire life had been lived at the whims of others, after all. But not for much longer. "You are wise, but a house party like the one Lord Waneborough used to hold, and like the one Lord Pentshire is hosting, would be quite an opportunity for our school. No knocking on doors or requesting invitations or accosting in the park to find funds for our school. All those likely to support it under one roof, their love for art at its peak for a fortnight."

"I do see how it would prove convenient to attend such a thing with our aims in sight. Perhaps you should attend it, Lady Cordelia."

"Me? No. Lady Balantine said the earl was being quite persnickety about invitations. Only painters and their muses. I am neither."

"But we know a painter, do we not? Mr. Samuels."

"And Mr. Samuels has a wife who would likely not appreciate him attending a house party with another woman."

Miss Williams jumped to her feet again, and a few long steps brought her to the fireplace where she swung around, throwing her arms out wide then dropping them. "It just seems a waste. We should find you a painter to attend with. You can be a muse, surely. All it takes is sitting there and being pretty, two things you do well."

Cordelia's hands, hidden by her skirts, raked lines into the silk of the chair cushion, but she kept her face from twisting into a portrait of disgust because she could not quite tell who disgusted her more—herself for having no talent or Miss Williams for saying so. She inhaled one almost calming breath and continued smiling, a steady show of optimism and good spirit.

"Yes, surely I could do even that. But what man would we find willing to travel with me, paint me, pretend to be enraptured with me, and whom ... whom I could trust." The idea of traveling with a man she did not know sent a shiver of unease through her.

"Quite right." Miss Williams pounded a fist on the fireplace mantel. "He must be trustworthy. Or a eunuch."

"Miss Williams!"

She showed wide eyes behind her spectacles. "It is not true? Those who know *of* you likely think you a ... a tart, but those who are actually acquainted with you realize you're innocent indeed."

Innocent. Ha. If only they knew. She'd had to accept Lord Waneborough's help for several reasons. But the most pressing had been fear. She could have been with child, after all. She'd been set to marry Simon, had not thought much about giving into her—their—desires a few months before the wedding. She should have. She truly should have. Then she'd not have stood on the doorstep of a man who'd rejected her looking at a man offering her a safe harbor and thought only of how her friends would spurn her once they knew. If her belly swelled. Thank heavens there'd been no babe.

The screech of violin notes stopped, and Miss Williams's attention snapped toward the door. "I must go. This is a paying client, and we clearly cannot afford to anger one of those."

"No. We can't. You're right. Go."

Miss Williams grabbed the door handle but hesitated before opening it. "Well? What will you do?"

"Think on it. Today and tonight. And take action tomorrow. The party is clearly not an option, but I'll speak to Lady Balantine, see if she'll be the face of the school, a vocal supporter if nothing else." So that Cordelia could live in the shadows where no one would have to be reminded of her flaws, her mistakes.

"A good start. I'll speak with Mr. Spencer to see if he has any ideas." Then Miss Williams flung the door open and disappeared across the hall with the precise movements of a military officer.

Cordelia sighed, alone once more, the air buzzing again, her body heavy and jittery at the same time. What to do? How to move forward? She'd figure it out. She had to, despite her lack of talent. Because everything seemed to be falling apart. If she did not figure it out, she must leave in a month's time, and her instructors, who had flung themselves behind this project with as much passion as she had, would find themselves lost as well. Their dream of a school was dissolving before her eyes.

No. She must remain positive. Lady Balantine would help, and she would know others interested in financing the school. As the old marquess used to say, things would work out as they should. She must not give up hope.

Five

The thorn in his backside could remain thorny and immovable for a while longer. Theo had work to do revealing the corruption of powerful men. He set his steps toward White's and held his metaphorical lance tight to his side for the great battle lying ahead of him—securing an invitation to a house party.

He found the Earl of Pentshire in the coffee room drinking port.

Theo sat across from him. "I want in."

Pentshire jumped to his feet, port sloshing over the rim of his cup, and pressed a hand to his heart. He returned slowly to his seat. "Damn me. You're likely to kill a fellow that way." Pentshire was tall and lanky and golden, his brown eyes soft with, somehow, a puppy dog's innocence. He dressed in clothes too big and too out of fashion for a man of his youth. Couldn't be any older than Theo's own six and twenty years. He appeared to be a boy playing at manhood.

But Theo knew he harbored hidden depths. The house party would reveal every league beneath the placid surface.

"I want in," Theo demanded, slamming his templed

fingers on the tabletop to punctuate his points. Surely he wouldn't have to be more specific than that. Surely Pentshire wouldn't want him to be.

Pentshire fell into the back of his armchair and focused on his coffee cup. "I've no idea what you mean."

"You wish me to speak of your upcoming house party in public and"—Theo raised his voice—"quite loudly? Very well—"

"Desist." Pentshire's blond brows flew together.

"I want in."

"Hm." Pentshire studied him from boot to hat. "Your father had the greatest personal art collection in the country. And by all accounts was quite charitable. Radical, even, in his social attitudes."

"I'm aware."

"I've heard he taught his children to be the same, but ... do you paint? The party is a"—he rolled his hand between them as if searching for the right term—"an artist's retreat, a way of filling the gap created by the loss of your parents' yearly house party. A place for like-minded individuals stifled by too-stringent social rules to ... exist. Without judgment."

Theo blinked. He'd never considered the party his parents held each year in that particular light. He'd loved it at one time, considered it a learning experience from those more skilled than himself. He knew better now, celebrated his brother's abolishment of the event. Every artist with any talent and every patron with any intent to nurture that talent had attended. And all had drained their pantry and their coffers for weeks on end to their father and mother's great delight, and to the detriment of those who relied on them. After each party, a new batch of servants lost their jobs, the family unable to afford them.

Felt right to sneak into a similar party and reveal the bad

things done there. With his own art, nonetheless. Something poetic about that.

"I paint," Theo said. "Until now it's been a private hobby. But I'm considering submitting to a gallery next year, and I need to create my best work." A good enough lie, that.

Pentshire rubbed his knuckles up and down the bridge of his nose. "Bold. But ... what is your subject?"

"My subject?"

"What sorts of things do you paint?"

Hell. "The usual. Still lifes." Pentshire wrinkled his nose, his hand stilling. "Portraits too."

The nose unwrinkled. "Hm. All those in attendance will be portrait artists as well. What ... *kind* of portraits do you paint?"

Theo blinked. "People?" The proper subject of all portraits, and—oh. Hell. Lady Balantine had mentioned something about muses, mistresses. "Women. I prefer to paint women."

Pentshire nodded, and each nod seemed to shed the look of the innocence he wore like a cloak. "Bring your model, then. When you come." He sipped his port.

What model? He had none. Damn. He searched for an excuse. "She's ... busy. It would be best if I came alone."

Half tipped, the wine not to his lips yet, the glass stilled, then Pentshire lowered it slowly, setting it on the table with a soft clink. "No model, no invitation. This house party is meant to celebrate the joy of two bodies coming together in love. If you cannot magnify that theme with your art and your presence, then—"

"Why?" Theo demanded.

Pentshire shrugged. "I would love to extend an invitation to Lord Waneborough's son, but I won't. The guests who have confirmed are bound to secrecy and promise their own secrecy. You will too if I deign to extend an invitation."

The opportunity slipped through his fingers like spilled ink from a pot. He couldn't let it because the more this man talked the more Theo knew ... whatever he discovered at this house party would be big, would allow him to draw a cartoon the printshops would fight over. It could well make his career, allow him to rent a house of his own instead of living with his sister ... a house, not a single room, and maybe one day, start his life with a—

No. He didn't want domestic felicity, no matter how lovely his siblings made it look. He wanted to reveal this man's secrets.

Pentshire downed his port and rose to leave.

Theo caught his wrist. "She'll rearrange her schedule. I'm sure she's as keen to attend as I am."

"Invitation extended then. But if you show up without your model, I'll turn you away. Do you understand?"

A profitable scandal indeed awaited Theo. If he could find a model to pretend to be his mistress, his muse. Theo rolled his eyes, tossed Pentshire's wrist away. "Of course."

"I'll see you there, then. Holloway House just outside of Manchester."

Theo crossed his arms over his chest as he watched Pentshire disappear into the hallway. "Damn," he hissed. He'd received an invitation, but it mattered not if he could not find a woman.

What now?

No answer came as he left White's and made his way toward Maggie's. When he reached her townhouse, he slammed the door behind him more loudly than he'd intended. The slam rang in the empty hall, the walls shook, and two heads appeared out of different doorways.

"What," Maggie asked, blinking, fingers wrapping around the doorframe.

"Was that?" Zander finished, stepping into the hallway from the dining room.

"*Grrgglll.*" The growl turned into a gurgle as if his throat couldn't decide which emotion strung him tighter—frustration or despondence. Theo stood tall, though, despite the fact he really felt like drooping. Perhaps even lying prone on the floor like a rug to be stepped on.

Maggie and Zander exchanged a look and rushed toward him. They each took one of his arms and propelled him toward Maggie's parlor. Maggie sat him down and Zander filled a family of tumblers with a decanter of port from a cabinet.

"Do tell." Zander handed Theo a glass and sat across from him.

Maggie curled up on the opposite side of Theo's sofa.

Theo's head grew heavier every moment till he could not keep it up any longer. He dropped it to the back of the sofa with a groan he muffled with his palm.

"Are you still in the doldrums about the Lady Cordelia problem?" Maggie asked.

"No. It's not that," he snapped.

Maggie looked up at the ceiling and Zander down at his shoes.

He approached an answer to the Lady Cordelia problem as easily as he might approach the sun. That is, not at all, reaching it an utter impossibility. And now he had the added difficulty of finding a model to bring with him to Holloway House.

He leaned forward and rested his elbows on his knees, hung his head, lost his gaze in the vines swirling on the carpet beneath his boots. "Perhaps the two of you can help me in another way."

"Yes," Maggie said, "Let us help you."

Zander rubbed his palms together. "We'll not fail you."

Theo swirled the port in the glass before taking a sip. "I need a woman." He looked up at them.

They wore identical expressions of shock, then Zander broke into laughter. "We ..." He wheezed. "We know that!" He doubled over, shaking, wrapping his arms around his belly.

Maggie seemed to be holding herself in utter stillness to avoid laughter of her own, her lips rolled beneath her teeth as if she must pinch them together to keep a bit of humor from breaking free.

"What"—she closed her eyes, took a breath—"do you mean by that?"

He'd hashed it. Knew it as soon as the words had escaped his lips. "I mean there's a house party I need entrance to, but the only people receiving invitations are painters and their ... muses. I can pretend to paint. I *can* paint, if not that well. But the muse bit"—he took another slug of port—"I need a woman."

"Why do you wish to go to this painter's house party?" Maggie asked.

Zander appeared to be recovering but not quite enough to speak yet.

"I've had word the men attending are mostly titled, self-righteous prigs, and the muses they plan to bring with them are their mistresses. And their mistresses are unknown to their wives. I intend to reveal them for who they really are." Ruiners of families. Men with power who wielded it for pleasure instead of for the good of others.

"Out for blood again, brother," Zander finally said.

Theo nodded.

Zander scratched his jaw, darted a glance at Maggie. "Cover your ears, sister."

She glared, pulled her ears out wide.

Zander rolled his eyes. "Do you have a former mistress who might help you?"

"No." Theo shook his head. "I've not had a mistress since before Father's death, and even then, they weren't mistresses so much as friendly acquaintances who were *quite* friendly at times."

"You can"—Zander glanced at Maggie—"*hire* a woman, then. Mags, you really shouldn't be listening to this."

"I shall listen to what I please. I have been married longer than you, and I did grow up in the same family. I know what you know, brother."

Zander shivered.

"Focus," Theo pleaded. "I cannot ask a stranger to accompany me. What if they discover why I'm really there? Who I really am?" No one knew who Sir George was, the satirist who signed his drawings with the small sketch of a knight's helmet. A bit of egotistical fancy, that, but one that served to remind him of his purpose—to slay the dragons of London society.

"I don't like that," Maggie said, pulling her legs up under her skirts and wrapping her arms around them. "You've drawn some nasty things about powerful men. Your anonymity protects you."

"I've drawn *true* things—which makes them even nastier —about men with too much power. And I would like to continue doing so. But I would also like to continue doing so undetected."

"So, no, you can't trust a stranger," Maggie concluded. "Perhaps you should not go at all. There is enough for you to write about just here in London." She nodded, as if she'd decided it all.

Zander pushed off his legs to stand. "I think you should go. Sounds like an ... interesting event. Take if from a former slightly nefarious man, what you need is not just a woman, but a woman who wants something you have. Other than, naturally, your appealing personality." He winked then sauntered from the room. "Fiona!" he called out once in the hallway.

Maggie jumped to her feet, eyes wide, face drained of color. "Shh! You cad!" She rushed after him. "You'll wake the baby!"

Alone, Theo pondered the ceiling once more. Two failures in as many days. A woman who would not be moved though she must move and accept his help or find herself without a home in a month's time. Hell, he wanted to help her. The Sir George bit of him wanted to save her—find her a new home, financial backers for her school. Her every wink drove him wild, but the last few days had taught him to see her as more than a tease, more than a thorn. He saw now the intelligence in her eyes, the softness of her heart.

He could not help but melt a bit. Another problem, that.

Best to put all Cordelia-shaped problems behind him. He could do nothing about them if she refused to be sensible. The house party remained the more pressing problem. He needed to find a woman he could trust in half a day or a woman to exchange favors with. Her help and her silence for whatever she wanted. That he could give her.

His breath hitched and his hands, pushing through his hair, froze. Hell. The two problems, their solutions, knit together in his mind.

He couldn't.

He shouldn't.

But Lady Cordelia possessed beauty enough to be a muse, to be a mistress, and she wanted the one thing her attendance at such a house party could give—access to people ready and willing to spend all their money on art. Surrounded by artists and those who supported them, surely she could find someone to help her when his family no longer would.

Slowly, he rose to his feet, brain buzzing.

To solve all their problems at once, he need only ask her to pretend to be his mistress.

Six

Cordelia had been awake an hour when the sun poured through her bedroom window and a hellish banging started at her front door. She stuck her head out of her window, looked below. The gargoyle? He stood on her doorstep, knocking as if the hounds of Hell were nipping at his heels and her door remained his only sure way to safety.

She hissed. Then she ran. Into the hallway and down the stairs to fling open the front door. "What are you doing?" she demanded, pulling her wrapper tightly closed before her. "You'll wake the neighbors." He had likely brought more horrid news with him, and she did not currently have the emotional fortitude to endure it. "Go away."

"I've a proposition for you." His eyes glittered, and he braced a hand on the doorframe, high above her head and pushed forward. A lock of hair fell across one of his eyes and casting shadows over his sculpted, scruff-roughened face. He'd clearly not shaved that morning.

"A ... a proposition?" She pulled her wrapper tighter, her heart kicking up its rhythm.

"Let me in, and I'll tell you."

She looked down the street to the right then down the street to the left then finally across the street. Abandoned in all directions. They were alone, but inside *alone* would become somehow *more*. Particularly with the silence of the early morning wrapping tight around them. "You've never visited this early. You should wait for an appropriate hour." She slipped into the foyer and shoved the door closed.

Tried to. Barely got an inch. His booted foot stopped it.

He nudged the door with his toe and pressed closer as it swung wide. "It's important."

She retreated even farther, needing more space between herself and his lean frame, taut and stretched out so close to her own.

He took the step back as an invitation and pressed into the foyer, shutting the door behind him.

"I did not give you leave to—"

He strode down the hall.

After one breathless, furious moment, she hurried after him, followed him into her parlor. "You will leave *now*, my lord."

He'd walked to the window across the room, but he spun quick, curt, and returned to her. "I'll help you find supporters for your school."

That truly knocked her backward, stole her breath. If her heart had been racing before, it meant to win the race now. "Do not play with me," she managed to say.

"I don't, and I won't give you my help for free. I need a favor. And it is an unsavory one."

"What is it?"

"You won't like it."

"Tell me."

He opened his mouth, but offered no more insight. Hesitation crept into his gaze and his gestures as his hand pushed through his dark hair. "I don't like it."

"Tell me," she demanded, striding forward. "I will decide how unseemly it is." She would do anything, perform almost any favor, to keep her dream alive and herself safe within it.

"I need you to attend a house party with me. We'd leave today and be gone for a week. A fortnight possibly."

"A house party ..." Her still morning-tired mind tried to snatch at some memory, a recent one.

"And during that time, you must pretend to be my model, my ... muse. My"—he licked his lips—"mistress."

Surely he could not mean ... "The house party Lady Balantine spoke of?"

"I know asking you to do this makes me less than a gentleman, and in the minds of the other guests, you will be less than a lady." His words sounded strained, difficult to speak. "But I need this, and I can see no other way. If you help me, I will help you."

"The school. You'll help me woo the guests ...?"

"Yes."

All her goals and dreams—hers for the taking if she pretended to be what everyone had already thought her all these years. Ha. Not the only irony in this situation. Just yesterday she'd discussed the merits and dismissed the possibility of attending the party. She'd not thought to attend with any man let alone Lord Theodore.

But here he was, asking her to accept her infamy in order to gain supporters for her school.

She glanced at him. He stood tall and stiff with just a hint of worry lining his face. She'd known him for so few months, and he'd not once made an inappropriate advance, despite her constant teasing. She trusted him. She did not like him, except to poke fun at, but she felt she would be safe with him.

"Well?" he demanded.

"Yes, I'll go." Not a very difficult choice, but a complicated one, and her mind whirred with questions and concerns she could not quite organize into clear thoughts.

She pressed her hand to her belly. Oh. Curses. She wore only her shift and wrapper with her braid slung over one shoulder. The realization shot awkwardness through her limbs and heat through her cheeks, and she pulled her wrapper tighter about her. "I should dress."

"Be quick." He stood like a statue, still as the gargoyle they all accused him of being. So stony. What in heaven's name moved him to such lengths?

"Why?" she asked, backing toward the door, arms crossed protectively over her chest. "Why do you need to attend the house party so badly?"

His stone body cracked into action, his toe tapping with impatience on the rug. "I'll tell you, but not until we're on our way. I do not wish to waste time when we could be traveling, and I need your guarantee of secrecy. It is part of our bargain. You attend the party with me as my mistress *and* you keep my secret." He grimaced. "It sounds rather one-sided."

"There is plenty benefit for me." She hoped. Support for her school, and ... oddly, discovering more about the man before her. What kind of secrets did he have? She could not quite suppress her very unnecessary curiosity. They had, after all, come to the same solution for her problems. It seemed, at least in some ways, their brains walked similar paths.

She spoke with a confidence she felt in her very bones. "I'll do it."

It took her half an hour to pack, even though she rummaged through her old life for a precious five minutes, finding the old jewelry and gowns of her one season and throwing them in her trunk. She might need them for this playacting, and they were her only finery, though they were four years out of date. Who knew what clothing she'd need for such an event. Better to be prepared. She spent a few minutes scrawling a letter for Miss Williams, so she'd know where Cordelia was going, then another informing her housekeeper of her plans. Or, a version of them.

"Briarcliff?" Mrs. Barkley asked, brow furrowed. "The old marquess's residence? With that horrid man?"

Cordelia nodded, guilt pinching her ribs with the lie. "I've been invited, and Lord Theodore is to escort me. I hope to come back with the means to start my school." She smoothed Mrs. Barkley's brows with a finger, and the older woman swatted her hands away, then Cordelia stepped into the hallway. "I'll be fine, Barkley. And I'll return victorious."

"Yes, well, excellent, my lady. Safe travels."

"Keep things running while I'm away. Give Miss Williams the letter so she knows what to do in my absence."

"Yes, my lady."

She bounced toward the door like a lamb in spring. "Don't miss me too much, Barkley!" She threw the door open wide and stepped into the street.

The sun shone bright, and hope glowed in her soul. Lord Waneborough had been right after all—things did work out for the patient. Eventually.

Lord Theodore secured her trunk to the traveling coach, not bothering to look up as she joined him. When he'd finished, he opened the coach door with a grunt.

"So terribly gallant." Cordelia climbed inside and settled into the forward-facing seat. Soon after he sat across from her, the conveyance lurched into movement.

She closed her eyes and found a steady rhythm of breathing. So much had happened so quickly, and she'd made such a quick decision. She'd done so at another time, with another man named Bromley, and that had been the saving of her. This decision, too, would prove valuable. It had to.

No matter that it felt like utter foolishness.

She opened her eyes and jumped.

He watched her, his eyes clear and intelligent, his body unmoving and big. He'd stripped his hat from his head, and it sat like another passenger beside him. She knew nothing about this man, yet she must share a coach with him. For ... how long? She'd never been to Manchester before.

She smoothed her skirts and gathered her thoughts, then lifted her face and offered a smile ... which he did not return, though his eyes narrowed, and his muscles seemed to bunch tighter. "If, my lord, you stay silent and tight as a boulder for the next fortnight, you might ... break. Into gargoyle dust."

"You mustn't call me a gargoyle if we're to pretend to be lovers."

"It's a term of endearment."

He snorted and spun to look out the window.

"So ... how far is Manchester?" she asked.

"It will take at least two days of travel. If there's good weather."

Two days. Trapped. With him. And ... what about ... "What are your plans for the night? Will we travel all the way through?"

"'Tis better to sleep in the coach than to risk being seen."

Surprisingly thoughtful, but ... "Surely we do not need to worry about my reputation. There will be men there who return to London with us and think me a lightskirt. There are already those in London who think me a lightskirt."

He scratched his jaw and spoke to the world rolling away outside the window. "No use hiding your identity, then."

"None whatsoever. I've had contact with many in the art community during my time in the Drury Lane house. I can only assume they've gossiped about me. I may even know someone at the party. From my old life." She'd been engaged to a painter, after all, had met his friends and tried to fit into his world.

Theo's mouth thinned. "I'd not considered that. Will it bother you? Everyone thinking of you as my mistress?"

"No. But ... I may need to ask a favor of you while we are there."

His hands folded together, a tight web of bone. "What is it?"

"I had planned on finding a respectable patron for my school who did not mind my own situation, who could act as the school's face and seek out other patrons in my stead. I had thought, perhaps, Lady Balantine could fulfill that role. I would have asked her today had you not shown up, offering a quicker solution."

"Hm. A smart approach to a difficult complication."

She blinked. He'd just complimented her. How unexpected. Unexpected, too, her reaction to it. She wanted to puff up with pride, to let spill all her other ideas and see how he liked those. She swallowed the fever to do so and folded her hands in her lap as if they didn't want to flutter up into the air with delight. "Erm ... thank you. But the complication still exists at Holloway House, yes? Even at such a gathering, people will be more likely to sponsor a project headed by someone of slightly more respectable standing than myself."

"I had not considered before. Perhaps we should go back—"

"No!" She reached for him, laid her hand on top of his folded ones. "I have a solution—the favor I'm asking of you. We will simply tell everyone it's your school. It is named for *your* father, after all."

"Bloody hell. No."

"We must. What sins are considered unforgivable in me will be quite forgotten in you. Pretending the school belongs to a man with a mistress will not hurt its chances, while revealing it's run by a woman only pretending to be a mistress will. Unfair but true. And we must act accordingly unless ... Is there a way I can attend without pretending to be your mistress? We can't say I'm your sister because that implicates your father, and—"

"No. Not that. Perhaps we should bring a chaperone. No. Pentshire said he'd kept the guest list small and selective. He would not allow another woman with no artistic leanings in."

"What an odd man."

"His oddities are giving me a headache." Theo untangled his fingers and rubbed his temples.

"We'll present the school as yours," Cordelia said, "and I'll work to win them over so that when they find out I'm the headmistress, they'll be less likely to run off, taking their blunt with them."

Theo sighed. "This is proving more complicated than I anticipated. But I think it will work out. Pentshire is being rather rabid about secrecy. My hope is that the guests will remain silent if we do. They'll want their secrets kept, too." The corner of his lip twitched ever so slightly upward.

A smile? No. Never. She leaned forward, demolishing the space between them and poked the tip of her finger into that quirked corner of his lips. "What is that?"

He swatted her hand away, his limbs wheeling wildly. "You"—he pointed a finger at her—"remain on your side of the coach."

"The entire time?"

"The entire time."

She lifted a brow. "You are safe from me. But you must explain the quirk of your lip. You see, I did not think it possible for you to smile."

"I didn't."

"Not quite, true. But the potential was there, brimming in that"—she focused on his mouth and leaned forward once more, the finger unfurling from her loose fist—"corner."

"Lady Cordelia."

She grinned up at him.

"Desist."

She sighed and sank back into her seat. "As you wish, my lord."

He sniffed, trained his lips into a tight line once more. Momentarily. That corner popped back up.

She pointed. "Aha! Explain yourself, sir!"

"I'm amused, is all. I promised to tell you why I must attend this house party, and we've come to the point."

"Which you find amusing."

Something heavy in his gaze settled on her, making her squirm.

"Do you pay attention to satirical prints?" he asked.

"Yes, I suppose," she said. "There was one a few months back Mr. Spencer tried to hide from me. Regarding the Achilles statue in Hyde Park. Such a fuss about a fig leaf."

"The fuss was less about the fig leaf and more about the ladies' reaction to it. Yes, I know the print. It's quite good. I admit to some envy there."

"Envy? Wait." Surely not, but what other direction could the conversation be taking? "You're an illustrator, too? A satirist?"

"I am. But it is not well known. My family knows. And now you. I publish under the pseudonym Sir George."

She gripped the edge of the seat to keep from leaping out of it. "Oh! I've seen your work, and—"

"You'll not speak of it. Ever. We attend this house party to obtain secrets these men do not wish the world to know." The corner of his lips popped up again, impossible, it seemed, to suppress entirely. "Then reveal them."

The man used art as a weapon, and the knowledge of it made a wicked blade of his half smile. His work was good. It had the same blade edge to it, as if every stroke of the pen swiped at the jugular. She could not call it beautiful. Too grotesque, too angry, for beauty, but it showed immense talent. His curved lips no longer made her heart leap. He smiled for all the wrong reasons. But ... she wished to creep closer to him, to know why he wore a blade for a mouth and splashed bitterness across paper with such finesse and always to expose evils. She remembered one sketch quite well, published just yesterday. A man had sold his daughter into marriage to another man triple her age and known for his ill treatment of women. She hoped the two men were shunned, that they paid for their actions, perhaps shamed into better behavior.

But would it work that way? Or would the daughter pay the price of their public shame? Still, the motivation behind the caricature had been clear—the men were villains. And Cordelia admired the complicated man sitting across from her for putting the notion into the air. If Lord Theodore wielded art as a weapon, he did so for good reasons.

She shivered. "Very well. I'll help you acquire secrets."

"You'll pretend to be my mistress. I'll acquire the secrets myself." He spoke with utter certainty, each word a boulder like himself, immovable. "You woo the guests with talk of charitable art schools."

Yes, an excellent reminder. An excellent partnership. They may hate one another, but they'd help each other to victory.

Silence stretched between them once more, and soon the muddy, crowded streets of London gave way to fields, open and green and such as she hadn't seen since her father's funeral. A gray day, that, but still the colors of the country had glowed bright, spring flowers in early bloom, her father carried from the house, stiff and cold.

She peeked away from the window to find Lord Theodore resting in the opposite corner of the coach, shoulders squeezed by the confines at his back. His eyes were not closed in rest.

They studied her, though with what emotion she could not say.

He scratched his jaw, an idle gesture, then he spoke. "I'll protect you."

Not a response to her comment, not anything she could have ever expected to leap from his tongue.

He leaned forward, elbows bracing his wide-spread knees. "No harm will come to you or your name through me. If I can help it. I swear it."

There it was again—his honor, the valiant impulses driven by anger. The power of his words felt like a kick to the chest. He meant it. He'd protect her as he fished for secrets from unknowing men. And on top of his earlier compliment! The gargoyle had a heart. Or a conscience at the very least. And knowing that did curious things to her, made her want to study him more closely.

"Sir George indeed," she whispered, ducking her head and watching the shadows of the sun and tree boughs outside the carriage dapple her skirts. "It is not necessary, though. Everyone already thinks the worst of me." She could no longer hold his gaze. It felt too heavy and her own will too weak, so she avoided it, peering out the window at the sun shining there. Would he ask about her past?

She held her breath, but he asked no questions, so she breathed easy once more. This man had already seen her Gallery of Shame. No need to share her other shames with him, the ones that shaped her bones and carved her hollow.

No need for her own inspection of her faults and failures from here on out. In two weeks, she'd have the funds needed to purchase or rent a location for her school, and she'd be free of Lord Theodore for good.

Seven

⌒⌒

Almost twenty hours. That was how long he'd been terrorized by the red-haired banshee. The first three or so hours of the trip had been a trick. She'd spent most of the time looking out the window, seldom speaking. He'd thought himself lucky to have such a silent companion for such a long coach ride.

If she'd winked or teased, he'd blush, think of kissing, and have to spend his time cowering in the shadowed corners of the coach, hoping she didn't notice. He'd thanked God and all the angels for her silence.

Lies.

She'd babbled on for hours after that, only stopping her constant prattle to sleep. But then, in the late hours of the dark night, he'd been sleeping too, squashed on a seat much too small for him. She'd lain out with only a little bend in her knees and had woken up with only a little drool on her cheek and a little confusion in her eyes.

He should have insisted they stop to sleep at an inn.

His body hated him for that poor decision, wanted to toss him from the carriage for it. They'd passed an inn around sunset. They could have had *beds*. But he'd insisted on pushing on. To protect a reputation she insisted didn't need protecting. And because what the hell would his body do with the notion of her in a bed so close to him in a bed? He'd never sleep. At least the coach provided almost constant discomfort to keep his imagination from undressing her.

Bloody inconvenient bout of lust. Should have been gone by now. He knew beauty held only deceit, but his body quite disagreed, and ever since their visit to Lady Balantine's, he'd seen her as more than merely a beautiful woman and leech on the family coffers. He'd begun to see beyond her body to her intellect, her cunning, her courage.

Even though he didn't want to see those things.

"What do you think?" she asked him now, tapping her pencil on her notebook.

"I'm not listening to you any longer." He held his small notebook tighter on his thigh and finished up the sketch he'd been working on slowly, to avoid the almost constant jolts and bumps of the swaying coach.

"Ah. Then I'll put that down as a yes." She flashed a brilliant smile, showing white even teeth through pink lips.

Hell. What did she think he'd agreed to? Dare he ask? He must. "Yes ... what?"

She grinned. "Thank you, my lord, for agreeing to teach a class in satirical sketches to—"

"No." He snapped the notebook closed.

Her grin dissolved. "But you just said yes."

"I didn't know what I was agreeing to."

"Your inattention to my conversation is no excuse." She sat taller, threw her shoulders back.

"Are we there yet?" He pressed his hands into the small of his back and arched, producing a crack that felt like relief.

"Almost. Surely." She craned her neck to look out the

window. "There are buildings up ahead. Several of them. Tall too."

He looked, saw the buildings in the distance. *Finally.* "Yes, almost." He'd traveled the road many times to visit Drew. "And we must make a stop first."

"Oh? Where? Why?" She snapped her notebook closed and held it primly in her lap, mostly hidden by her folded hands.

"My brother lives here, Lord Andrew. He owns an agency that hires out tutors and governesses to work with Manchester's wealthiest families."

"Ah. A nice little family reunion. With the mistress."

"You're not my mistress," he growled.

"You'd better improve at saying 'Yes, she's my mistress' in the upcoming weeks or you'll ruin your own cover." She batted her lashes.

If the damn woman knew how the mere sight of her was a goddamn tease, she wouldn't torment him so. She'd run away. As she should.

He busied his hands straightening his jacket and hair and brushing lint from his trousers. He was a rumpled mess, but so was she, and Drew would notice, but Theo didn't care. "I need information about Pentshire, and since Drew lives in Manchester, a short jaunt from Holloway House, he'll have heard whatever there is to hear."

She tilted her head to the side. Rumpled gown, hair falling despite her earlier efforts to tame it, bonnet gone long ago—a perfect fright. Yet, somehow, at the same exact damn time, plain *perfect* as well. Perfectly poised, perfectly calm, perfectly in control. Did no emotion simmer beneath her skin as it did his? Did the deeper passions never threaten to erupt from her bones? Even when she flirted, she did so in a coldly observant way, as if she wished merely to see how he might react.

"Your brother is a gossip?" she asked.

"Yes. But he calls it information gathering. In that way, we're rather in the same business. But we dispose of the information in different ways."

"You expose sins."

"And he places tutors and governesses in the perfect positions to support the families who seek his help."

She perked up, her eyes brightening. "Do you think he'll help me? Find the right instructors for my school? I'm sure to need more, and once I can afford to pay the instructors, I would be able to hire more."

"You can't afford him."

Her face scrunched together. "If he's so well-off, why does your family not rely on him to solve the coffers problem?"

"Because the lion's share of his commission goes right to the tutors and governesses who work for him. Most of them do not wish to teach their entire lives. They're gentlemen and ladies, poor relations, third and fourth sons, orphans and unwanted daughters who require a means of moving forward, of surviving the moment. His agency helps them. Trains them, connects them with the right households, negotiates their salaries. And he gets a cut. But refuses to take a large one." He wasn't living off Maggie's hospitality, at least, like Theo.

Lady Cordelia's lips quivered. If she attempted to suppress a smile, she failed. It broke her lips apart and plumped up her cheeks anyway. "Your brother is an angel, and you're a gargoyle."

"If you insist."

"I do." She pressed her palms flat against the glass. "We're here."

And they were. Buildings grew around them in size and number, and people appeared, spilling from every direction.

"Have you ever been to Manchester before?" he asked.

She shook her head. "I spent my life in Kent until my first season five years ago. And I have been in London since then."

She cast a glance at him before looking out the window once more. "It's so large. And crowded."

"Not much different from London. We don't have to travel far. Drew lives close. Here. This is Drew. Lord Andrew." He opened his notebook to his most recent sketch and handed it to her. "The shaking from the travel has all but ruined it."

She held the small book between gloved fingers and with a tilted head. Her face began to glow with merriment. "I see the resemblance to you. In the nose. And eyes. Does he truly wear his shirt points so high?"

"He can be a bit of a dandy. Very meticulous in his dress. The shirt points might be an exaggeration, though. Just a little."

She leaned toward him to hand the notebook back and their knees almost kissed in the small space between their bodies. She did not seem to notice, her gaze seeking his. "Is your brother like you?"

"No."

"Could you offer more details?"

"Why? I gave you a sketch."

She pursed her lips together. "And that is all you think I need?"

"A sketch can tell you many things the true person can hide. The sketch reveals what they wish to keep hidden."

"And what secrets is Lord Andrew hiding?"

"You can find out for yourself in a few minutes."

"Don't you believe in helping a lady be prepared?" she asked.

Yes, he did, actually, and he'd avoided preparation for two whole close-quarter days. Now though, only a quarter of an hour remained for such activities. Showing her the sketch— another distraction, a means of prolonging the inevitable. Best to have it done with.

"You wish for preparation?" he asked.

She nodded.

"Then you must call me Theo."

A light flared, briefly, in her eyes then she licked her lips. "I see how that might be necessary."

"You are to be my mistress, my muse. We must be less formal than we are now."

She laughed, a brittle sound. "Much less formal, my lord."

"Theo."

"Theo," she whispered. Then she cleared her throat and spoke with more confidence. "Theo. Yes, and you must call me Cordelia."

"Cordelia."

Her breath hitched, and she pressed a palm to her chest. "It is only an excision of a simple *lady*, but it is ... it is ... oh, I'm being silly. It is nothing."

She had the right of it. Dropping the "Lady" made the name sound different, feel different as it twisted his tongue up in it. "There is more to prepare for, Cordelia."

She must have heard something in his voice to take as a warning because she scooted farther from him. Attempting to escape? No. Not when she'd asked for it. Not when it needed doing.

He lunged across the coach and caught her in his arms, sat her on his lap. Where she went statue still; even her little round arse, perched upon his legs, clenched tight.

He tightened, too, in places he knew he would. He'd steadied his arms around her like shackles in case she decided to run back to her corner. She wouldn't be able to run once they reached Holloway House, so he'd not let her run now.

She cleared her throat, intent on speaking no doubt. As she had done their entire journey.

"No," he whispered in her ear, one hand wrapping round her neck at that slender sloped bit of her body where it became her shoulder, covered now by her high-necked, lavender spencer. Best not to touch skin, so why he stroked his thumb upward, finding skin anyway, his roughened thumbpad flirting with the velvet of her earlobe, he could not say. But he did.

And then she flinched, so he did not anymore.

"You must become used to this," he said, keeping his voice low. "Me touching you. Me ... kissing you."

"Kissing? Ah, yes." She swallowed hard and turned from statue to bird, a ruffled little thing beating its wings against the bars of its cage in vain. "The mistress bit does suggest ... Ahem. Yes. I see. Kissing."

"Yes." He wouldn't kiss her now, though. Not when they were alone. Never when they were alone. Privacy wove an intimate space where real kisses and caresses lived, shadows and locked rooms. And he'd promised to protect her as far as he could. "In front of the others. We must. Will you be able to bear it?"

A tight nod, and beneath his hand, her pulse fluttered. More wings against a cage, the bars his fingers. His own heart kicked into a rapid pace against his ribs.

"Good." He set her aside, his body cold without her firm weight, her lush curves. He'd known they were there, hidden beneath high bodices and gowns without much shape, had seen them in the silk-and-feather ball gown she'd worn months ago at the art auction. He hardly needed a reminder of their existence. His body seemed to thrum to life around her, no matter what she wore. But pulling her onto his lap had turned the thrum into a bone-shattering vibration. It had branded new information into his muscles. He not only knew his body liked the *look* of her, he knew his body craved the *feel* of her.

Another benefit of thorough preparation. He would not be surprised by her feel, by his own heated reaction to it, when they touched in the coming days, when they embraced, when they kissed.

~

Cordelia did not like admitting she had jumped into a lake without knowing how to swim and might need just a bit of help. Someone to swim out to her, or perhaps row a boat in her direction. But here she sat, placid on the seat where she'd slept last night, feeling a bit odiferous, and looking out a window, *drowning*. And all because a domineering man had carted her up onto his lap and promised—no, threatened —kisses.

Of course, they'd have to kiss. Of course, they'd have to touch, even sit as they had sat mere minutes ago, so close, so terribly bone-singingly *close*. And naturally, her body had melted entirely. Become wet, doughy clay for him to shape as he pleased so long as he did so around those firm thighs of his, that hard abdomen, those chain-like arms.

She'd always known him to be handsome, but touching him changed things, granted her knowledge she shouldn't have, woke something inside her that asked for more, that wished to reach out and take it. It had been too long since a man had touched her. She'd thought to never desire the touch of a man again.

But now that he'd touched her, the desire prickled along her skin and tingled in her fingers.

How did an illustrator cultivate such a hard body? Shouldn't he be the doughy one from sitting all day at a table, hunched over a pot of ink and sheaf of paper? Her betrothed's body had been slight and slender and almost soft as her own, a painter with unfashionably long hair and eyes with a dreamy haze about them. She could no longer remember their color. Odd, that. They must not have been a memorable shade to begin with. Unlike Lord Theodore's eyes—pale gray and piercing, memorable.

But deuced inconvenient, like the rest of him, hard body

included. How would she remain composed, focused, alert with those large hands on her? How would she keep from fainting dead away if he kissed her? At least such reactions would sell their lie. If she seemed a woman affected by her lover's touch, it would be because she *was* a woman affected by this man's touch.

The coach slowed, and Lord Theodore—Theo she must remember to call him—was on his feet and out the door before it fully stopped. He disappeared into the daylight of the street, then his hand appeared in the entry. She hesitated. The shock of his touch, after all ... Yet, because of that, she must touch him. Touching him now, before they arrived at their destination, was a preparation she sorely needed. She took his hand and a tingle of awareness skittered across her skin. She'd known it would and still it shocked her. She wore gloves and yet they offered no barrier. Of course not when layers of clothing had not protected her from the heat of his lap. It must be that he did not wear gloves, and she could see his knuckles, the scar on his thumb, the ropey veins like netting across the backs of his hands.

She ... liked hands. Had liked to watch her betrothed's hands while he painted. Had liked the look of them on her bare skin. She'd thought them paintbrushes then, and now she knew she'd liked them so well for the beauty they created, liked them for the sake of his art, which she'd loved. Loved him for the sake of his art as well.

Lord Theodore's hands were different, as were the feelings they elicited. So much larger, tanned and beaten, offered a stark contrast to the other man who'd touched her with such familiarity. They were not beautiful. They were brutal. And the art they created did not rouse Cordelia's aesthetic appreciation so much as her discomfort. Yes, she liked the caricature artist's hands better than she liked his art. If Theo's hands were to splay across the span of her naked belly—

"Lady Cordelia." Lord Theodore snapped his fingers before her face. "You're not attending me."

She shook the vision, wanton and wrong, away and focused on his face. Ah, the gargoyle had returned, stony and expressionless. No, not expressionless. Pure annoyance vibrated round the edges. Excellent. That doused her rising lust quite handily.

"No, I am not, my lord." She studied the doorstep they stood on in a small but respectable street. The door they stood before, painted a vibrant blue, was framed by a gothic arch with sharp points soaring high above. "Shall we knock? This is the address, I assume."

He glared, and he did not knock. He strode right in, yelling, "Andrew, you cur, where are you? Andrew!"

"Stop yelling," she hissed, following him into the house.

He shrugged. "Best way to get his attention."

"You have no finesse."

"I have finesse when it counts." The words, low and dark, came with the hint of a growl that made her ache between her legs. What moments counted to him? She had to know. *When* did finesse count?

She leapt away from him, burned. Who was this man? A week ago, she'd been able to send him running with a saucy wink and a well-placed innuendo. Now he hauled her onto his lap and made suggestions that froze her like a single drop of air on a winter wind. From liquid to ice in a moment. But an ice with a molten core.

A woman appeared in the hallway, a furrow between her dark brows. "Lord Theodore. Only you would make such an entrance. You're lucky we are alone at the moment." Despite her stern expression, the woman had a warm voice, and she stepped to the side to usher them both into a room.

"Good afternoon, Mrs. Dart." Lord Theodore bowed before her, then passed through the door.

Mrs. Dart studied Cordelia. Cordelia studied her, following slowly behind him. Mrs. Dart was as neat and pressed as Cordelia was rumpled, not a fold of her brown muslin gown out of alignment, and not a hair out of place. A considerable accomplishment considering the sheer volume of said hair, the wildness of the tiny corkscrew curls. Somehow the woman had tamed them. Likely just by looking at them in the mirror and telling them to behave. She'd likely banish the freckles scattered across her nose and cheeks to permanent exile with a quirk of her brow if possible. She seemed the sort, tidy and organized in a way Cordelia deeply admired but could not quite emulate.

Cordelia bobbed a curtsy, then rushed into the room.

Mrs. Dart followed at a more sedate pace and circled a large desk in front of a curtained window, coming to a stop next to the chair. A man sat there, and if he hadn't been sitting, if he'd been standing like Lord Theodore on the other side of the desk, they'd have seemed mirror images. Same hair, though his eyes were blue, same broad shoulders and serious mouth. But the other man dressed better, as sharply as Mrs. Dart in fact. And his dark hair tended more toward sandy brown than black.

"Do you visit your tailor each week or each month?" Cordelia asked.

From behind the desk, Lord Andrew's gaze slid, slow yet steady, from his brother to Cordelia. "What is that you've brought with you?" He flicked his fingers in Cordelia's direction.

She bristled, felt like a cat, and wanted to claw him. Did she ... prefer the gargoyle to this other man? Surely not. But Lord Andrew was, impossible to believe, colder than Lord Theodore—Theo. Her Bromley brother at least had a simmering passion just beneath his stony exterior. This

Bromley brother had ... nothing. Pure ice, he was, and she shivered.

"That," Lord Theodore said without even a glance in her direction, "is Lady Cordelia Trent."

"Ah." Lord Andrew thrummed his fingers on the top of the desk. "The last of the leeches."

Her mouth dropped open. "I am *not* a leech." At least she was trying her best not to be. She tapped Lord Theodore, Theo, on the shoulder twice in quick succession. Hard. "And I'm *a woman*, not a *that*."

Mrs. Dart made a gurgling sound she quickly dominated before beaming at Cordelia. As if she'd said just the right thing to please her.

Lord Theodore acted as if she'd never spoken, as if her finger digging into his shoulder had been nothing but the brush of a fly. "Besides, what's the matter if I have a woman with me? You have a woman, too." He gestured, open palmed, toward the woman in question.

Mrs. Dart inspected her fingernails as if she refused to honor such a conversation with her attention.

Lord Andrew scowled, glanced over his shoulder? "Oh. Her? That's not a woman. That's my secretary." He grunted. "And the agency's face. You know that."

Mrs. Dart's expression, so indicative of happiness moments before, turned wild for a brief instant during which Cordelia feared Lord Andrew would soon be bludgeoned with a nearby vase. Thankfully, her expression quickly descended into scorn. She settled her scowl on her employer.

"The agency's face?" Cordelia asked Mrs. Dart.

"Everyone thinks I run it. He actually does. Needless to say, you should not reveal the truth to anyone outside of this room."

Cordelia pulled herself up tall. "Certainly not."

Lord Andrew stood and rounded the desk, ignoring

everyone but his brother, his arms wide and welcoming. "What brings you to Manchester, barging about like a bull?"

The brothers clapped one another on the back, rare and breathtaking smiles breaking across their faces. Unfair. They should warn a woman before doing that.

"I've business nearby," Lord Theodore said.

His brother sat him at a sofa near the room and then sat on the opposite side, leaving Cordelia and Mrs. Dart to stare at one another.

Cordelia inched closer to her. "We've been forgotten."

"Can one be forgotten if one is never noticed to begin with?"

"Ah, I see," Cordelia said. "You're a wise one."

Mrs. Dart sliced her a look like a blade that softened as her gaze wandered its way around the room and settled on the two men talking on the sofa. "I'm a foolish one." She faced Cordelia and stuck out her hand. "I'm Mrs. Amelia Dart."

Cordelia released the other woman's grasp. "I've never shaken anyone's hand before. How ... American."

"I spent part of my life there when I was young. Certain things stuck."

"Not the accent, though?"

"I can do that if it pleases me." Mrs. Dart spoke with a flat American accent and held an arm out toward the sofa. "Shall we join them?"

"Actually, if you do not mind, I would like to clean up. We have been traveling for two days, and we slept in the coach. I would like to be more presentable when we arrive at our destination." She'd like to look more desirable, too, like the type of woman who inspired sin and art at the same time. "Is there a place I could do so here? My valise is in the coach—"

"Of course. I'll have James, our footman, bring it indoors. You can go upstairs to the second room on the right."

"Thank you." Cordelia wanted to thank her, as well, for

not asking questions. She had her own questions for Mrs. Dart. A widowed female secretary pretending to run an agency? Fascinating. Thrilling. Terrifying. Cordelia wanted to be friends with her.

She found the stairs, then she found the room and slipped inside, followed quickly after by a maid with a pitcher of water, which she poured into a washing bowl on a dresser.

"Thank you," Cordelia said as the maid retreated through the open door, almost bumping into the footman who clutched her valise in his hands. "My, what an efficient household." The footman left, acknowledging her existence with nothing more than a nod. The door clicked closed, and she was alone for the first time in two days.

Unease crept up her spine, and she closed her eyes, listening for the sounds of movement in the house, the sounds of life, evidence she was not entirely alone—a door opening and closing in the hall, steps on the stairs, muffled yet deep male voices in conversation with one another, their words undecipherable. Good enough. She hauled in a breath. Not entirely alone.

She disrobed and washed as thoroughly as possible with the water from the bowl before donning the wrinkled gown from her valise. Wrinkled but clean. An improvement. By the time she'd dressed, but for the tapes at her back, a knock sounded on the door.

With flying steps across the room, Cordelia opened the door and found Mrs. Dart. "You are just in time to help me." She presented her back, relief coursing through her. Not alone. "Do you mind?"

"You *are* forward." Mrs. Dart stepped into the room and shut the door behind her.

"No use in being otherwise."

Mrs. Dart's fingers worked quickly at Cordelia's back. "There."

"Thank you."

"Shall we return downstairs?"

Cordelia nodded and followed the other woman. At the top of the stairs, she said, "I see you have a gargoyle, too."

Mrs. Dart did not miss a step. "What do you mean?"

"Lord Andrew. He's a stony sort. Like his brother."

"Ah. I see. I would compare Lord Andrew more to a block of ice. An entire tundra. But he can be charming when it pleases him. He is not mine, though. Rather, I am his. His secretary. As he explained." Did her voice take on an edge there?

"I think mine might possibly, deep down, be soft on the inside."

"Mine is not. Pure ice all the way through."

"A pity for you, I think. I look forward to cracking mine open." A surprising truth, that. The heat of lust that had wrapped her up earlier when he'd held her tight on his lap should have terrified her, sent her running, but her curiosity had been roused instead. Had he been as impacted as she had? He always blushed when she teased ... did that blush carry emotions other than anger?

Just outside the door to the room where they'd left the men, Mrs. Dart stopped, stopped Cordelia, too, with a light palm to her shoulder, which she quickly dropped. "*Is* he yours? Lord Theodore, I mean. I thought you were one of his father's projects."

"I ... I joke. He is, of course, not mine." Why did she feel so flustered? By the question, by the answer. "Not really mine. We are traveling together in a scheme that will be mutually beneficial. Nothing more." Nothing like, oh, planning to act as his mistress for the next fortnight. "And you? How did a woman come to be a secretary at an agency for educators?"

"I thought to be a governess. Lord Andrew recognized my many talents and kept them for himself. And when he realized expanding the agency required more discretion, he hired me to act the proprietress for him. He stepped out of the spotlight, and I entered it."

"Do you like your work here?"

Mrs. Dart glanced at the closed door at her back briefly. "I do."

"Very well. I shall not try to steal you away then."

A quizzical look.

"I'm organizing a charitable art school, and you would be wonderful help. I can tell already. Are you sure I cannot steal you away?"

Another glance at the door. "No. Thank you. It sounds a wonderful project." Mrs. Dart pushed into the room.

Cordelia followed.

Lord Andrew jumped to his feet. "You've returned. Excellent. I need the files on the woman we sent to Pentshire's estate a year or so ago."

Mrs. Dart bustled across the room, knelt behind the large desk, pulled open a drawer, and stood just as quick, file ready. She snapped it into her employer's hand. "Here you are, my lord."

"Excellent," he mumbled, opening the file. "The governess's name is Miss Sue Carter. She worked there until two and half months ago when she requested a change." He peered over the papers, sliding a pair of spectacles resting in his hair onto the bridge of his nose. "She did not say why."

Lord Theodore—Theo—leaned forward, attempting to view the documents.

His brother snapped the folder closed and held it out to Mrs. Dart who whipped it away and replaced it in the drawer. "Confidential."

"Of course," Theo grumbled.

"But I can contact her and see if she has any information on Pentshire she's willing to share with you." His lips thinned.

"I don't like it, though. I've not opened an agency to provide you with gossip."

Theo rolled his eyes and stood, scratching his fingers through his hair and seeing Cordelia for the first time. "You look better."

"Your compliments quite make me giddy, my lord."

He grunted, and it almost sounded like a laugh. "I'll clean up too, then we'll be out of your hair, brother."

Lord Andrew wrinkled his nose. "Please do. Clean up, that is. I can smell you from here. Once you're less odiferous you may stay for a meal if you'd like."

"No. We must be on our way."

"The house party, yes." Lord Andrew rounded his desk, sat once more, and Mrs. Dart took up a position that looked rather like her home behind him, a position she sank into with ease. "Be careful, brother. You're good at keeping secrets, and revealing them, but you've never been very good at lying." His gaze flashed to Cordelia, and he gave a tight nod.

Lying. Yes. She'd never been very good at it either. Withholding information, yes. Lying ... Her stomach flipped and she took a steadying breath. She'd do what she must, though, to win her home back. Even walk into a world she used to think she'd live in, a painter, her future husband by her side. That future had never come to be, and she'd grown grateful for it. But she could no longer be a *leech* as Lord Andrew had called her. She would not let a few weeks and a few naughty noblemen keep her from shaping her future for herself, from becoming a woman who saved herself.

Eight

T heo always hoped for gossip, but this time none had come his way. Still, Drew had promised to contact Miss Sue Carter, and that could provide insight into Lord Pentshire and his family. If they were anything like Theo's own family, there would be more than a few rumors to sift through.

He peered down at his notebook, open to a ripped page. He'd pulled an illustration from it just before they'd re-entered the coach in Manchester, given it to a flower girl selling wares on the street in front of Drew's offices. None remained now. His well had dried up. His pencil rested above his ear, ready, as ever, but he could think of nothing, not even a tiny sketch to hand to a Manchester child when they next passed through.

He'd barely had an idea, barely drawn a single scene since his father's death. Only a handful of satires drawn and published.

A problem soon to be quelled.

"Is that a moat?" Cordelia—why did he find it so easy to use her Christian name only?—kicked him in the shin with an outstretched leg. "Look, Theo, look. It's a moat!" She'd changed into a lavender gown of some sort and had knotted her hair simply at the nape of her neck below her bonnet. She appeared young and innocent, and he was carting her into a den of iniquity to parade her as his mistress.

If he didn't need this so much, he'd never do it. She had her own reasons for coming here, though. A reassurance, that.

Yet he hated his soul anyway and peered out the window, feeling darker than a storm cloud. "What in blazes is that?"

"A moat," she offered.

"Not that. The *house*."

"Well, you've rather answered your own question there, haven't you." She tried to suppress her grin. The corners of her lips bounced up, eager to escape.

"Yes, it's a house, but good God, what kind of house?"

"Old. And surrounded by a moat."

The house likely dated to the sixteenth century or older and had been built in the timber-frame construction of that time period, the wood used to make a dizzying array of patterns that made the house seem like something out of a fairy story. The first floor extended wider than the ground floor, and it ... leaned, looking rather like a cake about to topple.

"A witch lives there," Theo grumbled. "It's absurd."

"Absurdly charming."

"You just like moats."

"And who doesn't? That's what I'd like to know." Her grin escaped, made a wild landscape of joy out of her face, and the coach crossed a narrow rock bridge to cross the small body of water and entered an empty courtyard.

"Are you prepared for this?" he asked as her ease disappeared, and she lifted her hand to chew on her thumbnail, a nervous gesture he had the strange compulsion to soothe.

She dropped her hand heavy to her lap with an almost determined exhale. "I am."

"As soon as we disembark, we—"

"I know. The playacting begins."

"If I do anything that goes too far, tell me. I won't ... I do not wish to hurt you."

She gave him a smile, a curious little quirk of a thing that made his stomach flip over. "I know, you soft thing, you. And never worry"—she winked—"I'll let you know if you do something I cannot abide. Do you know, you're quite easy to imagine in armor, sitting atop a horse. Have you ever tried? You'd make an impressive sight."

She mocked him. But before Theo could do a damn thing about it, a footman opened the door and held his hand out to help Cordelia down.

She reached for it, but Theo reached her first, taking her hand for his own and holding it tight.

"Apologies," Theo grumbled at the footman, lifting her hand to his lips. "No one touches my muse but me." He kissed her knuckles. Covered by thin cotton gloves, the warmth of her skin still bled through, and her scent, too, tickled his nose.

Her hand fisted for a moment before loosening. She did not shake him away. "My apologies as well, Mr. ..."

"Mr. Trembly," the footman said.

"Mr. Trembly. Lord Theo can be a bit of a bear when it comes to me." She patted his arm, squeezed it.

And Theo tried to respond with some pleasant expression, but he found the muscles rusty. Thank God he had no mirror to view the spectacle that must be his tortured face.

Cordelia saw, though. Her eyes widened, and she coughed. To cover a laugh?

Theo addressed the footman. "I'm Lord Theodore Bromley, and this is Lady Cordelia, my ... wife."

The footman snorted and spun toward the house. "They

all say that. Follow me, please. At least you didn't try to claim her as your sister. One fellow did that this morning. Then kissed the woman right on the lips. Not even trying, is he?" The footman, long strides eating the distance across the entry hall, snorted again. Wood paneling soared upward on all sides, and windowless walls gathered shadows around them.

"It's rather dark," Cordelia whispered, her body shifting closer to his.

He squeezed her hand, still holding it, using it to wrap their arms together as if they were accustomed to closeness with one another. He touched her, held her, to protect her. Nothing else. His body, relishing every damn minute of the closeness, ignored good sense and pulled her nearer.

Mr. Trembly glanced at them without breaking stride. "Lord Pentshire is in the withdrawing room. This way."

The withdrawing room proved brighter with more modern windows that looked out onto a knot garden. Three couples sat scattered across the room in little groups.

"Lord Theodore and Lady Cordelia," the footman announced. "Husband and wife." Another snort, his words drawn out with all the suspicion he likely possessed in his entire body.

And all six of the room's inhabitants looked up, including Pentshire, who stood and bowed. "Lord Theodore, welcome. With your arrival, our party is complete." He crossed the room, bowed so low he almost kissed his knees, then popped up with puppy dog grin for Cordelia. "Quite lovely, aren't you?"

"Don't you have your own muse?" Theo drawled.

"Certainly. Come meet her." He led them across the room, and the woman he'd been sitting with stood. She had yellow hair and delicate features and a low-cut bodice threatening to rip under pressure. Buxom was an understatement.

"This is Miss Mires. Maria, my love, meet Lord Theodore and Lady Cordelia."

Theo bowed, Cordelia curtsied, and Miss Mires giggled.

"She's a farmer's daughter."

"I am." Miss Mires frowned, regarded Lord Pentshire with narrowed eyes and downturned lips. "But I'm *more* than that, Tommy."

Pentshire kissed the top of her head. "Indeed you are." He turned to Theo. "Do you wish to meet the others?"

Introductions happened quickly. Baron Armquist and his mistress Mrs. Meredith Bexford, an actress. Mr. Trevor Castle and his wife. A merchant and a lover of oil paints.

"The other guests," Pentshire said, "are about somewhere, and I am sure you will meet them in time." Lines bracketed his mouth as if something displeased him. "Everyone has already begun to break into little groups. There's one walking the grounds and another in the gallery above stairs."

Mr. Castle bowed deeply when introduced. "I apologize for my rather tame circumstances. No mistress to speak of." He took his wife's hand and smiled softly at her. "I found it best to secure my inspiration by taking my muse as wife when the opportunity arose."

Unless the man hid a deviant spirit behind a jovial façade, he seemed a trustworthy fellow. Theo would keep close to Mr. and Mrs. Castle, leave Cordelia in their care so he could rummage about the estate, spy a bit, keep his focus where it should be—on his work. And hopefully they would prove not only protection for Cordelia, but the sort of connection she'd need to fund her school quickly.

"Did Pentshire say your name is Bromley?" Mr. Castle sidled up to Theo, glass of wine in hand.

Theo stiffened. "He did."

"And was the Marquess of Waneborough your father?"

Theo nodded. "We attended his house party the last year of his life. He was a kind man. Brilliant too."

"It is so good to hear someone else praise the marquess." Cordelia finally stepped away from Theo's side, close to Mr. Castle.

"Did you know him?" Mrs. Castle asked Cordelia.

Theo knew two things in that moment. His initial instinct about the couple had been true. And if he didn't find a corner to hide in or a glass of wine to pour down his throat, the deluge of praise for his father would kill him. Absolutely not an exaggeration.

"Pardon me, Mr. Castle," Theo said, "but where's the wine?"

Mr. Castle gestured to a bottle on a long table at the side of the room, and Theo found it, poured a glass, and returned. Too soon, apparently.

"I've never met a kinder man," Cordelia said. "So full of passion and generosity."

"Full of something," Theo mumbled into his wineglass.

Cordelia raised a copper brow, stole his wine, sipped some between her full pink lips, then handed it back with a wink.

The Castles and Cordelia ignored him.

And her wink muddled him, as it always did, so Theo sipped his drink, his lips touching the glass where hers had, and studied the others—Pentshire with his armful of a farm lass and Lord Armquist and his actress. Theo had read about her in the papers. Used to scandal, she was.

He wished the other guests were close to hand to see how likely it would be to gather usable gossip from them. But if Armquist and his actress were any indication, the other guests would prove just as scandalous. The house party itself would prove so beyond the pale he'd be able to live off the gossip gathered from it for years.

"Pentshire," Theo called out, "what is this to be like, then? This little gathering?"

He smelled Cordelia before he heard her, felt her arm brush against his. "Be less obvious, Theo darling." She spoke so low through gritted teeth he barely heard her.

Pentshire strolled over, his arm around Miss Mire's waist, and the baron and his actress joined them.

"Yes," Armquist said, "do tell. Where are we to set up our easels?"

"Wherever you'd like," Pentshire assured them.

"When we were guests at the Marquess of Waneborough's party," Mr. Castle said, "we were provided much entertainment."

Theo snorted. That entertainment had cost more money than they'd actually had. Maggie's dowry had been poured into the pockets of violinists and tightrope walkers. His tuition money for Oxford had similarly disappeared, as had his future as a clergyman. Not that he'd been overly excited about it.

Cordelia pinched him. He glared at her. She smiled in return. He downed the rest of his wine because he wanted to kiss her. *Kiss her.* And why? He couldn't rightly say but that her every grin and tease and wink crept beneath his skin. He swore she tried to make him *laugh*. And he ... almost felt like he could, even with the conversation of his *dear sainted papa* echoing about the room. He should have left his father's final letter at home, or better yet, slipped it into Zander's luggage so he could take it back to Briarcliff. But he'd put it in his satchel, resting it against the charcoals and sketchbook. With all this conversation of his father, he'd not be able to move without thinking of the letter burning a hole through the worn leather of the bag. At least he'd left the satchel in the coach to be unpacked by the footmen.

The drink had clearly gone to his head. Why else would he

be obsessing over the dual plagues of Cordelia's lips and his father's letter? He finished the drink and slammed the glass down on a nearby table.

"Yes," Mrs. Castle said, "we were also given tasks, challenges, and opportunities to learn from and teach one another. Will we have the same here?"

Pentshire nodded. "In all ways, this will be a better experience than that provided by the late marquess, and the only of its kind now that the new marquess refuses to continue the tradition." Raph inviting all of England's artists into his own home. Not bloody likely. Raph *hated* artists. "But," Pentshire continued, "we shall have a more intimate group here, with all the challenges and intellectual pursuits you could desire. Our first challenge, for instance ... Would you like to hear it?"

"Absolutely." Mrs. Castle leaned forward, her eyes lighting with anticipation.

Theo rolled his eyes.

Cordelia tugged on his arm, drawing him closer and cupping her hand around his ear. Her breath tickled, and he tried not to think of tongues and teeth and sensitive skin.

And failed.

"You must act," she whispered while he died of desire, "as if you enjoy these sorts of things."

Her breasts brushed against his side, and he snapped, control gone in an instant as he cupped her neck and crashed her body into his then crashed his lips onto hers. What reason had he to do so? None. But what had he to stop him? Nothing.

A gasp rose up around them in six different voices, then settled into chuckles. To hell with them. They'd all done worse, and he couldn't currently remember why this was bad. Kissing her. In a room full of people.

She'd likely remember, though.

She froze. For a mere moment. Then she melted, her lips

parting on her own small gasp, an inhalation and exhalation that introduced her taste to him. The spice of the wine they'd shared. She should taste that way—rich and tart and ... hell ... *wonderful*. Soft lips, the perfect shape, and when she leaned into his hand cupped at her cheek, when she made a little mewling sound hopefully only he could hear, his body urged him on faster, harder, begging to take her bottom lip between his teeth.

This he enjoyed. So much more than he should. This he'd been aching for since the day he met her, and she'd put the idea into his head—she could be his mistress. A quite unfunny joke. Because to have her under him would be a bloody miracle. To have her body lying alongside his at night, keeping the lonely away, a heaven.

But solitude he enjoyed too. Solitude he *needed*.

So he ended the kiss, pulling away just enough to rest his forehead against hers. Their hands still tangled, he held her tight, watched her with open, wary eyes until she opened hers.

She made a sound—half choke, half gurgle—and stared at him with wide, wondering eyes. "What was ... that?"

"The wine." Only excuse he could offer that didn't reveal his eternal weakness—things of beauty held him in thrall, and she had more beauty in a single eyelash than he'd seen anywhere else in the world. And every damn moment he spent near her increased it.

"Forget the challenge I had planned," Pentshire said, his words shattering the hold Theo had on her. "Let's do *that*."

"What do you mean?" Miss Mires asked.

Pentshire stood beside Theo and Cordelia, arms spread wide, lips wide, too, in a never-ending grin. "Kiss, of course. But better than that. Let us *paint* a kiss."

Mrs. Castle scratched his temple. "Would be difficult for two models to stay arranged just so for such a length of time."

"No." Pentshire's head shook with vigor. "Let us kiss, then paint what it *feels* like."

Lord Armquist groaned. "I don't paint feelings. I paint things. And people. The proper subject of paintings."

"I like the idea," Mr. Castle countered. "I'll do it." He took his wife's hands and pulled her close, kissed her. "There. Now, to my paints!" He dragged his wife out of the room, the both of them laughing like children.

Theo released Cordelia entirely and pulled in a breath to clear his kiss-crazed mind. Focus. He must focus on his purpose. And these people were making achieving that purpose rather ... easy. They seemed to feel safe here and with one another, behaving with ease in ways the ton would censure. Theo would merely have to be present to collect his gossip.

"What about you, Lord Theodore?" Pentshire waggled his brows. "Will you kiss again or—"

"No." Theo strode for the door, leaving Cordelia behind him. "I'll retrieve my charcoals." He couldn't kiss her again. He might never stop. Gathering gossip might prove easy in the next fortnight, but danger still threatened in the warm sighs and soft lips of Cordelia's kisses.

When he returned to the entry hall, charcoals in hand, he followed a couple slipping into a small side door and found himself in a narrow spiral staircase, stuffy and smelling of dust and stone and bodies pressed too close. The very top opened up to a long gallery, windows stretching the entire length. Cordelia sat at the far end near Mr. and Mrs. Castle, pointing to something on Mr. Castle's canvas.

He almost hated to intrude. She looked happy. He was a frowning imposition on anyone in a good mood. How many years had it been since he'd created anything other than satirical drawings? The art he'd done before, the type of art he'd learned from his father and used to love—it had no true meaning and purpose. It existed, was beautiful, but achieved nothing. He pressed the heel of his hand to his chest where it ached. He had to paint without purpose for two weeks. No more. He could pretend he enjoyed it as he had then. Theo marched through the milling throng of artists. Cordelia was acting. So could he.

She looked up, and her happy smile slipped slightly, her breath catching, the teeth darting out to bite at her bottom lip. Thinking about the kiss? Hell. He shouldn't have done it. But two days of travel and the way she'd sipped from his wine-glass ... he'd crumbled.

"I'm glad you've joined us," she said when he reached her side. She nodded at Mr. Castle's canvas. "He's already begun. What will you draw, my lord? To depict a kiss?" Her words existed somewhere between flirtation and curiosity, and he wanted to keep her guessing a bit longer.

He took a seat beside her, opened the beaten box that held his notebook and charcoals, and set everything up to his convenience. Then he looked at her, charcoal in hand, and considered the challenge. To draw a kiss without drawing a kiss. An impossible task created merely to drive him mad with longing. What good did it do to paint the feeling of a kiss?

"What do you think a kiss looks like if not two bodies pressed together?" he asked.

"You ask me?" She laughed. "You know I cannot help you."

"You may not be able to draw a straight line, but you have a brain. Tell me."

She looked startled for a moment, her lashes fluttering swiftly, then she swallowed hard but held his gaze until her eyelids closed, pale and striated with the dark red-gold of her eyelashes. That. That was a kiss—the close of an eye, the discovery of sensation and raw possibility in the dark of the self. His hand dropped to the notebook and began its movement across the page, needing to draw, no matter how useless, how silly.

Here—in the sweep of his hand across the page—the real danger: he had a bit of his father in him still, a bit that enjoyed beauty and the creation of it. But he'd long since put his talents to better use. He would not at the end of two weeks find himself trapped.

"I think," she said as he sketched, "a kiss might look like a ... a pause. The moment just before lips touch." Each word more breathless than the last as his own hand flew faster with the charcoal, leaving the shape of her eye, the strokes of her lashes, the idea of movement, the eye having just fluttered closed. "A pause between the lips, too. That makes no sense. I mean that the lips open. Just a breath. Anticipating ... They pause before the storm arrives."

A kiss as a storm then. Theo threw the page he'd been working on aside and scratched his charcoal against a new page, smudging its clean surface with the flat of his hand as well as with the chalk. Thunderclouds and lightning. No. Wrong somehow. He threw it away.

"A kiss is not a storm," he grumbled.

Her brows drew together. "No? Hm. No. Perhaps you're right. It's warmer, isn't it? Like a blanket wrapped round you."

"Hell. I've no idea how to draw that." He threw his charcoal into his box and flopped backward in his seat, flipping the page with her eye over to study it.

Her eyes popped open, and she leaned over. "Oh. Is that ... my eye?"

"It is."

"It's so large."

Mrs. Castle peeked over Cordelia's shoulder and pointed. "Rough, Lord Theodore, but clever. You caught the lover's form in the reflection of the eye. So we see the kiss coming as she does."

Cordelia leaned closer to the paper, gasped, and shot upright. "How immensely clever."

He ruffled a hand through his hair. "It's nothing."

Several others wandered by to look at his work, and Cordelia beamed at him the entire time. How could he converse with her staring at him as if he'd just pulled the moon out of the heavens and gifted her with it. And over a damn drawing. Nothing more. Nothing good or—

"Do you know Mr. Simon Oakley, Lord Theodore?"

Theo looked up. He did not recognize the man who spoke to him. "No."

"Ah, well, he's a friend of mine. A painter, and I've seen him use this trick—using a reflection to show something unexpected."

"Anyone could do it," Theo said. And they had. It was nothing special.

"Did *she* tell you about it?" The man's focus narrowed on Cordelia.

"No. Why would she?"

"Ah. Well, excellent interpretation of a kiss." The man backed away, eyes scanning the crowd for a conversation to join, an easy escape from the uncomfortable Lord Theodore.

Cordelia would tell him to be nicer. He turned to face her lecture head-on and found her frozen, her mouth slightly open, no easy breath lifting and dropping her chest. She'd paled.

He placed a hand on her wrist where her pulse beat rapid as a rabbit's run. "Cordelia?" No reply. No movement. He wrapped his hand around her wrist, squeezed. "Cordelia. Are you unwell?" Words spoken in a gruff tone that turned to gravel the next he spoke. "What's happened? Do you know that man? Tell me or I'll—"

"I do not know that man. But I know Mr. Simon Oakley." Her lips barely moved when she spoke, and her voice wavered.

He knelt before her, taking both her hands in his. Cold, they were, and trembling. He cupped her cheek in one hand, forced her to meet his gaze. "Tell me."

She licked her lips, and her eyes darted side to side before settling back on him, heavy as a winter coat. In the end she stood her ground, as he'd come to expect from her. "He was my betrothed."

Betrothed. The word a slap in the face. No, a hole in the street he'd stepped into with no warning, the one that twisted his ankle and threw him face-first into a pile of horse dung. The word a secret blown wide open. He unclenched his fingers, realizing with the small flinch of her lips that he squeezed her too tight, and sat back on his heels.

He'd been worried about bringing her here, guilt-ridden they could not hide her identity in some way. He'd told her about Sir George. And the entire time she'd been hiding something from him. She'd been betrothed. What other secrets did she have that could harm their purpose here?

"I want to know more," he finally said, keeping his voice low and his touch light. She nodded, and he returned to his seat, picked up his notebook and chalk and stared at the blank page.

"Yes. Of course."

She'd been engaged, but that told Theo nothing. Had she cared for the man? Why were they not now husband and wife? Had this happened before or after his father had all but adopted her? He had no information of much value. But he could be patient. He set his charcoal to the paper and pretended to watch the lines he drew there. Her eye the shape of a kiss? Ha. For some other man, perhaps, but not for him. He should remember that. Beauty always deceived.

He would not let the siren call of beauty distract him from

his purpose here. He would not lose himself in art and creation. He watched the others, waiting for something explosive, something that would make the ton twitter.

When he felt like the explosion had happened right beside him, inside the body of the calm beauty with the regal tilt to her chin who he couldn't look at without thinking about a kiss.

Damn.

Nine

The clink of cutlery and the flicker of candles in the chandelier above the long table cast a golden glow over the dinner guests, and though everyone around Cordelia chatted and laughed, she did not. Could not. Was too busy plotting, planning—panicking, truth be told.

Was London too far away for walking? Perhaps Lord Pentshire would not care if she stole—erm, borrowed—a horse. Yes, she'd contemplate larceny to escape her current predicament, to escape the cold, calculating, sharp-as-a-pin gaze of Lord Theodore. Theo.

The man who'd kissed her before God and every guest of the house party. For no particular reason. Perhaps he meant to throw her off balance, to prepare her, as he'd said in the coach. Perhaps it had been meant as revenge for all her winks and innuendos. She regretted them now.

She'd thought she'd been prepared for a kiss. She'd not been. Not for the warmth and strength of it, the patience and the brimming promise burning just beneath that. Not for the firm shape of his lips or for the hush of his breath. Not just on her lips. But everywhere too, somehow. She'd suspected it before—a softness in him, hidden well. And the kiss had given her a peek at it. Because he'd kissed her to calm her. It had felt like protection, and she'd wanted to grasp his lapels and haul him closer, to part his lips with her tongue and show him she knew more than he likely thought she did.

It had been much too long since she'd last been kissed. A clear conclusion considering her reaction to such a tame offering. She should kiss men more often, so she did not become so obsessed afterward. She glanced at the lips of the guests. There were more assembled for dinner than she'd met that afternoon. At least a dozen guests sat on one side of the table and another dozen on the other. None of the lips she could see from her seat beneath the chandelier compared to Theo's. She snuck a glance at them—chiseled, a lovely pale pink, quite soft, she now knew, yet firm. Kissing him had been an experience in contradictions.

Much like knowing the man was proving to be.

Why did she feel so compelled to seek out the hidden softness in him? Even if she did discover a lonely, longing center similar to her own, what good would it do? No good at all. But a gargoyle high above, perched upon a ledge, always watching but never participating must be lonely, and she knew loneliness well, hated to see it calcify anyone's heart.

If only his heart was truly calcified, but she did not believe that to be true. She pressed a hand to her heated cheek and reached for her wineglass, passing her arm over plates and cutlery as the guests at the dinner table chatted on every side.

A tinkling of glass as Pentshire stood, clinking his knife on his wineglass. "Attention!" The low roar of dinner chatter quieted as everyone turned to their host. "Thank you," he said. "I believe we should all retire to the parlor for drinks and joviality, but first, I would like to explain the schedule for the next few days. I have taken the initiative to fill the gap caused by the loss of the late Lord Waneborough's yearly art party. I even have one of his sons here to help christen the event." He lifted his glass to Theo, who tried to smile but ended up merely looking like he'd smelled something horrid.

"As many of you know, I am a patron of the arts, though not one nearly so generous as old Waneborough was." A chorus of disagreement rose from the guests, and Pentshire settled them down with open palms and a gently raised voice. "I do what I can, and while you are here, what is mine is yours. If there is anything you need, do not hesitate to let my—to let Miss Mires know, and she'll make sure your stay is one of utmost comfort."

An awkward silence, then Pentshire started again. "I give to you all not only these two weeks of learning and creating before us, but also"—he paused much longer than necessary—"a prize."

Gasps, discomfort forgotten.

"What kind of prize, Pentshire?" Armquist demanded.

"A rather large one," the earl said. "A thousand pounds to the artist who produces the most stunning body of artwork from our two weeks together."

Whistles and murmurs and whispers rose around them.

Cordelia leaned close to Theo and whispered, "If only I had an ounce of talent, I would go after the prize myself."

He grunted, studying his wineglass, around which his long, nimble fingers wrapped, spinning the glass by the thin stem and making light dance around the dark wine.

"But"—Pentshire raised his voice and his arms to quiet them all down—"your work must come from the challenges set daily to be considered for the prize."

Theo's fingers tightened around the stem of his glass, his knuckles showing as white as the tablecloth they rested on. "Do you think," he hissed from the side of his mouth, "that he has the funds to offer such an enormous sum without beggaring his family?"

The poor man wore his every emotion on his sleeve though he tried heroically not to. Of course he'd feel sensitive about such expenditures. But her endeavor—her school— required them.

Pentshire downed the rest of his wine. "Nothing adds fire to artistic creation more than a little bit of competition. Now, if we're done here, drinks in the parlor!"

He led the rest of them out, Theo and Cordelia trailing at the back of the group. Her arm had hooked into his, and though she looked up at him, she did not fully turn, so she saw only his stubbled jaw, tight and sharp against his black cravat.

"Theo?" Her voice a whisper.

"Yes?"

"I think I'd like to retire now." She should stay and converse, begin discussion of her school and see who showed the most interest. But the discussion of Simon Oakley had shattered her a bit, had stolen her focus away, her confidence too. "Do you think anyone would be offended if I, *we*, retired early?"

Hopefully he understood what the *we* meant. That she had to tell him about her past. She should have told him the moment she knew she traveled toward a house filled with people who might know her former betrothed.

She made her way up the narrow spiral staircase they'd used before dinner to find their rooms and freshen up. Each couple had been put in a corner of the house, secreted away for privacy, and though she and Theo had been given separate rooms, their doors sat at the same corner of the house and practically opened into each other. They reached the top of the staircase, and he opened the door to her bedchamber, ushered her through then followed, shutting the door tight behind him.

She paced away from him to the end of the low-eaved room and sat on her traveling trunk. Her feet ached. Her shoulders ached. Her head hurt a bit. The narrow bed in the corner had room enough for two, and it called to her. She toed her slippers off one by one. Who cared that she should not do so in a man's presence. Especially when that man was not her husband. She'd done far worse in her life.

Simon Oakley, for one.

Theo leaned against a bedpost. His gaze, steady and strong, felt like a physical touch. She squirmed beneath it, stretching her toes and wiggling them within her stockings. She did not want to relive this, but she must.

"How come you've never insisted I tell you how I came to be under your father's care?" she asked.

He shrugged a single shoulder, scratched at the back of his neck, and provided no answer.

Very well, then. If this was not to be a conversation, she could handle a monologue. "Every tutor and instructor your father sent to the house assumed the same thing at first—that I was his mistress. Then, I think, their minds wandered toward the idea that I was his illegitimate daughter. They became a tad kinder to me at that point. But they remained suspicious. Naturally, I suppose. Eventually, thankfully, they did not appear to care about the truth of my identity. They merely liked ... *me*."

She paused, pointing her toes and rolling them under on the hard floor. Lord Waneborough had always sent her kind people. Even when they'd been suspicious, they'd never hurt her with words or actions, never gossiped about her with others, at least in her hearing. They'd protected her.

"For their kindness," she continued, "I am ever thankful. I'm grateful, too, for your father's kindness in finding patient instructors to teach me." She snorted. "*Attempting* to teach me. It is not their fault they had such a talentless student." She interlocked her fingers together and looked to him.

He watched her, stony as ever, arms crossed over his chest, looking too big for the small room.

"You have never suspected the same of me?" she asked.

"I know my parents." His voice sounded gruffer than usual. Enriched by the wine? He scratched his jaw and let his arm fall. "I can see how others, who did not know my parents well, would think you were his mistress or the product of his liaison with a mistress. But anyone who had intimate knowledge of them would never think that."

She smiled. "I understand. He brought your mother to meet me once, and they were so wrapped up in one another, they never stopped touching each other. Little touches. And when they couldn't, their gazes always found another." As if they were each other's home.

"I'm bitter about many things."

What an odd response to her observation. "No! Never say, my lord."

"And one of the things I can find no faith in is love. It is too much like beauty—deceiving, blinding. That's the kind of love my parents had—blind, loyal to a fault. My parents loved one another so much they could not say no to one another. My mother wanted a house party, my father gave it to her. No matter the strain on our finances. My father wished for another statue, and my mother did not say no, even if it meant they had to dip into my sister's dowry. You do not love someone that much—to the point of destruction—and then give yourself to another."

She flattened her feet on the floor. When he put it that way, it didn't sound much like love. But what did she know, never having experienced it?

"My brothers," he said, "all look on that relationship as the one good thing our parents ever did for us. I don't see it that way. Their love ruined us. Had either of them loved each other slightly less, perhaps my father could not have done so much damage."

"And I am a part of that damage. With my two hundred pounds a year and my lovely little townhouse?" Not hers for long.

Silence, as loud as a roaring river rushed between them.

He did not have to respond. They both knew the answer to her question.

She swallowed and tucked her feet beneath her skirt. She couldn't stop there. "Even though they wondered—all of my instructors, you understand—about my relationship to your father, and why he supported me as he did, I never told them. Not a single one of them. Not because I'm ashamed, though I'm supposed to be, I know. But ..." Heat flushed across her cheeks, and she cupped them to hide the blush, took a deep breath before continuing. "I did not tell them because I liked the idea that they might think me his daughter." She winced. How mortifying. She'd been missing her own father terribly when the marquess had found her and saved her.

"If you had been his daughter," Theo said, "he would have brought you home to Briarcliff. Had you been alone and in need ..."

She risked looking up at him.

His eyes were softer than she'd ever seen them before. "I'm frankly surprised he did not bring you to Briarcliff, daughter or not."

"Better to be in London and attempting to do something to earn my keep." Did she truly believe that? London had been so very lonely, even with instructors marching in and out every day. The two remaining people who had professed to care for her—the marquess and his wife—had lived so far away, visited so seldom. She curled her toes and swept the questions away. "Though I admit ... it has been a bit lonely at times."

He grunted. "You? Lonely? Every time I step foot in that

house, you've a circle of people around you, every room filled." She liked to keep it that way, keep voices always echoing nearby so she did not have to remember how she belonged to no one, and no one to her. Not really. "You're not telling all." His jaw twitched. He'd grown impatient. "You've gone in circles round the real story. Your betrothed?"

"Simon Oakley. Four years ago. My father contracted the union at my request. And then ... we anticipated the wedding night." Best said without hesitation.

She waited for the reprimand to come, for him to storm out of the room. A man who lived to reveal others' weaknesses and secrets ... she should be running, hiding her secrets where he could never see, never draw them up to lay before greedy ton eyes. Not an option any longer. She held his gaze, daring him, showing him his judgment would not faze her.

He bounced off the bedpost, stalked toward her, and with a slight spin, sat next to her on the trunk. He braced his elbows on his knees and steepled his fingers together before him, hanging his head. His hair hid his eyes, and she could not see what truths his face might hold.

"And then?" he asked.

And then. Such simple words, a gentle request. No judgment or name calling. No haughtiness or abandonment. Just simple human curiosity.

She breathed deep, letting the air fill her lungs, letting his two words—*and then*—guide her forward.

"And then my father died," she said with a shaky exhale, "and Simon wanted nothing more to do with me."

Theo's knuckles turned white as his steepled fingers wove together to make a praying fist. "Why?"

"My father had many connections, but no heir. The title died with him. And I learned that Simon had wanted more to be the Earl of Crossly's son-in-law than Lady Cordelia's husband. Simon wanted connections to the ton. Young and promising painters with little money and no connections of their own must start somewhere. He'd thought marriage to an earl's daughter a miracle, a blessing. But marriage to an orphan with no living family ... a burden."

Theo cursed and shook out his hands.

She continued. "When an alliance with me could no longer provide him with what he wanted, needed, he did not wish for the alliance."

"And how does my father fit into this?"

"Your father supported Simon, who prided in telling me—and anyone who would listen—that Lord Waneborough had called him a 'rising genius.' It was all a happy coincidence, really. The day Simon told me he would not marry me, your father happened to visit. He found me sitting outside Simon's front door, crying." There's where the shame rushed in. She'd been so weak, so alone and helpless. "He asked what ailed me, and when I told him ... I wasn't really thinking. I just poured all my troubles out to him. I should not have, I know. I expected nothing from it. But after I did, your father marched into the house, and a quarter hour later, marched right out again, picked me up, and told me that everything he'd promised Simon as his new patron was now mine. The two hundred a year, the house ... what was meant to support a rising talent in the art world was wasted on talentless me. I suppose your father thought it fitting retribution."

The sinewy hands resting on Theo's thighs bunched into fists. "Let me see if I understand this correctly." She held her breath. Here it came. The censure. The lecture. The venomous disapproval. "Simon Oakley slept with you." She nodded. "Then your father died." She nodded. "And then Simon Oakley abandoned you?"

She didn't nod this time. She ducked her head to hide her tears. Silly things. Silly her. She had not cried over this in years. "You see," she said, speaking into her shoulder, "I am, in the end, the perfect woman to bring to this house party. Fallen quite thoroughly. All the way down. The only reason every bone in my body is not broken from the fall, the only reason I do not currently work in a brothel or as a pampered mistress in the demimonde, is because your father saved me. At the risk of his own reputation, really. I understand why you hate him. I think if I'd had a father so careless with our blessings, I, too, would wear a scowl as you do."

"*If* you'd had a careless father?" He stood slowly and glared down at her. "What about your dowry? Where were the close friends to look after you? Did he truly leave you so unprotected?"

She swallowed, bit her lip to rival the pain of the truth in her heart. "He had a solicitor."

"Why didn't you turn to him? I assume no one knew you'd laid with your betrothed."

The frustration, loneliness, despair from four years ago welled up within her as if it were new. She jumped to her feet. "Have you ever felt desperation? I have! My lover had thrown me out. My father dead. No family to speak of. Simon told me everyone knew I'd ruined myself, said he'd told many and no one would want me. And"—she began pacing—"I was a naïve girl. A fool perhaps, but I believed him. Have four years taught me the truth, taught me he is a lying scoundrel not fit to hold a woman's heart? Yes, but I can still feel that girl in here." She stopped before him and pounded a fist to her chest. "And she was *so scared*. And there before her, like a good fairy, stood a kind man promising to do her no harm. Should I have thought of the solicitor? Oh, yes, of course. Absolutely." Her words were crisp and practical and could not even begin to hold back disdain cut through with burning pain.

Silence, then he said, "He ruined you." No need to say who *he* was. His father.

"He didn't mean to, Theo. And I am as much at fault as

he was, as I've so recently explained. I have done as best I could in the intervening years to educate myself, to arm myself so I do not fall prey to young artists and philanthropic marquesses. Do not pity me."

"I don't. But I blame him—both of them—whatever you might say. Does this Mr. Oakley yet live?"

Something in his voice spoke of fists and bones, of blood and blades, and she almost lied to him. But he would not seek out her former betrothed. For what reason would he do so? To punish him? Ha. Lord Theodore? Who had a soft center he hid quite well ...

"Yes, he does. As far as I'm aware. We've exchanged not a word since that last day together. You know, now I speak of it out loud, it's rather ironic, is it not?"

His head tilted, his jaw hard. "How so?"

"He left me to cultivate social connections, and now I must cultivate my own. We are rather alike in the end."

"No, you're not." Theo stood. "Will you be well? Will knowing his acquaintances are about, may bring word of you back to him, keep you from doing the work you came to do here?"

What had she expected from him? Comfort? Ha. Men like him did not know how, no matter how soft their centers.

"Of course," she assured him. "I will not let you down." She should stand and press close, wink and ask for another kiss, disarm him as she always did, but she slipped away from him, showed him her back. "You do not have to worry about me."

For several moments, he did not move, then bootsteps stomped toward the door, which opened then closed, and he left. Without even a good night.

She collapsed on the bed, too tired to undress. But sleep never came. It never could in new places where she felt most alone. When she'd first come to Lord Waneborough's house, she'd not slept for weeks. So she'd lay in the dark and repeat the same words over and over—Simon does not matter, and she would win her house. She lost count of the number of times she'd said it, thought it, prayed it, when the sun appeared as a dark-orange glow on the horizon below an early-morning navy sky.

Boots outside her chamber door snapped her upright, but no knock came. Instead, a square of paper slipped beneath her door. The floor felt cool on the soles of her feet as she padded over to retrieve the paper, then found the window to inspect it. A note, no name on it, but clearly meant for her. Shoved under her door and all. In the dim morning light, she unfolded it.

And she laughed.

She ran her fingers over the detailed sketch—a scene from *A Midsummer Night's Dream*. Titania, the fairy queen, and Bottom in the moment she realizes he's nothing more than a braying ass. And while it clearly depicted Titania, it also clearly resembled Cordelia. Though the illustration of Bottom looked nothing like her former lover, a name had been scrawled beneath the illustration—Mr. Bottom Oakley. The man's teeth had been exaggerated out of all proportion, and donkey ears grew out of his hair, which had been styled fashionably but ridiculously so, a mockery of the style the man who had spoken to her about Simon yesterday had worn.

Titania's hair was exaggerated as well, but not in a way that mocked her. It curled round the entire scene, ensnaring a small figure in the bottom corner of the page—a knight on horseback holding a lance. He'd included the small mole she had on her right temple, too. And Queen Titania spoke to someone out of frame, not drawn but hinted at. Oberon, perhaps? She said, "Has he always been an ass?"

Oberon, if she spoke to him, likely nodded yes.

Cordelia laughed again.

Had this truly come from Theo's hand? From his imagination? It must have. It could only have come from him. But there was such a lightness to it, a levity he never showed in person, no matter how much she teased. The dark, angry strokes curved around the sketch of Bottom, but every other object on the page had been penned with a light touch, graceful, playful, light—something she'd never expected from him.

The humor of the sketch was the least of its wonders, though. Yes, it was expertly drawn, but more important than that as well, was the *why* of it, its reason for existence. He'd drawn it for her. To make her feel better, to put into the world the ideas he could not speak out loud. He'd left her room last night in silence, asking only reassurance that she would keep her end of the bargain, but then ... this. She'd glimpsed his softness before, but the drawing offered proof. She should be pleased for the man, for his immortal soul. But she found herself more pleased for herself.

She hugged the drawing to her chest. Lovely little thing. And made just for her. And after the unrelieved loneliness of last night, it shone like a ray of sun right into the loneliest regions of her heart.

Ten

P lans had changed. Theo had known he'd have to play protector, and he'd known he had in some way dedicated himself to Lady Cordelia's cause by bringing her here. But now that he knew why his father had picked her up and wrapped her up safe, now that he understood how utterly careless her betrothed and his father (despite his best intentions) had been with her, he wouldn't, *couldn't*, treat her so carelessly himself.

He must protect her until she found another to do so.

And he would win her that damn prize money.

He checked the position of the sun in the sky as he marched back toward Holloway House. Still early morning, and hopefully his investigations in the nearby village had not kept him from the party's next challenge. He'd let the curate keep him too long at the garden gate with hints of scandalous gossip that had proven to be nothing Theo didn't already know—the Earl of Pentshire had taken up with the dairy farmer's daughter. Ruined her. Certainly the perfect subject for a caricature. He could envision something with cows in it. But he could do better. He'd not settle on anything yet, would sketch multiple options to see which *Ackermann's* preferred.

Too bad he'd not yet found evidence of financial mismanagement, servant abuse, or baby-blanket stealing. After he'd slipped his drawing under Cordelia's door, he'd searched every room not occupied to no avail, even Pentshire's personal study. He'd found only perfectly kept account books that showed an estate in fine shape, particularly its dairy farm. Suspicious, that. Was Pentshire paying the farmer for ... *use* of his daughter?

He'd find out.

But first he needed to find Cordelia and the others and see what artistic challenge faced him today. And see if Cordelia had liked his drawing. He'd not known what to say last night. Still didn't. But when he'd lain down to sleep, he'd begun sketching in his mind instead. Then his fingers had itched, and he'd been unable to let the idea remain in his brain. As he'd put it on paper, he'd discovered what he should have said —*Oakley is an arse, and you deserve better.*

Did he really believe that? It appeared he did. He'd been wrong about her all this time. She was the woman his father saved instead of saving his children, yes. But she'd not controlled his actions. She'd been in need, deserted and alone. And his father had given her what he could. An odd surge of gratitude rose in him. He wasn't used to it. He preferred to think only of the man's ills. But he'd done something *good.*

Theo cracked his knuckles, his steps quickening.

He was headed toward the house when he heard laughter from the gardens around the side. It was a nice day, an abundance of sun, the guests were all artists, and the house, with its old windows, was shadowy and dark. They had probably set themselves up under the open sky. Theo rounded the house and found an arbor with climbing rose vines set behind a knot garden and guests scattered about in various positions. The men stood at easels, and the woman stood or sat in front of the easels however, Theo assumed, the men had placed them.

Cordelia sat in what appeared to be a comfortable wicker chair in a small circle of guests who'd made an island for themselves amongst the rest. As they worked, she regaled them. "And then, when it became clear he would not tell me just how bad my efforts had turned out to be, I went along with it. So for two months, my watercolor instructor thought that *I thought* I was a genius."

"How did it come to an end?" Lord Pentshire asked, flicking his paintbrush into the air so that a drop of paint hit his model, Miss Mires, on the cheek.

She flinched and glared at the earl. He winked, wiped it away with the pad of his thumb, his soft gaze melting hers.

"I could not bear," Cordelia said, "to let him know I had been making fun the whole time. So, I let him go, told him my genius no longer needed instruction."

Pentshire threw his head back with a guffaw and wiped a tear from his eye. "That's rich."

"Poor man," Theo said, stomping through the gaggle of artists and striding straight for Cordelia. "I've seen your watercolors, and they—"

"Are more water than color?" she provided.

He grunted, grabbed an easel leaning against a tree, and popped it open before connecting a bit of paper to it.

"Watercolors are not for everyone," Mrs. Castle said. "A woman as bold as you should find a bold medium."

"Life is her medium," Theo said, kneeling near Cordelia's chair and retrieving his box of charcoal. "Thank you," he said looking up at her, "for bringing my supplies down. My apologies for my lateness."

"I expected you to keep your distance," she said, voice low and a bit wavering, "after last night."

"Not at all. I merely needed a walk this morning.

Cordelia ..." He gripped the edge of her chair just next to her leg. He could feel the heat of her but did not dare touch her. No one here would bat an eye. Beside them, Lord Armquist pushed a tendril of hair from his muse's face and took his damn time about it, fingers lingering on her jawline. To the other side, Pentshire's muse smoldered at her baron, pressing her breasts together with her upper arms. No one would care if Theo touched Cordelia. But he could not because she was to be protected, not used.

He cleared his throat and tried again to say what he needed to say. "Cordelia, we are going to win that prize money. For you." He'd find his scandal here. Of that he had no worries. But her ... everything about her situation worried him. More and more every damn day.

She raised a brow, and it flew like a stroke of red paint up her forehead. "Are we? You are that good an artist?"

Frankly, he had no idea how good he was. He'd done nothing but caricatures for years now. Was he good at sketching ridiculously, exaggerated things? Yes. No doubt of that. But could he do what Pentshire needed the winning artist to do—show the soul with a brushstroke—perhaps not. The thought terrified him. He'd long since attempted to cut his work off from the soul, from beauty, from those things his father used to rhapsodize about. Those things he had once taken seriously himself.

He could flirt with them once more to help Cordelia win.

"Well?" she prompted.

He had no answer he could give her, so he stood, the garden air rippling over his exposed skin like her breath had across his neck—fragrant and warm. He returned to face his easel, which he placed right before the chair. He pulled a pocket watch from his waistcoat pocket. "There's still a quarter hour till noon, so morning will do. Now be still, Delia my dear. Pentshire, what is the assignment?"

"We've decided to keep it simple after last night's more difficult challenge. A portrait is all. That captures your muse's best quality."

He stared at her, frowned. Best quality? He liked her hair, all wild and long and that deep, deep shade of copper that seemed impossible.

Cordelia laughed, throwing her head back and exposing the long, strong column of her throat, elegant and creamy. Perhaps that was her best feature. He certainly seemed fixated with it. He opened his box and placed a bit of charcoal in his holder, and started there, putting the line of her neck onto the paper then, when she tipped her chin back down to stare at him with amused eyes, he sketched the round dip of her chin. That bit of her good too. Somehow quite, *quite* kissable.

Hell, he should not be thinking about kissing her.

"What amuses you so?" he demanded. Better to grouch than lust.

"Why, you of course. You're looking at me as if you cannot find one thing to approve of."

His turn to laugh because he couldn't find a damn thing in her to disapprove of. "The exact opposite is true. I cannot decide which good quality to emphasize."

"Shocking! Do tell."

What a mischief maker she was. He suppressed a sudden, unwanted smile.

"What can you find to approve of in a talentless woman like me?"

How many times had he heard her call herself talentless? He'd seen her room. He knew she had not an artistic bone in her body, but to so carelessly and ceaselessly throw herself away as she did just because she couldn't draw ... It made him want to rip something in two.

"Talent comes in many forms," he said. He faced the Castles, who sat just behind his right shoulder. "My muse,

Mrs. Castle, may not be able to count art as one of her skills, but she is an artist nonetheless. She shapes the world around her till it gives her delight and satisfaction. She needs no tools as we do. She uses her wit and her cunning and her charm."

Mrs. Bexford chuckled. "Do you tread the boards as I do, then, Lady Cordelia? Are you an actress?"

"Not at all," Cordelia assured her. "Lord Theo is ..." Her gaze softened yet still somehow bore a hole right through him. "He is teasing me." Said as if she could hardly believe it.

"I'm not," Theo assured her. "It's precisely what you do. You meddle until things are as you wish."

She huffed. "I prefer the way you said it the first time."

"You organize," he continued, "and you inspire."

Her chest stilled on an inhale, and her lashes fluttered as a rose-scented wind stole across her cheeks.

He stepped back and studied the drawing so far. He'd caught her eyes when she'd been gazing at him intently, shocked he'd teased her. No tease, though. Mere truth, and something he rather liked about her, too.

"Can I see?" she asked.

He nodded, and she stood, joined him on the other side of the canvas. She stretched out a hand and traced the lines of herself without touching the charcoal. "It's ... lovely," she said. "But you've made my hair a bit wild."

He leaned down to speak into her ear, pushing a tendril of that wild hair out of the way. "I deal in exaggerations. And that's the best bit of you I wanted to bring out." Just one of them, the one that featured in his dreams, waking and sleeping.

Her breath caught.

He pulled away an inch to see her eyes, those brown pools like honey in the sunlight then stood and returned to his easel, picking up the charcoal and revisiting the lines of her face. He focused on finding the perfect curve for her eyes and the bow of her upper lips, tried to capture the slight upward flight of her brows, the gleam in her eye just before she winked at him.

"Theo." Her voice husky, begging.

"Hell." He dragged in a raw breath, then faced her.

Her smile broke, likely because of his grim expression, but she pressed on. "Thank you."

"For what?" he asked, ripping the charcoal down the page as he returned his attention to the deepening sketch.

"*A Midsummer Night's Dream* is not my favorite. I prefer *Much Ado About Nothing*. Yet ... it eased the pain of old memories. Thank you." Such sincerity in her voice.

His hand trembled, and he stared into the eyes of the Cordelia taking shape beneath his hand. The scent of flowers climbing into his lungs like clinging vines—did that come from the garden flowers or from her? She always smelled of some sort of flower, fresh and warm.

"Lord Theodore, do you not use color?" Mrs. Bexford asked from nearby.

"No," Theo answered.

Mrs. Bexford chuckled. "Do you smile at anyone but your muse?"

He threw a glance at Cordelia and frowned. "No." He'd not even meant to smile at Cordelia, but he'd not been able to stop it. Rather like indigestion.

"A shame," Mrs. Bexford said. "You'd have a lovely face if you smiled."

"You're not supposed to appreciate the loveliness of any face but mine, Meredith." The baron stabbed his paintbrush into an orange square of watercolor and then stabbed that onto his paper.

"Use the jealousy as inspiration, darling," Mrs. Bexford said. "You do your best work when under its influence."

"No need for jealousy," Theo assured the man.

"Mrs. Bexford," Cordelia called out, "I saw you in London at the Theatre Royal ages ago. *Macbeth*."

"And? What did you think?" The actress said it as if she didn't care for Cordelia's opinion. When she clearly did, taking peeks at her though she sat with her profile to them.

"Magnificent."

"Don't grin like that, Delia," Theo said. "You're throwing the portrait off."

She stuck her tongue out at him, and his cock jumped with interest. Damn it all to hell.

Mrs. Bexford's cheeks glowed pink. "Thank you. I am rather proud of that run. Though you mustn't call that play by its name in my presence."

"What shall I call it, then?" Cordelia asked.

"The Scottish play. Old superstition."

"I'll abide by your wishes."

Mrs. Bexford narrowed her eyes at Cordelia. "Will you run away if I tell you, my lady, that we were all talking about you last night?"

"I shan't run. What were you saying?"

"That"—she leaned in close and looked about the garden —"Mr. Bradley told us about his friend, Mr. Simon Oakley, your former betrothed. Quite the scandal." She spoke in a whisper with quick glances thrown over her shoulder toward another group of artists, Mr. Bradley at their center.

"I would appreciate it if all of you minded your own damn business," Theo growled. "Particularly Mr. Bradley."

Cordelia reached a hand out to him. "No, Theo, it's of no matter. Better to be out with it. Yes, Mrs. Bexford, it was scandalous."

"The way he treated you is the scandal," Theo muttered.

"Mr. Bradley," Lord Armquist said, "had ungentlemanly words to say about the matter. But I don't believe them."

"That's right, dear." Mrs. Bexford beamed at her paramour. "We cannot judge when we are not perfect ourselves. It's why we've settled our easels over here with Pentshire and the Castles. Bradley's a good artist but not the kind of man we associate with. Our scandal is miles above your own, as I'm sure you've heard, Lady Cordelia."

Cordelia shook her head. "No, I've not heard. I'm rather ... isolated ... socially. I've acquaintances but no true friends to gossip with. Ah, er, but for Lord Theodore, of course, and he does not gossip a bit."

Theo snorted. The vixen. Of course he gossiped, but he did so with ink and paper and for a reason.

"You don't know?" Mrs. Bexford asked. "Shall we tell her, Ronny?" She blinked at Lord Armquist.

He shrugged. "As it pleases you."

"Should you wish to know?" Mrs. Bexford asked Cordelia.

She grinned. "I shall take Lord Armquist's strategy and say as it pleases you."

The actress beamed. "The baroness introduced us."

Theo slung his head around to look at her. "There are many. Which one?"

"*Lady Armquist.*"

"H-his wife?" Cordelia tried not to look shocked, but the growing circumference of her eyes gave it away. "Or his mother?"

"Wife." Mrs. Bexford's head bobbed like an apple in a bucket of water. "Theirs had been a union of convenience, and she and I were girlhood friends. She thought we would suit, and she wanted to see the both of us happy. I suppose we are now. In our own unconventional way."

Theo picked up a new piece of charcoal. "You're saying you have his wife's blessing?"

Mrs. Bexford made a purring sound, a hand brushing the bare skin above her bodice. "Oh my, yes. I tell you only because it's a very well-known secret already."

Lord Armquist stepped back from his painting and tilted his head, studying it. "Elsie—my wife, that is—travels with a *personal footman*. A fellow she's known for a decade."

"And I travel with Ronny here," Mrs. Bexford added, "and but for small, occasional visits in London, we live our separate lives. You did not know? You had not heard the whispers?"

Hell. He hadn't. The charcoal became dust in his fist. "What about children?" Theo demanded. To put them into such a situation—

"We don't have any," the baron replied, "and never will. Any of us."

"But your estates—"

"Will go to my younger brother. And then to his son."

"Ronny's brother has three beautiful boys," Mrs. Bexford said with a gentler tone than he'd heard from here before now. "Though we don't get to see them. Except from afar. In the park if we happen to meet." Her gaze sharped and the dreamlike haze she'd sunk into dropped away. "Ronny married for money so that his brother could marry for love." She looked down at the knitting frozen in her lap. "All is as it should be."

Perhaps in some ways. Not in others, though. Mrs. Bexford clearly did not approve of all aspects of the situation.

"But surely," Theo said, "your brother was not trained to manage the estates."

"Of course he was!" Behind his mustache, Lord Armquist bristled. "We were trained since childhood. Together at Father's knee. Taught to do what was best for the estate, for those in our care. For me, that meant giving it all up to my brother." He reached for his lover's hand, and she reached back until their fingers tangled together, wove a deep pattern, a heart beating outside of their bodies.

"You're sure you didn't know all this?" Mrs. Bexford asked. "You're not very good at gossip are you? I must not be either, or I'd have heard of the marquess's son sleeping with his dead father's mistress."

Another lump of charcoal gone to dust, his palm a dusty, dark cemetery. "Where did you hear *that*?"

Cordelia laughed, a brittle thing like a leaf in autumn. "Is that what Mr. Bradley has been saying?"

"Everyone here is talking of it. I'd heard rumors before that the Marquess of Waneborough had a pretty little thing hidden away, but with no evidence, I scarcely believed it. But now ..." One of her brows lifted high.

"What else is Bradley saying?" Theo asked. He pinned his gaze to the man, imagining the ground opening up and swallowing him. No, Theo did not wish that. He wanted to pummel the man into the ground himself. No sudden geological shifts required.

Bradley must have felt Theo watching him; he turned toward Theo, nodded an acknowledgment, then leaned close to his mistress and whispered something in her ear. Then his attention flitted to Cordelia, and the mistress's did, too. Her hand flew to her mouth, and they laughed, not even trying to hide their mirth nor the object of its arousal. Cordelia.

Theo's fists itched. "Tell me what he's saying," he demanded again.

"That she stole the marquess's patronage from Simon Oakley," Armquist said, his face a scant inch from his paper, paint splattered across his cheek.

"I did not." Cordelia did not drop her gaze or let her shoulders droop.

How could he protect her from this? She clearly did not wish to discuss her past, nor to discuss Simon, but if she did not, the rumors would continue.

"It's horrid falsehoods," Mrs. Castle cried. "I've known your late father, Lord Theodore, and he was not the sort to have a mistress."

Mrs. Bexford hummed. "And a man so old with a mistress so pretty doesn't leave her to rot alone in London 364 days of the year. And my dear friend Sophie, who gives voice lessons, worked with Lady Cordelia for an entire year. Said the marquess visited only once that she could tell. And everyone knows he rarely left the country."

"Just so." Mrs. Castle looked like she might spit if she saw Mr. Bradley.

Cordelia's hands gripped the arms of her chair like claws. "Mr. Bradley does not understand the true story, but I will not speak unkindly of Mr. Oakley."

"That's sweet," Miss Mires said. "You're kind, Lady Cordelia."

"Just the sort we want here," Pentshire said.

"I'm done." Theo snapped his chalk down.

Mrs. Bexford on his one side and Mrs. Castle on his other craned their necks to view his work.

"Admirable," Mrs. Castle said.

"You're no Turner," Mrs. Bexford added, "but there's a fierceness to your style that catches the eye. You've expressed something vulnerable in her, I think."

Mrs. Castle nodded.

"No!" Cordelia leapt from her seat and joined him, almost pressed her face entirely to the paper. "I don't see it."

Had he caught something fragile about her? He'd not meant to. He did not see her that way. Except for last night when she'd laid her past before him, her stockinged feet peeking out from beneath the hem of her skirt, her toes curling and uncurling when she could not meet his eye.

Perhaps he'd put a bit of that in her.

But was that the best thing about her? Did the drawing fulfill the requirements? Hell if he knew.

"I don't think we should worry about Lord Theodore,

Ronny dear," Mrs. Bexford said. "He's good, but he'll not provide much competition for the money."

Pentshire threw his head back with an obnoxious but merry guffaw. "God, but I love a good cutthroat competition."

Theo wanted to hit him after he was done with Bradley. What would giving a thousand pounds to some artist achieve except for amusing the earl?

A hand slipped around his wrist, a slight presence then a squeeze. Cordelia looked up at him, squeezed his wrist again. "Breathe, Lord Theo. I think it's an excellent drawing." She followed the outline of her eye in the drawing with her thumb then tugged him toward the edges of the garden, away from the others, stopping beneath a shady bower, wisteria hanging over their heads.

"It *is* good," she said, letting go of his wrist and pacing away from him. "I've produced enough bad art to know good when I see it. I think you've made me look rather dreamy, not vulnerable. As if I were in love." She gave a huff of laughter. "Vulnerable. In love. They may be something of the same thing."

Theo stuffed his hands in his pockets. "I don't believe in love."

She startled, tilted her head, and the wind picked up a strand by the slope of her neck, played with it before it died down and dropped it to rest a red splash against her pale skin. "Do you know ... I'm not sure I do either. Romantic love, that is. But ... I would like to find evidence of it. And I think perhaps they are it." She pointed her chin toward the group they'd just left. "Lord Armquist and his actress. They took long looks at one another at different times all morning long. As if they could not stand to look away from the one they love. 'Tis a pity their lives are so complicated."

"They do not seem to care."

"Do you often draw as you did this morning?" A bit of purple flower fluttered from above to land in her hair.

He picked it off and flicked it to the ground. "No. I used to. When I was young. I gave it up when I realized it was no good."

"I think you're very good."

He shook his head. "Not me. Art itself. It does nothing."

"It creates beauty, does it not?"

"What does beauty matter when the world is so ugly?"

She ducked her head and toyed with the cuff of his jacket. "Do you truly believe that? I know there is much injustice in the world. I lost everything when my father died, and I had no power to take care of myself outside of doing what I am glad I did not have to do. I think I tease about being your mistress, about joining the demimonde, because it could have been my reality, and teasing about it takes its power away. I know the world is not as I would like it to be, but ... I'd like to think there are happy endings, too. Even if they do not happen for me."

Everything about what she'd just said—utterly wrong. She should not have lost everything. She should not have lacked the power to fend for herself.

He snapped a bit of wisteria from a branch and twirled it. "I gave up on happy endings long ago. At the same time I gave up on the sort of art they expect here. But I ... I used to think as they do. What a fool I was, a selfish fool to spend the first sixteen years of my life thinking I could be an artist." He found the end of the bower, putting more space between them.

"What happened? To convince you otherwise?"

"I found out about my father. My older brother had kept the reality of our situation from me until I was, to his estimation, old enough to know the full extent of our debt." Theo scratched his jaw. "Perhaps my grandfather shares some of the guilt. He did not train my father to care for the estate, believing his eldest son would always be safe. A foolish optimism."

"Why must optimism be foolish? And why must you blame anyone? Living as if you expect those you love to die is silly indeed. Assigning blame will not change the past. Nor will it change the present that you live in."

"You're an optimist, too, aren't you?"

A silly half grin popped up the corner of her lips. "I am."

"I am not. Optimism has proved a waste of time in the face of reality. I was sixteen when I found out about my father, and my brothers had all taken on various work to keep the family afloat. Raph did what he could to keep the estate running despite not yet being the marquess, Atlas joined the army and fought his way up the ranks, Drew was working as a tutor and organizing his agency. And there I was, thinking I could spend my life painting, being *optimistic*, thinking I might live out my father's dream of attending the Royal Academy of Arts. Ha."

"Creating something beautiful hurts no one, Theo." She stepped toward him, her hands rigid at her sides as if she could not determine what to do with them—wrap them round herself or reach for him.

"Perhaps not. But it doesn't keep a family fed and housed. My father put art above his family, and I'll not do the same. I'd rather die than waste my life as he did."

"Your family has not conceded defeat. They've not given up. That's optimism at its finest." Her face sobered, and she looked away, back toward the group of gathered artists, her rigid arms softening as she clasped her hands together before her. "I do not think your father's life a waste."

Theo hissed a curse and flicked the wisteria away. He'd hurt her saying that. "Not an entire waste." He stepped forward and held out an arm. The man had saved Cordelia, after all, and Theo could not deny the value of that. Not any longer.

She took his offered arm, and he drew her closer, close enough to tip her chin up with his knuckles and drop his lips to hers.

Somewhere nearby, a bee buzzed, but it felt like the buzzing of his blood along his veins as he sipped from her. A ruse. The others looked on, and they stood in a picturesque location. A kiss was a necessity. For the ruse. He'd been soft the first time, and he remained so now, but deepened the kiss nonetheless, licking the seam of her lips until they parted, then he stroked his tongue inside gently. Her body swayed toward his, and he wanted to crush her to him, to double—triple— the points of contact on their bodies, until no space remained between them.

His sign to end it. He took one last nip at her bottom lip, then lifted from the kiss. Her eyes were closed, her breath soft, as she tilted her face up to him, wearing a dreamy smile. What had she said about the painting? That he'd made her look dreamy? As if she were in love?

Hell.

No. Not a worry. Neither of them believed in such a state.

Not waiting for her eyes to open, he drew her arm through his and led her back to the group. He collected his charcoals before leaving her with the Castles. He wanted her someplace safe when he hunted down Mr. Bradley.

Eleven

Why did Mr. Bradley stare at her as if she'd just belched loudly enough to knock the room from the house? A touch of disgust there she could not ignore. Was he still upset about Simon? He seemed to have quieted his gossiping tongue since the first day of the party, but she'd had to endure his silent looks since then, and on two nights of fitful—at best—sleep.

She should have retired after dinner when Theo had, but the prospect of another sleepless night staring at the ceiling had sent her running for the parlor with the other women, sent her bouncing into a chair near the window of the crowded room because that was infinitely safer than not sleeping in a room so close to his. Each night she'd stared at the ceiling, some wicked voice inside her had whispered that she did not have to be alone, that a man slept just beyond the thin wall, and that if she asked for his help, he'd likely give it. Because he was the secret Sir George, slayer of dragons; not a saint, but still a knight of stout heart and fierce courage.

But she knew the wicked whispers' motivations—the kiss in the bower beneath the wisteria. It had been too much and

136

too little at the same time, had made her crave more. Though what use was more? She'd learned the hard way that pleasure was a delight, but it meant nothing in the end. Men gave their bodies without promises, and a woman such as her, with no clear future in sight, needed promises more than pleasure.

Best to avoid her bedchamber as long as possible.

Even if it meant she must suffer Bradley's uncomfortable stares. Could he not focus, instead, on the woman draped across his lap? Or the cards he played with three other fellows?

"Do you know," Mrs. Castle said, settling into a chair beside her, "Mr. Castle and I discussed Lord Theodore's school last night, and we are both terribly excited. We do not have much, but we would like to donate enough for a yearly scholarship for one child. I know that does not help Lord Theo fund a new building, but it takes a bit of the worry off, yes?"

Cordelia blinked her attention away from Bradley and pressed her hands to her heart. "Oh, how wonderful. Yes, that is more than enough. You are so very generous."

"I'm sure Lord Armquist and Pentshire will help as they can, too."

"Lord Pentshire has already pledged an amount to go for a scholarship as well." Lovely to find so many who admired her scheme, but none of it helpful for her pressing needs. They seemed to want the honor of having a scholarship named for them, and as the house, the school itself, would take its name from the late Lord Waneborough, their donations could not bring them notoriety in that way. "I was just about to speak with the viscount, Lord Ellsby." She nodded toward the man sitting in the corner, his muse near to hand, both of them reading. "Do you mind if I abandon you here?"

Mrs. Castle waved her away. "Do as you need. And good luck! Though if you ask me, Lord Theodore should be the one soliciting donations, since it's his school." She sniffed.

"Yes, well," Cordelia said as she stood, "I am terribly excited about it."

"I suspect you are his muse in this, too."

She opened her mouth but found nothing to say so forced her silent lips into a smile. "Just so."

Lord Ellsby did not look up as she approached, though his muse did. A little blonde woman with spectacles perched on her nose. She blinked, and the glass magnified her large brown eyes.

"Ellsby, that woman's here."

"I see," Ellsby said, his nose still deep in paper and ink.

"Lord Ellsby, I just wanted to tell you how lovely your paintings of Mrs. Pruitt are."

"Thank you," Lord Ellsby said, but the words were cold. He did not mean them.

But Cordelia would persevere. "And Mrs. Pruitt, I am in awe of your ability to sit still for so long. It quite astounds me. I'm so very fidgety—"

"It's no accomplishment," Mrs. Pruitt said. "I am an artist's model. I must sit still." She rolled her eyes up to look at Cordelia. "And so must you learn to do or find yourself out on the streets."

"Out of Lord Theodore's bed," Lord Ellsby muttered, "but not on the streets. She has that house."

"Ah. Yes." Mrs. Pruitt returned her attention to her book. "If only all of us were so lucky."

Bradley's gossip, no doubt, had poisoned them against her, but they did not know her yet. Surely she could win them over. She sat in a nearby chair and folded her hands in her lap. "The house you speak of is truly only mine until it is made into a school." Mrs. Pruitt's eyes flashed to her, a hint of curiosity there. "An art school for those less fortunate. For anyone, truly, but our mission is—"

"Our?" the viscount asked.

"Lord Theodore's actually." Blast. She must train her tongue better. But she was so very tired, she could not get her tongue to do anything particularly articulate. "It is his school. I am merely an enthusiastic supporter." What an injustice that he could champion a school and she could not, that her association with him might make her an inappropriate headmistress for a school while his with her did not harm him at all.

It did not matter that the associations were pretend only. Theo should draw a caricature about *that*.

"If you wish the school to succeed, Lady Cordelia," Lord Ellsby drawled, "then it would be best if *you* stopped speaking of it."

A gasp rose in her chest with a sharp breath, but she refused to let it out. She knew well his implications. "Have I offended you, my lord?" she asked instead. "If so, please tell me how, so I may make up for it."

He waved a hand at her. "Your presence offends."

Not much she could do about that but leave, and that she would not do. At least not until the party ended. Naturally. But that hardly signified at the moment. She swallowed a yawn and forced her mind back on task.

But time, like her opportunities, drained away as Ellsby rose to his feet on creaky knees and held out his hand for Mrs. Pruitt. "Come, my dear, let us join Mr. Bradley for cards."

Then Cordelia was alone. She searched the room for another corner of conversation, another opportunity for her school, but everywhere she looked, others looked away. The cold shoulder. The cut direct. Perfection.

She rejoined Lady Castle and sank back into her chair. "It seems I am not welcome here."

Mrs. Castle patted her shoulder. "All of us have felt the sting of disapproval at one time or another. Ellsby and Pruitt are not free of scandal. They merely think theirs is less scandalous than others." Mrs. Castle sniffed. "They are not worth knowing."

"People generally like me. I try hard to make it so."

"Don't mind them. No one here is better than anyone else, though some of us have titles and some do not. We all live a middling sort of life. The things we create admired by the ton, but our own selves cast off. You seem to have accrued the things they want—house, funds, protection—without possessing the skill they do."

"Lord Waneborough did not save me for my talent," Cordelia whispered, guilt curling her insides.

"I know. It was impossible to meet the man and not see the kindness simmering in him. He could be a bit flighty and forgetful, but he wished to make the world better. Thought art the way to do that."

"He made my world better." Art had as well. No matter the man's faults, he'd got that part right.

"Ah, yes. But also, perhaps, put you in a difficult position. Your association with him, vague as it is, hinders your ability to marry within the sphere you were born to. And his treatment of Simon Oakley colors how those in *this* sphere view you. I do not envy you." She placed a hand on Cordelia's shoulder again, squeezed it this time. "You look exhausted. Retire now and get some sleep. I've no doubt your Lord Theodore will champion you, whatever happens."

Cordelia stood, nodding and smiling, though her very soul trembled. Lord Theodore was not her champion, not really.

Yet, as she marched up the ever-spiraling stone staircase, she could not shake the feeling—like a ghost—that he *was*. That if she told him she needed him, he'd give of himself to do so. It must be the lack of sleep that made her feel such falsehoods were true. Her door creaked open, and she slipped out of her gown and into her shift with the ease of cream pouring into a teacup. Her body had become liquid, malleable, but as soon as her head lay on the pillow and she closed her eyes, her body popped awake. She pressed her eyes tight, attempted, as she had every night since coming here, to empty her mind and find some peace.

She found only the buzzing electricity of loneliness. She rolled onto her back and opened her eyes. No use closing them now. The ceiling above her bed remained the same as it had been the last three sleepless nights. Dark, still—the perfect surface to play over the moments of her greatest loneliness in life. When her father had died. When Simon had abandoned her. When she'd agreed to live in a house alone with no friends nearby to keep her company. When the first art instructor quit after three weeks of tutoring. When she'd heard of Lord Waneborough's death. When she'd met Lord Theodore, and he'd told her she must leave her life behind.

He'd brought with him news of change. But only of scenery because, for her, nothing could ever truly change. She would always be alone; would never have the husband and children she'd once dreamed of. When she'd been an earl's daughter and not a marquess's mysterious scandal.

She might not even have a school. She'd amassed promises of donations, but not enough. And if the others banded with Mr. Bradley as Lord Ellsby had ... She'd likely end up a companion to Lady Balantine after all. Unwanted, accepted only out of charity and pity.

Lord Theodore would help her, though. Theo. Who kissed like welcome sin. And suddenly, she wanted kissing very much. Kissing to ease the ache of loneliness. Kissing to drown out thoughts of solitude. But if he kissed her now, she might very well fall asleep on him.

Horrid thought, that.

Kissing would be nice, but she desired nothing more at that very moment than sleep.

She slipped her legs over the edge of the bed and grabbed

her wrapper, donned it, and rested her bare feet against the cold floor. They took her into the hallway after the deafening creak of her opening door, and they took her to stand before his bedchamber door, holding her wrapper tight across the front of her body with a white-knuckled fist. She took a deep breath. She must do this. She had no one else to ask for help, and in her current state, she could not continue playacting for him or charming the other guests for herself.

She knocked, a sharp rap before she let her hand hover just inches from the door, waiting. Then she knocked again, and before she could finish, the door swung open, and Theo stood tall and—she swallowed hard—shirtless in the frame, his hair falling over his brow, his eyes hazy from sleep, ink smudged on his large hands.

She pushed past him, taking advantage of his confusion to gain entry.

"Cordelia?" He closed the door—no squeak from his hinges, only the barest click of the lock in the frame. "What are you doing here? Are you well?"

The night outside his window glowed black as pitch, the clouds from a dreary day blocking the stars. She faced him. "I would like to sleep with you. Or you with me. Doesn't matter, really, as long as I'm not alone."

No moonlight in the room to see his reaction. He offered a dark outline only. Unmoving. Then he cursed and crooked an arm, lifted it, the outline of a bunched bicep popped into view as he ran a hand through his hair.

"You're not alone. Your room shares a wall with mine. There are dozens of guests nearby."

She shook her head. "Not enough. When I first moved to your father's house, a housekeeper, maid, and cook were all employed, and one of them slept in the house every night. I was never alone, but ... I did not know anyone. No one knew me well enough to care what happened to me. If I died in my sleep ..." She shook her head, wrapped her arms around her, and turned back toward the window. "When I'm alone like that, my mind runs away with me. No, that's not quite right. It locks me up inside myself, reminding me that alone is all I'll ever be. It's ... suffocating."

The warmth of a body pressed against her back, and Theo's voice rumbled near her ear. "I would care." A huff. "Get in the bed, then, damn you."

She turned.

Horrid idea.

Because his chest was *just there* now, his collarbone at eye level, the broad expanse of shoulder so much clearer so close up. Despite the dark. She dug her fingers into her forearms to keep from doing as she wished—reaching out, touching, placing a kiss.

She ducked and darted around him, dove into the bed, and that, too, was a mistake. The pillow, the sheets, the quilt—they all smelled of Theo. She inhaled, held the scent of charcoal and paper and soap in her lungs, waited for the weight of his body to join her.

Instead, she heard the rustle of paper as he put away his drawings and then the scratch of chair legs across the floor.

"Theo? A-aren't you going to ... join me?" Perhaps just one kiss before she sank into oblivion.

He stopped the chair by the bed and propped his feet up. "I'll sleep here. Near enough you can find me if you need me." He crossed his arms over his chest and slumped lower, letting his head fall backward to rest on the slight cushion.

"Theo, I think—"

"Sleep," he grumbled.

She sat up, fighting the pull of the warmth, his scent, his presence. Irritation had banished the desire for a kiss. "I *will* be listened to."

"*Humph.*" His eyes still closed, his arms till crossed.

"I am asking you this favor, but I will not deny you comfort. If you do not get in this bed this instant, I will march back to my room." To prove her point, she swung her legs off the side of the bed.

His hand clamped around her wrist, and his body half stood, hovering over her. Then he moved, slowly, pushing her back into the bed, stealing her breath.

"Fine." His hold loosened, and she scurried away, curling herself up at the very far side of the mattress as he stretched out across from her. He folded his hands behind his head. "My father hurt you badly."

She startled—his voice like midnight come to life.

"No. He saved me." How many times would she be forced to take up for the man?

"He kept you locked away like a cursed princess when he could have brought you home. You could have had family. Bloody hell. I'll never understand why that man did the things he did. Just like when I asked him about ... everything. When Raph told me, finally, all those little puzzle pieces clicked together in my imbecilic brain. I demanded to know why he'd spent everything on dead paints and paper."

"What did he say?"

Theo snorted. "The man had tears in his eyes. They never fell. Just made it seem like he was looking at me from behind a pane of glass. Said he thought I understood better than the others. That money didn't matter. Only beauty did. And love." Theo turned onto his side. His back curled toward her like a wall. "I won't touch you. I promise."

And so far, he'd kept every promise he'd made her. Made her want to cry, that did. Perhaps she would have, too, had sleep not claimed her surely as a tide rushing to the shore.

Twelve

༄

ordelia snored.

Damn it all to hell, the woman snored, and he found it adorable. And he never used that word —*adorable*. But there existed none other to describe her freckled nose snuggled against his chest, her lips slightly open, that rumble of a snore sneaking out of her and shivering across his skin.

Adorable. And endearing. And he couldn't tell ... did it break something inside him or heal something jagged?

He should not have allowed her into his bed to bring with her such words as *adorable* and to make him think anything about him needed healing. It did not. But she'd been so beaten by exhaustion last night, he'd been unable to say no, and he did not dare wake her to tell her to leave. She needed sleep like he needed ... like he needed ...

Hell. Who bloody knew anymore.

The morning sun peeked through the window, and the heat of its rays would wake her soon enough. He'd let her snore and enjoy the feel of her in his arms while it lasted. Soft and supple, strong and sensuous, vulnerable and fragile. Her hair as silky as he'd always thought it would be. An unexpected smattering of freckles across her shoulders he had to bite his lip to keep from kissing.

He should not be holding her thus—her head resting perfectly on his chest, his arm wrapped tight around her. He wanted to be a gentleman, to protect her, and seducing her would throw all that wanting away. His cock was hard as a damn rock, though, liked the idea of seduction. He should roll away from her and take himself off to perdition for stealing this embrace, for taking while she slept something she would never give him while awake. But he'd wanted her for months now, and while she slept ... he had her.

Different than he'd imagined it. He'd thought it would be a passionate storm of an embrace built from animosity and frustration. It proved something much more dangerous.

Didn't want to leave her, did he? Wanted to kiss her shoulder, no, *those freckles*, didn't he? Wanted to slip from the bed only to get his notebook before returning to her and drawing her something to make her laugh.

Mocking truths.

He'd always had too much of his father in him, and he'd sworn he'd purged the worst of it. He'd been wrong. The worst of it remained—preoccupation with beautiful things. Obsession.

He ripped his body from hers and dressed quickly, silently. Other than a slight hesitation in her light snoring, she did not seem to notice his absence. Good. He grabbed his satchel with his charcoals and paper, closed the door quietly behind him, and made his way downstairs to the great hall where all meals were served. Reminded him of Arthurian legend, and if the table there were round instead of rectangular, he'd imagine himself a knight ready to do the king's bidding.

No. He grimaced. *Cordelia's* bidding. This was why he'd grouched and grumbled at her, why he'd fixated on the task of removing her from the house. Because he'd known how it would be if he let himself get close. Obsession with the beautiful, desire to save those in need. He'd be hers.

Might already be becoming hers. He'd have to close himself off again, keep his distance.

From a sideboard at the far end of the room, he piled a plate with food and poured himself a too-full cup of coffee, then joined a corner of the long table where Castle, Armquist, and Pentshire already sat.

Pentshire slapped him on the back as he lifted the cup to his lips, making the coffee slosh over the rim.

Theo glared.

Pentshire laughed. "I'm glad you requested an invitation, Lord Theodore. You and your lady have made an interesting addition to the party. I can guess now why you wished to attend."

Theo froze, his cup halfway to the table. "Oh?" He could not know about Sir George, about Theo's purpose for being there.

"That school of yours. Lady Cordelia can talk of nothing else."

"You're all making donations, I hope." Relief tumbled through him like a cool winter spring, washing away his fear.

"Mrs. Castle would roast me over a spit if I didn't," Mr. Castle said. "I fear she'll want to have a guiding hand in it. You and the lady wife will accept her meddling, I hope."

Theo bit a toast point in half then spoke around his chewing. "The lady wife?"

"You're marrying Lady Cordelia, aren't you?" Lord Armquist asked. "The footman announced you as married, though we all know that's as true as anyone else's marriage here this week."

Pentshire barked a laugh that sounded more like a yelp and downed his tea.

Theo swallowed hard. "Why do you think I'll marry her in truth?"

"Because she's the one championing your school." Armquist stabbed a bit of bacon with a fork. "She makes it sound as much hers as yours. I figured the two of you would run it together, and it wouldn't work if she remained your mistress."

Theo raised a hand. "Well—"

"And she's a lady, despite the gossip surrounding her circumstances." Pentshire snapped his own fork to the table. "You *can* marry her."

"I suppose," Theo said, "But—"

"Besides," Mr. Castle added, "she's lovely. Why wouldn't you?"

"Of course she's—"

"If I could marry Meredith"—bacon sputtered out from between the baron's teeth—"I would in a heartbeat. But I needed the wife's money. You know how it is."

"Yes, but—"

"But what?" Mr. Castle asked, his eyes narrowed on Theo.

Armquist and Pentshire also tore him to shreds with critical gazes, the earl's fingers drummed a rhythm on the tabletop while the baron polished a butter knife to a shine on a serviette.

Theo reached for excuses to appease these men with threats in their eyes and found several within easy reach, as if he'd lately chewed on them himself.

"I have little money to start a family. And I cannot count on my family to support me. I'm sure you've heard of my father's financial troubles."

Armquist settled the knife on the table and leaned back in his chair. "Yes, I'd heard that. A difficult situation for all involved."

Pentshire continued his tapping. "I've met your brother,

in parliament. He seems a reliable sort, intent on setting things right. I'm sure your family would help you make ends meet should the right woman snag your heart."

The very truth of the matter. They would. Had they not done so for Zander and Fiona? Yes, and gladly.

"And I heard you have an inheritance of some value," Pentshire continued, though his tapping stopped.

All three men looked at him again, this time with a shared light of curiosity in their eyes.

Theo cleared his throat, pushed his plate away, suddenly not hungry. "Yes. A Rubens. Unfinished but highly sought after."

"Sounds," Pentshire said, dragging the word out, "as if your father set you up for happiness, to choose your own way, which is more than mine did for me." More than a little bitterness there. "Smooth ways are hard to come by," he muttered.

Mr. Castle patted Pentshire on the shoulder. "Me and Mrs. Castle had much less starting out." He shrugged. "Love provided." Theo rolled his eyes. How often had his father said similar things? "And a bit of hard work." Mr. Castle leaned over the table and tucked into his eggs.

Theo watched him. He knew little about the man. "I know you are a merchant, Mr. Castle, but what is it, exactly, you do when you're not painting? If you do not mind me asking."

The man took one more large bite of eggs and pushed his plate away. "Not at all. I'm a colourman. It's how I knew your father. He bought paints from me for his parties. I have less custom now than I did before he died. Yet another reason to regret his loss."

"He wasn't ever … short on funds with you? I imagine he racked up quite the debt in your shop."

"There were times he could not pay, yes. But he offered other means of recompense. He helped Sally, our daughter, find a position as a watercolor instructor in a well-to-do school for girls. And he sent everyone he knew to our shop." Mr. Castle chuckled. "Quite put that old Samuels out of business. He diluted the colors anyway, didn't care about quality. And your father helped us start out. Loaned us the money to open our shop. When he couldn't pay"—Mr. Castle shrugged—"everyone falls on hard times. He was a good man and deserved lenience here and there."

Theo pushed the food around his plate, poured scalding coffee down his throat.

Armquist elbowed him in the ribs. "You'll marry her, though, yes? Because if you don't, I have a cousin, just turning thirty years of age this year and in need of a wife. I think she'd make an excellent—"

"No. She wouldn't." Theo stood. "Now, would you leave my personal matters to rest?"

Pentshire stood too. "It's time for today's challenge, anyway." He made for the door and called out over the clatter of cutlery and chatter. "To the parlor when you're done! Make haste!"

Theo gathered his satchel and followed him out. Better to face a blank expanse of paper than to face how others saw his father—a hero. He slipped into the parlor and found it already occupied. He found Cordelia, too, looking fresh and well-rested. After a night in his bed. His feet moved toward her, two, three steps without intention but to hold her, see if his scent still lingered on her.

But to what end?

He stopped himself, held back, and took up position on the opposite side of the room so he could watch her.

Pentshire calmed the masses, and once silence reigned, he broke into it. "My guests, today's challenge is a surprising one, but I hope you'll find it enjoyable. Today, we will let the muses make the art."

"What?" Miss Mire's voice, high and shrill, rang out. "I can't paint or draw or anything!"

The earl ambled toward his mistress, stroked his hand down her hair. "It will be fun, darling. You'll see. I'll teach you."

Theo locked the image away in his memory to draw later —the earl petting his muse before one and all, promising to *teach* her. Suggestive, that.

"Get to work," Pentshire said. "As always, the work must be completed by the end of the day. A difficulty for all but Lord Theodore, whose work is so simple and sparse that he can finish it in an hour." Amid the gentle rumble of laughter, Pentshire found Theo in the crowd, lifted a brow. In challenge?

Theo shrugged. Not a challenge he would accept. He liked the stark black-and-white of his art. Truth was that way—one or the other without any in between. He took in a steadying breath then made his way toward Cordelia. She looked terrified, her face drained of all color, her posture stiff, and her terror eased his own stiffness, lust draining away in the greater desire to put her at ease.

He sat on the sofa next to her. "You can do it."

She shook her head. "If you had any chance of winning before, it's over and done with now. I can't—"

Likely true, but that worry achieved nothing.

He placed a finger to her lips, silencing her. "No. Perhaps you can't. But you can try, and whatever you end up with will be fine. I'll teach you." An echo of Pentshire's words. He dropped his hand to rest between them.

"And you think you'll be the teacher who finally breaks through?"

"Probably not. But you need the money, so we'll try."

She huffed, slumped into the back of the sofa, and lifted anxious eyes to him. "Must we?" A whine.

He rummaged in his satchel for his notebook and opened it up, pulling a pencil from between its pages. He placed both on her lap.

She made a face that looked as if she only just managed not to stick her tongue out at him.

He swallowed a grin. "You're feeling better today."

"Yes." She sat up with a sigh. "Despite our current task, I am feeling considerably better. After last night." Her voice lowered. "Thank you."

He lifted the pencil from where it rested between the angled pages of the notebook and handed it to her.

She stared at it, mouth slightly agape, body rigid, as if he'd thrust a snake into her palm. "I ... I do not wish to disappoint you." Her words almost silent.

"You cannot. I merely wish you to have fun. To create something that makes you smile." He snorted. "Perhaps you should have a different model than I."

"No! You make me smile." She jumped at him, her hands fluttering birds at his shoulders, her cheeks blazing with color. "I mean ... I enjoy teasing you. Sit just there. Do not go anywhere. I'll draw you as you are. If you insist I do so, that is. But I have warned you, so ... be warned. It will be no good."

"It will be fine." He drew himself up tall, pulled the lapels of his jacket tight, and straightened his shoulders, gave her his profile. "Do you want me like this?"

"Yes." So much mirth in a single word.

Why was he doing this? He should keep his distance after the troubling emotions brought on by waking with her in his arms, after the conversation in the great hall. In her he seemed to be rediscovering some joy he'd lost years ago. But joy was a dangerous thing. He'd used to love his art, find joy in it. He'd learned what a folly that was. When you saw art as beauty instead of truth you wandered down a path of selfishness.

Cordelia would draw him, and the drawing would do no

concrete good. But it might make her happy for a time, and wasn't *that* good?

"You've gone stony, Lord Theo," Cordelia said. "I cannot get the line of your jaw right because just moments ago it was slack and now it's hard as rock."

"Do not focus on the actual line. Then you'll get it right."

Her brow furrowed. "Pardon me? Do not focus on the actual line? I have had many an instructor, and I can assure you, they all say—"

"They're all wrong. To focus on the actual line is a good way to be technically proficient, but what truth is there in the technical?"

Her brow remained furrowed.

He looked about the room. The Castles were closest, but they seemed to be flirting with one another. He unwrapped his cravat, and she lifted her brows suggestively. Theo didn't dare peek at her drawing. No telling what provocative images it held.

Perhaps he should peek, to reveal it in his drawings later. But they were not who he was after. A colourman and his wife? Middling people when he wanted to expose the shadows at the top.

He leaned in closer to Cordelia and lowered his voice. "Consider satirical drawings."

Her hand slipped into the pocket of her gown. "Like the one here?"

Which one did she have there? The first he'd drawn her or one of the other three he'd given her since, slid beneath her door while she slept and before he crept into the morning light of the narrow hallway they shared.

It did not matter. He shouldn't be drawing them. What good did they do?

They made her smile. They filled her pockets, apparently. Damn. Focus.

"In satirical drawings," he said, "you do not represent things, people, accurately. You exaggerate them."

"Like my hair?"

He nodded. "And even though the reality of the drawing is not there, everyone knows what it means with a single look."

"Yes."

"You must pick up on that thing that defines the subject of the drawing and put your effort there. You've met my brother Zander, and he's very tall, so if I were to draw him, I'd make him a giant. I cannot explain it further. In many ways it makes no sense. But—"

"No. I understand. You portray the inner self, the hidden reality, by exaggerating the outer bits as much as you can without entirely negating a resemblance. You focus on the part of the outer resemblance we most associate with a certain individual, and by focusing there, you communicate the identity best."

He leaned into the sofa's back. "Precisely so."

"I cannot do so well as you, but I shall try."

She set his pencil to the page, and the sounds of scribbling, scratching, filled the air between them. Now and then, she glanced up at him, and sometimes the very tip of her tongue flicked out in concentration.

Hell. He was in hell, having her full concentration on him, her body so near and his to touch according to every mind in the room.

"There," she finally said. "Oh, it's a masterpiece fit for my Gallery of Shame, but I rather like it. Would you like to see it?"

"Yes."

She handed him the notebook. She'd drawn a statue hewn from hard rock—Theo. Even the curve of his hair was chunky and chiseled. "My jaw is huge, Cordelia."

"I have made it so, yes, but only because when I look at

you that's what I most see—that hard and unforgiving jaw, always clenched. But look there. Can you tell?"

He followed the line of her finger further down the page, past the rugged cliffs that were his shoulders and to the ... melting expanse of his chest? The cliffs of his head and shoulders dropped steep into the ocean of his body, a stormy ocean. The lines of the drawing were not practiced, but the eye that had drawn it was observant, the mind that conceived it thoughtful.

"Have you ever seen the Cliffs of Dover?"

"Yes."

"You remind me of them. Hard and craggy cliffs dropping into the sea. A week ago, I would have thought you all cliffs and edges, but now I do not think so. Is that truth?"

He ripped the paper from the notebook, and she gasped, clutched at it. But he waved her hands away and folded it, dropped it into the pocket of his jacket. It might be truth. "It's mine now. You cannot have it for your gallery." Nor could Pentshire have it for his little competition.

She leaned away from him with a pout. Then a yawn, her hand coming up to cover her mouth, her eyes fluttering closed.

"Still tired," he said. "Go back to bed."

"I can't." She ducked her head and whispered, "Not without you. *Can't* without you."

He would have picked her up then, carried her up those damn dangerous, spiraling stairs, laid her on his bed, and done much more than sleep with her there. But he wouldn't because no matter what Pentshire and the others thought, he could not make her his wife. And he refused to make her his true mistress.

"Try," he growled, standing. He left her alone on the sofa, his last glimpse of her one of slight dismay, her eyes having shot open, her mouth parted with an affronted and damn adorable gasp.

The first deserted room he found contained books on every wall from floor to ceiling. Distraction. Good. He grabbed the nearest one to hand and fell into a chair with it. But try as he might, the words floated before him, refusing to make sense, to march to the order he bade them to.

They moved aside to make way for the memory of her small gasp and for visions of all the things he could do to her to make her gasp again.

Thirteen

He'd done it again, shown her in the most abrupt way possible that she was a hindrance, not someone he delighted in being around, but a burden he would be glad to be done with in ten or so days' time.

Needing something to do with her hands to hopefully distract her from the roaring in her ears, she picked up the pencil and drew useless lines across the paper—up and down, back and forth, over the bumps left behind from her drawing on the paper above it. Which now resided in his pocket. How could he look at her as she sometimes caught him doing, hold her as he had this morning, and then stride away from her as if she were no more to him than ... than a stranger on the street.

The pencil's tip snapped, and she tossed it to the sofa cushion and buried her face in her hands with a tiny, almost silent groan. She knew she should not want him, shouldn't want to be wanted by him, but he'd turned her inside out. She stood, tired of being alone in the room full of partners, tired of feeling like a burden, and—

Tripped over his satchel.

She cursed, steadied herself, and yanked the satchel off the floor, threw the pencil and notebook inside, and slung it over her shoulder as she stormed from the room. Where had he gone?

"Theo!" she cried out as she marched down the hall. "Theodore Bromley!" She poked her head into the three rooms on the right side of the hall, called his name again, without the honorific, again, so he *knew* where he stood with her. Then she moved to the other side and threw open the first door there. "Theod—oh. There you are."

He sat in a chair by the window, slumped low, legs spread wide, one booted ankle crossed over his knee and his arms slung across the chair's arms. He lifted his gaze above the edge of the book. What simmered there?

He snapped the book shut. "You were looking for me?"

She threw the satchel at him, and it landed mere inches from his foot. "You left that." She held out her hand. "Give me my drawing back. I must have it to win the prize."

"No." He kicked his satchel under a nearby table.

She clutched her hands in her skirts. She could tackle him, pull the drawing from his pocket. A temptation, indeed. But she *was* a lady. Still. Somehow, after all this time. So she relaxed her hands and pulled a chair to face him, stole the notebook and pencil— No, it was broken, and she did not feel like mending it to a point. She grabbed the box of charcoal instead and laid everything out on the table next to her.

"Stay still," she demanded. "If you will not give me that drawing, I will make a new one."

He folded his hands together, studied her over his knuckles. "Few of the muses have any training in art. I doubt Pentshire will count having your work amongst mine against us. To my great shock and dismay, he seems a mostly honest fellow. Not that I've stopped looking for his faults."

"You be quiet. I must concentrate." She'd draw him in the

manner he'd taught her mere minutes ago—exaggerations and truth. But she'd not let her partiality to him soften her sketching this time.

She would not draw the man with a soft, hidden heart. She'd draw the gargoyle.

He chuckled and sank lower in his seat, drawing his propped leg off his knee and setting his foot to the floor, legs spread wide.

Her tummy flipped, and her breasts ached, and why did that man's pose seem intentionally designed to set her body aflame? Intentionally designed to draw her gaze to the apex of his legs, so clearly displayed by his stance.

She licked her lips and held on to her anger.

"You're spoiled," she said, scraping the charcoal across the page.

"Oh?"

"Yes. You were a pampered marquess's son who didn't get to attend a grand tour or whatever it is you expected, and now you hold a grudge."

His slight smile hardened and broke away. "I never wanted a grand tour."

"Then what do you care about? Other than making fools of those you hate for, apparently, having more money than you do?"

His hands on the ends of the chair arms became claws, white-knuckled and vicious. "Do you know who I target in my satires, Lady Cordelia?" All his *Delia my dears* gone. Ice in his voice now. "I target men who mistreat the women they should protect. I target men who ruin their families with their selfish actions. I drew a caricature of the masquerade months ago, to show the vultures picking over a dying man's luxuries. I expose men like my father, hoping that shame will curtail their activities before their families lose everything."

She slashed the charcoal in the opposite direction, creating a crosshatch effect to shade the gargoyle's marble skin. She'd learned a thing or two during her lessons, even if she couldn't do those things well. "Why does everyone insist Lord Waneborough was a louse?"

"Why do you insist he was a hero?"

She added devil's horns, claws like his fingers curved over the ends of his chair.

He stood, slowly.

"Sit back down," she barked. "I am not done yet."

He decimated the short distance between them and knelt in front of her. "He hurt you, though you will not admit it, and I will not let it happen again. I do not know why"—his hand appeared over the top of her drawing, and his knuckles nuzzled the sensitive flesh beneath her chin as he pushed her face up to meet his gaze—"you have come in here like a fury ready to strike me down, but tell me how I can help."

She threw his hand away as she leapt to her feet, the notebook and charcoals spilling to the floor. "I do not want your help. I do not want to be your burden as I was your father's. Do you not think I know? He did not want me! He felt pity for me." She beat her fist against her chest. "So he locked me away in a tower and sent servants to care for me, but they did not want me either, because I had no talent. Only my father ever wanted me, and he died. But I choose to see the best in your father because to see only bad would drive me mad, would leave me in a puddle of my own tears from morning to night. There is more to life than night-mares, Theo." She shook her finger at him as he rose to standing. "But some nightmares cannot be ignored, I suppose." She shot him a look that said everything she'd left unsaid.

"You think I'm a nightmare, I suppose."

"Just like your father, you don't really want me. You only want me about so I can help you hurt all these people."

He took a tentative step toward her. "If they are harming others, they deserve to be harmed themselves."

Why did tears sting her eyes? She hated them, and she flung them away with the heels of her hands. "You despise me and cannot wait to be rid of me and I ... oh, heavens, I cannot help it ... but I cannot stop thinking of your kisses. Only two, but they've entirely ruined me." She shook as she spoke, a hopeless, bitter sort of laughter rising up out of her with each word. "I've become obsessed with a man who hates me!" She clutched her belly and laughed until every ounce of energy she'd gained from sleep the night before had drained from her, and her limbs, loose and heavy and numb, threatened to give out, to drop her to the floor. She turned to find a row of windows and pressed a palm against the glass, seeking steadiness.

Into the shivering silence between them, he spoke. "God, Cordelia." A tremble ripped through his usually steady voice. "Hate you? *Hate* you? How many times have I shoved a mask on just in time to hide my *wanting*?"

Another variable to add to her confusion. She turned from the window.

He strode across the room, his steps multiplying and lengthening until he swung her into his arms. Then a shudder rippled through his entire body, and it was as if a mask had fallen from his face entirely, leaving his every emotion raw and visible there. She'd seen hints. Now she saw it all—the pain, the fear, the loss, and yes, the wanting. Her anger dropped away, though she *should* clutch it to her. She'd never been good at being bitter.

She reached a hand up to cup his cheek, and he leaned into it, closing his eyes and muttering a curse at the same time. How very ... Theo. She smiled.

"You have been a thorn in my backside since I met you," he said. "Since before I met you." Hardly promising, that, and yet something straining in his voice told her to hold her judgment, to stay in his embrace. His hands tightened on her waist. "There have been moments I would have sold my soul to purge you from that townhouse and be done with you."

"I'm not sure you should continue," she said.

"But the entire time, I've *wanted* you, too. Wanted your curves beneath my hand and your lips pressed to mine, wanted your hair wrapped like silk rope around my fingers."

"Ah." She stiffened, her brief wonder turning bitter. "I can do nothing well but be pretty." She did not even try to hide the poison in her words.

"Pretty? Yes, but I wish to God that was the beginning and end of it. But you must insist on being more than that. Each day, you show me how strong you are, how brave and cunning. And damn, but that makes me want you *more*."

Her heart felt like a bird in a cage, fluttering, fluttering, needing out. She licked her lips, and his eyes sparked with all the colors of wanting, of desire.

"Do not ever think you are unwanted," he said, "because I want you day and night."

"Show me." She went up on tiptoe, sliding her belly across his taut abdomen as she lifted her face closer to his. "*Show* me."

The room became a blur as he whirled her, pushed her backward into an alcove lined with books. Her back hit the shelves, and books thudded to the floor, but all she felt, heard, and saw was Theo—his face descending to hers, his lips sipping along her jaw, his hair hiding the lust-hazed gray of his eyes, and his shoulders blocking out the world beyond.

His hands were everywhere on her—hair, jaw, neck, shoulders, and then down her spine and around the curve of her ribs to cup her breasts as his lips left hers to trace kisses along her modest neckline, low enough to show a hint of her curves. She sent up a silent prayer she'd not worn her high-necked gown today. She regretted any muslin that kept his skin away from hers.

She threaded her hands through his hair, silky and thick and just as marvelous as she'd always thought it would be. She fisted her hands in the strands, just a bit, and he moaned, nipped at her the sensitive flesh of her breast. Her head fell back onto the bookshelf behind her with her own moan, the hard edge of the board slicing into her neck. The slight pain only seemed to add to her pleasure as his fingers dipped beneath her bodice's edge and pulled it low, low, so low her nipple first pebbled in the cool air and then beneath the ministrations of his skilled tongue.

She scratched her fingernails down the back of his skull to his neck, then along his spine as far as she could reach. Not enough. Wool and linen too much in the way. She ripped at his shoulders, wanting the jacket off, but his arms curved round her backside, lifted her, and she had no choice but to hold on, to wind her arms about his neck, past the snowy folds of his increasingly mangled cravat, and wind her legs around his waist. Beneath her rear, she felt the press of something hard as he pinned her to the bookshelves.

"Do you feel how I want you?" he asked, his harsh voice close to her ear. "Do you feel it? Feel me?"

"Yes," she breathed, "yes." And she wanted him, too, fiercely and with no doubts. As if every pretend touch and kiss and glance over the last week had wound her up tight and set her in this direction, as if every time he put her likeness on paper, he made her anew with a heartbeat and pulse and need tuned to him. Only him.

Perhaps she'd not been able to sleep because she'd wanted to sleep with him. Her loneliness, this time, a lonely yearning for a single man—Theo.

The man who snagged his teeth along her neck and nipped at her ear, who held her close and groaned her name. Then he lifted his mouth to hers once more, and they drank from one another until their hearts found the same rhythm.

He set her back on her feet.

"No." She clutched at his shoulders, trying to pull herself back up.

But he sank to his knees, one hand finding a home at the curve of her waist while the other slipped beneath the hem of her gown and found her leg, cupped her calf, and smoothed a pathway up past the back of her knee and over her thigh. As his arm rose, so too did her skirt, then her shift, revealing—as her gown pooled in waves like waterfalls from where he'd pinned it at the hip of one leg—her pale-blue stockings and the little black ribbons that held them tight. Would he like them?

He must because he kissed the skin above the ribbons then squeezed her rear and kissed her still-covered belly. Low. Scandalously low, his lips burned her through worn silk and the muslin of her shift.

She tangled her hands in his hair once more, tugged, and he looked up at her, a grin on his face. The first full smile she'd ever seen from him—wicked and wonderful and only for her.

"Theo," she breathed.

"Finally," he said. "I should not."

"Whatever it is, you're wrong. Please *do*."

"Delia, I've wanted to touch you like this since I met you. I know it's wrong, but—"

"It's not." She tightened her grip in his hair. Kneeling before her, looking up at her with something like adoration shining in his eyes, she no longer wanted words. Only action. "No more words. Show me what you've wanted to do. *Show* me."

That wicked smile flashed again, and he pressed his lips to her belly once more before ducking his head beneath her skirts. His hand on her backside slid around the side of her hip to splay low on her naked belly, his thumb extending into her curls between her legs as he placed hot kisses along the inside of her thighs. He trailed tingling sensations along every inch of skin he stroked, kissed, and when he lowered his mouth to her very center, she almost shattered.

So long. It had been so long since anyone had touched her like they wanted her, and no one like this, kissing there. She clutched the bookshelves behind her, fingernails digging into soft wood, elbows digging into the spines of books packed tight in rows at her back.

He licked her, trailing his tongue up her inner thigh then higher, replacing his thumb where it circled in her curls at the exact spot where she sometimes ached when she thought of him. The place that sparked when he kissed her, even if that kiss had been fake. *This* kiss—intimate and dangerous—was quite, quite real. It threatened to undo her. With every stroke of his tongue deeper into her, every slash of it against that aching bud, her pleasure wound her tighter and tighter. And when she glanced down with heavy eyelids barely open to see her skirt, her shift, draped across his broad, strong body, the tiny thrill of a single word ripped through her—*mine*.

She clutched at him, fingers reveling in his hair as she bit her lip, exposed breasts aching for his touch, so that when his hand slid up her body to knead her breast, to flick that always excellent thumb over her taut nipple, she shattered with a scream. He rushed to standing in one fluid movement, his mouth covering hers, taking the scream as she arched her hips into him, feeling the press of his hard manhood against her belly. She tasted herself on his tongue, and his hands in her hair, at her nape, undid with ease the simple knot she'd wound her hair into that morning. When she'd left his bed. When she'd thought he'd left her behind, unwanted like all the others.

But he did want her. He'd not only told her so, he'd shown

her. As she'd asked. And she'd never been happier to be wrong in her life.

He kissed her passionately at first, his lips slanting hard and needy against her own somehow to the rhythm he'd set her body to with his tongue and hands, the same rhythm pulsing pleasure through her. But as the pulses receded like ocean waves, leaving her heavy and drowsy, the kisses changed, became slower, softer, still incomparably lovely. When his body fell against her own, pressing her harder into the shelves, he dipped his head and traced kisses along her neck, her shoulder, murmuring ... what did he murmur? She rustled herself out of her fog to listen.

"Shouldn't have done it. Don't care. Can't care. I should protect you, though. Not *this*." He groaned. "But *this* is all I want."

She shifted so she could cup his face in her hands and lift his head away from her body. His eyes held worlds and all of them aflame, and she swallowed and blinked to put them away. For now.

"I do not want a knight in shining armor, Theo. I have long since learned I must save myself. I cannot rely on anyone to do it for me. Not even you. I do want ..." She licked her lips. "I do want someone to spend the hours with." Lonely as they were, as they had always been. With his body pressed against her, that loneliness receded, washed away in the ocean of pleasure he'd dipped her in.

She slipped one hand between their bodies, finding the long, hard ridge of his shaft pressing against the fall of his trousers. "Does it hurt?"

He hissed, rolled his hips against her hand. "It's a sweet pain."

She rubbed him, adding more pressure to the action, and he ground harder into her hand.

"We shouldn't." His voice guttural.

"You keep saying that."

"I shouldn't let you do this."

She kissed the hard line of his jaw. "And you think you can stop me?"

Truthfully, she could not say what would happen if she continued. *When* she continued, for continue she would. She touched him out of curiosity and a need to reciprocate. When she'd touched Simon years ago, he'd enjoyed it quite a bit, and though their three times together could not be considered adventurous, she'd learned enough to know the basics of how it all worked. She'd learned enough to know men liked to be touched where she currently touched Theo.

"Do you like it?" she asked. Just to be sure.

"God, yes." He nipped at her neck.

She stopped her up-and-down rubbing briefly to squeeze him through the wool of his trousers, and he moaned, kissing her deeply on the mouth. So she continued, up and down, faster and faster until his hips rocked into her hand, until his body shuttered and he kissed her name into her mouth. Never before had the sound of her name made her feel less like a burden. This time, she felt like a queen. A warrior queen with sword in hand. His sword in hand. She chuckled.

"Nothing funny." He groaned the words into her shoulder where his breath came in ragged huffs. She erupted into full-throated laughter, and he pinned her tighter to bookshelves at her back, straightened to regard her with glittering eyes. "Care to share what—"

The shelves behind them collapsed, the books spilling everywhere and three planks clattering to the floor with them. Theo yanked her into his arms and away from the paper and ink avalanche as the sound of disaster echoed around them. She covered her mouth to silence her scream and looked up at Theo, his arms wrapped tight around her waist. His eyes wide as saucers, his face granite. But then stone twitched and trembled, a smile breaking through.

"Don't you laugh," she warned, pressing her palms to his chest.

But that part of his body rumbled deep and true, and he threw his head back in great guffaws.

"Theo!" she admonished.

But he wasn't listening. He was laughing, his face red with mirth, unaware of the footsteps running down the hall.

"Quick!" She pulled him out of the room, and they ran, hand in hand, Theo laughing like a fool. Though they were sure to be discovered, she didn't ask him to stop. She loved the sound too much. Rare as it was, Theo's laughter seemed the truest thing about him, his soul made plain. And she didn't want him to hide it ever again.

Fourteen

Theo had never tried drawing directly after climax, but when he reached his room, he cleaned himself up and found the writing desk, and lines and shapes poured forth as easily from his fingers as the pleasure had poured through him not a half hour before. Not his usual stuff—the lines lighter, thinner, more elegant, the shapes designed to draw a smile instead of frown. He scratched his hands through his hair and studied his newest sketch when the knock on the door came.

"Yes?" he asked, though barely aware he'd spoken. He added another thin line to the drawing. Better.

The door creaked open then quickly clicked shut.

"I've brought your satchel," Cordelia said.

Her voice shivered through him, and she clutched his satchel to her belly wearing the shyest smile he'd ever seen from her. Even when they'd first met, she'd been bold and unafraid. Now she acted timid? After she'd come on his tongue and rubbed him to completion with her clever hand? *Now?* He almost laughed again when his belly still ached from the last time.

She placed the satchel by the small writing desk he sat at and tilted her head as she studied his work spread across it. "I secured the satchel before Pentshire saw it and submitted my sketch of you to him before coming here. These are wonderful." Her fingers air-traced the outlines of his drawings. "They're so funny."

"Well, I do have a sense of humor, if you can imagine it."

"You hide it well, but I know. I have discovered your secret."

He pulled her down onto his lap. "Should we return to the others?" Not that he wished to do so.

"No. Tell me about these." She nodded toward his work. "That one is Pentshire and Mr. Castle, and ... Lord Armquist?"

"Yes. They cornered me this morning. I decided they'd make a perfect trio of judges."

"But their robes are covered in hearts."

"So was their conversation."

She let her body relax into his and rested her head on his chest. "They would not like to see how silly you've made them look. Those wigs, Theo. Are they made of ... sausages?"

"Yes. Their court is located at the breakfast table."

Her chuckle rumbled through him. "And that one?" She pointed at another. "The vulture one."

"Ah. That's Mr. Bradley."

"But he doesn't look a vulture at all. It's a fine sketch, but I'm afraid you've missed the mark."

"You don't see the resemblance? Hm." He shrugged.

She shifted her body away from him to move the papers around, stopping abruptly and sitting up stiffly. "Is that ... Miss Mires? And Lord Pentshire?"

He looked over her shoulder, grimaced. "Yes. Not my best."

"I hate it."

"Pardon me?" She hated it? It wasn't horrid. Far from, actually.

She twisted to look up at him. "Miss Mires is nice. And Lord Pentshire is ... jovial. But you've made them look wicked. Are they in a dairy farm? And is that joke about udders a joke about her—"

"Yes." The word sounded like rock breaking on his tongue. He reached around her and hid the drawing under others. "It's not my best. I'll likely not use it."

"Do you ever feel bad about your drawings?"

"No." They were necessary.

"I think I like the funnier ones better."

"They sell the best, too. I sketch one now and again, put my signature upon it, and give it to a child, a sweep, or a flower girl with instructions to take them to the printshops. To be paid for it."

"That is terribly sweet, Theo." He snorted, shifted, wrapped one arm more tightly about her. "What's this?" She picked up a small wooden cylinder with a bit of paper peeping out of its side, lying crooked at the far corner of the table.

"Open it and look closely. It's called *Going to a Fight*."

She unrolled it carefully and leaned closer, wanting to see every little detail. "Those two are fighting already. And look at that man's face. So angry! And the sweet little dog. I could look for hours and find something different with each pass. How delightful. Did you—"

"No. Robert Cruikshank. Pull again. There's more."

She did. Then again and again, laughing because she could not now imagine the paper having an end. "Is that a ... a bull? And a tiger? When do we get to the fight?"

"I suppose every new scene is a fight in a way, but soon. Keep at it."

She did and finally found the men facing one another within the boxing ropes. "This is amazing. But I cannot imagine why you have it. It's not terribly serious." She dropped her tone low on the last bit, mocking him just a smidge.

"It's only slightly satirical, you're right. But it makes me laugh, and I like how clever it is."

"You're not entirely made of grunts and growls and scowls, then?" She smiled to show the tease and pecked him on the cheek.

He rolled the painting back into the tube and replaced it on the edge of the desk before reaching for another of his own drawings. "Here. Look at this one."

She leaned forward for a closer view. "That's me. And you. And we're ..."

"Not nearly careful enough of the books behind us."

Her cheeks flushed. "This is *not* a satirical drawing."

He kissed the soft skin just below her ear. "No. It's not. It's a drawing just for you. To keep in your pocket." He snorted. "I'll have to pay Pentshire for those shelves."

"I certainly hope those books were not valuable."

"If they were, he shouldn't keep them out in the open like that."

"Mm. Yes. Such activities against bookshelves are likely a common occurrence. The books are best locked up tight."

She was so damn beautiful, and he lost the thread of the conversation in the exploration of the freckles scattered across her nose, her cheeks. Her smile fell, but when he reached through the thickening silence between them to stroke his knuckles down the side of her face, it returned.

He kissed it.

She gave into him, melting against him once more. But for too short a time because she pulled herself out of his lap and strode to the window. After a moment of looking out, she spoke. "I'll be returning to your bed tonight."

He hadn't dared hope for it, and he certainly had not planned to ask for it, but his body loosened in relief.

Her hand stroked down the curve of the curtain, pulled to the side. "I think, for the duration of our stay, we should be in truth what we've only pretended to be so far." She looked over her shoulder, caught his gaze. "Lovers." She turned fully and folded her hands before her. "And before you refuse, let me say I care not for your notions of protecting me. I am a woman who knows what she wants. It would not be wise to continue such an association when we return to London, but as I do not plan to wed, and you are currently without a mistress and we both, it appears, enjoy the thrill of pleasure in one another's arms ... why not?"

Why not indeed. He couldn't think of a single reason ... except.

"There is the risk of pregnancy, of course," she said.

That. The reason. "I don't have a French letter."

Her brow furrowed. "What is that?"

"Did the other fellow not use one? Did he not put a ... a sheath on his sword?"

Her furrowed brow arched upward. "Oh. No, he did not. Should he have? I only barely understand what you're saying, I'm afraid."

Theo stood and took measured, controlled steps toward her. "A French letter covers a man's cock, prevents him from spilling his seed inside you."

"Ah. No. He did nothing like that."

"He risked getting you with child, then abandoned you?"

"I risked it as well. The act was mutual. As it was, will be, between us."

Nothing between them would be as it had been between her and the other man. *Nothing*.

He stopped before her and pulled the braid from behind her back. She must have fixed it quickly after their interlude in the library. He wrapped his hand up in the silken rope and tugged her up against him. "I'll not treat you so carelessly."

She swallowed hard. "Then you'll not—"

"Oh, no. I will. We will. But I will be careful not to get you with child."

"How?"

"I will not spill my seed inside you."

"You can do that? Without a ... a French letter?"

"Yes." He tugged her braid to tilt her face up to him more. "Shall we begin tonight, when you slip into my bed once more?"

"No." A tremor in the single word. "I plan to sleep then, considering how little I've slept the last several days. I think ... I think I'd like to begin now." She raised up on tiptoe, dragging her body against his as she did so, and kissed him.

He ran his hand down her back and found the tapes of her wrinkled gown. He loosed them, and when the gown bunched, he pulled the sleeves low.

She gasped and broke the kiss.

He took the opportunity to circle her. "You are going to enjoy this." He would too. "I'm going to make your bones melt into the mattress then bury myself deep inside you and make you scream my name." Heat flushed across her cheeks, her shoulders, the tops of her breasts as he pushed the gown lower down her body. "But first, I want you naked. I want to look at you."

She raised her chin as the gown slipped to her waist. "You too. Every stitch of clothing, gone."

"As you wish," he whispered near her ear, rubbing a hand over her shoulder and down her arm as the gown puddled at her feet.

He made short work of her stays and shift, leaving only her stockings and slippers.

He angled the chair toward her and sat. "Take them off."

Covering her breasts with crossed arms, she huffed. "Truly? As if it's a ... a show?"

He nodded, his body hard already.

She looked about the room, somehow thoughtful and playful at the same time, and then she sat on the bed, wagged her eyebrows and lifted one leg, and bent toward her knee, revealing her full breasts as she pulled on the end of one ribbon holding her stockings up. Hell. Perfect in every damn way.

She dropped the black ribbon to the floor once she'd unknotted it and rolled the stocking down her leg, revealing the creamy, slender appendage beneath. She did the same with the other, and by the time she finished, entirely open to his view, he'd become almost too hard to move. Thick hips and thighs with deep-red curls between them. His mouth dried with need. No work of art more beautiful than her.

She moved then, slipping to her feet and padding back to him, taking his hands, she pulled him to standing. "Now. No show for me. I want to undress you myself. No help from you, thank you very much."

Had her voice always been so husky? Did he truly fill her with as much desire as she filled him? Hell, if he'd known it sooner, he would not have waited to begin this liaison. Neither of them believed in love, and he found with each of her kisses that he felt as she so openly did—he wanted to be wanted, too. Particularly by her. He wanted what she did—an affair that burned hot and quick.

He closed his eyes and held his arms out wide.

～

The first time Cordelia met Lord Theodore, someone had been undressing him in her drawing room. The widow in question hadn't gotten terribly far. He hadn't wished to be undressed, after all. He'd been stripped only to his shirtsleeves, his waistcoat, and cravat—all rumpled, but still in place.

Cordelia would get much, much further today, would see what the widows had wanted to see, what she had wanted to see, as well. At the time, she'd thought nothing of the wanting. The man filled out his trousers admirably, and curious women did not hire male models to disrobe before them without having a variety of reasons to lead them down that path. Curiosity one. Fun, another. The forbidden, too.

Theo certainly looked forbidden. Tall and strong with a scruffy shadow about his jaw. He must not have shaved that morning. Had he skipped his morning ablutions so he did not wake her? Emotion nipped at her heart. She quieted it. No room for any emotion but lust just now.

He dressed as he had that first day, tucked shirt and unbuttoned waistcoat, an unnecessary cravat. She tugged at it, unwound it, and eventually revealed the strong column of his throat. She kissed it, and his head fell back, offering better access. She slipped the waistcoat off both arms at the same time, pushing her hands over the muscle of his shoulders. When the waistcoat fell without a sound, her curious hands traveled south along his front to untuck the shirt from his waistband, to throw the shirt over his head where it could join its fallen compatriots.

She trailed her fingers down his chest, enjoying the crisp hair there, then down his abdomen to where a line of that hair disappeared beneath his trousers.

She licked her lips. "So well built for an artist."

"I like to box." His voice gruff.

"I am not surprised you enjoy hitting others in the face." She chuckled, though she did not feel like laughter. Her body thrummed only with desire, no room for anything else.

Hands trembling, she worked at his fall, only slightly distracted by the ripple of muscle above it. Well, perhaps more than slightly. She kept stealing another look, an impossible impulse to resist, so she gave into another and kissed the area just below his navel.

His hands slipped into her hair, and his fingers massaged her scalp as he spoke her name like a prayer.

Then the buttons were done with, and the long thick length of him strained against the thin linen of his smalls. What use was such a garment in the face of such a foe? She pushed the wool and linen down his slim hips, and he stepped out of them. Their bodies pressed together so close but not quite touching, and she took hold of him, wrapping her hand around his length. Silk and steel. She squeezed, and he arched against her, the muscles in his jaw working hard.

She released him and fell to her knees, trailed her fingernails down the muscles of his thighs, scattered with hair as well. His hands remained in her hair, and he tried to pull her back up.

"Beautiful," she whispered, resisting his efforts, liking it just fine where she was. All lean muscle and ropey sinew. All man.

"Those words are for me to say to you," he said.

"I shall say as I please, and this is the truth. You should be the model, not I." For he served as her muse in a way, inspiring her to mold her own life as she saw fit. "Can I do to you what you did to me?"

"Not today." The words sounded choked. "I will lose control."

She rather liked the sound of that—to drive a man with such control as he had quite to his wit's end. Hadn't she been trying to do that all this time anyway? She never suspected she would do it without her clothes on, but her teasing and her winking—all of it meant to ruffle him.

And because she was curious and did not like following commands, she kissed the tip of him and then tasted the length of him, drawing her tongue down the shaft. He had flicked his tongue inside her earlier, but she could not do that to him. Perhaps ... she took him into her mouth, and he hissed a curse. She removed her lips from his person and looked up at him. Had she hurt him?

But the gaze he cast down at her was one of intense pleasure, not pain, and before she could take her next breath, he hauled her to her feet and threw her over his shoulder. Three strides took him to the bed's edge, and he threw her down upon the mattress. He stood poised above her like a warrior, a victor—no, a king. Setting one knee on the mattress, he touched her everywhere, paying particular attention to the places where her curves were most ample—hips, breasts, thighs. He kissed and clutched and looked, and she kissed and touched him back.

"Oh, Theo." The words that had begun as a caress turned into a cry as he slipped his fingers inside her, his thumb going to that spiraling bud of need at her center and circling, pressing, in just the right way.

Then his hands bracketed her hips, and he flipped her, pulled her to the edge of the mattress until her feet hit the floor. She arched her back to see his intentions in his face and saw only a wild thing, no polished king, but a feral god of old.

He was everything she wanted, had ever wanted.

And he wanted her. He did not hide his desire. It rose long and throbbing between them, and it burned in his eyes. He pressed himself against her rear and cupped her breasts as she supported her weight on her arms, her hair a curtain spilling around her face, cutting her off from the world, cutting her off from everything but him.

This, *this*, felt wonderful. Her only complaint that she could not see him, touch him. But some deep corner of her enjoyed giving in to him this way, making herself entirely vulnerable and at his command as she never would be outside of the bedroom.

"Beautiful," he said, raking his fingernails down her back. He likely scored her skin, and she welcomed it. She wanted to score him, too. His hand reached between her legs. "Wet."

"Yes."

And then he pushed inside her slowly, and it had been so long, and he felt so big.

His body leaned over hers, holding her tight with strong arms, holding her up if she needed his strength. "Are you well? Is it fine? Shall I stop?"

"No." She hugged his arms with her own, keeping him connected to her. "Never stop." She dropped back to the bed, supporting her own weight with one hand and reached the other arm backward to draw his body closer, using her nails to hook him.

He hissed, but he came to her, did as she bade him, and he did not stop until he was buried in her to the hilt. "Perfection." He kissed her shoulder.

She agreed. Absolute perfection, the fit of their bodies together. How could it be so, when they were so opposite in every other way?

He withdrew, oh so slowly and almost entirely before he thrust back home. And then again and again, slow then faster, over and over, the same rhythm that had driven her to the same peak of delirium she'd experienced earlier in the library.

Almost there. Almost *there*, but not quite.

And then his hand appeared low on her belly, and his fingers worked at her center, stroking, circling, holding her tight to him at the same time, and as his hand worked, and as he thrust from behind, she gave in to him, gave in to the feeling, and let it sweep her entirely away.

She collapsed, her muscles no longer able to keep her upright, but her rear still lifted for him as he made his final thrusts and pulled entirely out, spilling his seed onto the mattress beside her.

His breaths were ragged pants, and as he crawled onto the bed beside her, he pulled her with him, held her close against him. The sun still shone beyond the window glass, but the bed curtains offered welcome shadows to hide herself in. He stroked his fingertips along her jaw and neck, down her arms and back up, making her shiver and burrow closer until he stopped and kissed the top of her head.

She should have taken a lover sooner. She never would have guessed that if she did it would be Lord Theodore. Now, she could not quite imagine it being anyone else.

Fifteen

Cordelia woke to a kiss. And as the five mornings since she first began her affair with Theo, she pretended to sleep just a moment longer. Because Theo adored her most when he thought her sleeping; when he thought she could not hear or feel his adoration.

"Hell, Delia," he whispered into the tingling skin over her spine. "What am I going to do with you?"

An odd question. Yesterday morning, it had been "Hell, Delia, when will you wake and let me have you once more?" And the morning before that had been "Delia, you damn vixen, wake, darling." And before that, in exasperated tones, "Why the bloody hell do you feel like forever, Delia dear?" Her favorite so far. In fact, the more he cursed, the more frustration filled his voice, the more she liked it.

Kisses planted on every unclothed bit of her. And every bit of her unclothed. When his prickly cheeks scratched against the sensitive skin of her inner thighs, she squirmed, unable any longer to pretend sleep.

He inched up her body, walking his fingers over her

abdomen like a soldier marching across a battlefield, eyes sleepy yet full of mischief. "Awake yet?"

"I am now. But I would still be sleeping if you had an ounce of self-restraint."

"You've slept plenty since coming to my bed."

"I've slept barely at all." She pretended grouchiness, put a pout in her words that teased his smile wider. It was truth. She was as sleepless as ever. But less upset about it. How could she be with this man in her bed, touching her, whispering curses to her each morning.

No gargoyle, her nighttime Theo. Wait till she told the others in London. They'd never believe it.

"What's wrong?" He frowned up at her.

"Nothing." A lie.

He scowled and laid his head beside hers on the pillow, gathering her tight to his chest. "Liar."

What was wrong? His arms felt much too good to give up in, what, less than a week now? How had she formed such a habit of him in so short a time?

He kissed her ear, her neck, her shoulder, trying to tease her into cheerfulness. An odd exchange of roles, and one that did not work. She pulled from his embrace and left the bed, feeling the weight of his gaze on her as she dressed in her shift and wrapper.

"I should dress for the day," she said. "And you as well. Meet you in the gallery with the others soon?"

He nodded, jaw hard, a rebellion jerking at the corner of his lips. He jumped out of bed, pulling the quilt with him, and before she could do more than admire the cut of his body, feel the heat, seeing it always pooled low in her belly, he had her pinned against the door, wrapped with him in the quilt, kissing her. Kissing her so softly she almost forgot the world outside of their six more days. She kissed him back as if the school did not exist, as if the townhouse would not go to someone with more money, as if no one had ever gossiped about her connection to his father, and as if Bradley were not turning guests against her.

With a sigh, she stopped the kiss and laid her cheek against his chest. His hand wound in her hair, as it always did when she wore it unbound and streaming down her back or plaited in a long rope.

"I'm nowhere near being able to rent a new location for the school. Those who offered to donate only wish to sponsor students, not buy buildings. I do not know what will happen to me when your brother sells the house."

His arms tightened around her as he rolled them so that he rested against the door, and she rested against him. He kissed the top of her head.

She pushed out of his embrace. "I have work to do still, that much is clear. No more lost sleep in your bed, Lord Theo. I must counter Mr. Bradley's nasty influence among the guests."

His mouth opened like a fish. "Bradley?"

"Yes." She tweaked his nose and slid through the door before he could catch her once more. When she gained the privacy of her own chamber and peered into the looking glass above the wash basin, her face looked bleak. No surprise. She'd not made as much progress as she'd have liked. Still, hope prevailed. There was always the competition. Theo had attended every single event in order to paint and try his hand at winning it. For her. She loved him for it.

Love?

She laughed. My, what a slip of the tongue. Er, mind? She didn't *love* him. Of course not. Certainly not. But she did *admire* him. His commitment to his causes, of which she'd become one. But she would not delude herself. While he had talent, his drawings often seemed to be missing something. He was technically proficient, but in many ways his work seemed ... flat. It did not have the emotional weight the others possessed in a single stroke of a single color across a canvas. The works he drew alone at night were better. Less technically proficient, sillier sometimes, garrulous others, ugly often, but purposefully so. Yet brimming with emotions—anger predominantly. But the ones he did not take seriously because he said they did nothing, the ones he drew for her were filled with something else—a playfulness of spirit, a generosity and optimism she'd not associated with him before. He might win if he shared those. He could not share those.

The fact remained: she could not rely on the prize money for her school, for her livelihood. Mr. Bradley's gossiping had done damage she could not undo, no matter how she tried.

Her face glowed pale and weary, shadowed and gaunt in the looking glass. She did not look like the teasing lady Theo had drawn in the garden at the start of the house party.

She had a purpose, and Mr. Bradley would not keep her from it. That purpose set her steps straight as she found the gallery. As soon as she stepped foot into the long, windowed room, an arm slipped into the crook of hers.

"Up late?" Theo asked, bending low and wiggling his brows.

"No teasing, Theo. I'm focusing."

"Now who's the gargoyle? Do you need tea? Food?"

"Absolutely, I do."

"Well, then." He dragged her toward a small table in the corner of the room, over which hung every work of art created so far at the party. Theo's were easy to spot in the chaotic mix. They were the only ones with bold black sweeps across charcoal-smudged white paper. Odd to see herself continually in each of his works. Odder still that he always made her look so alone, that he caught something in her she did not share with anyone. Ever. How did he see it? Likely because she'd cornered him in his room and insisted she sleep inside it. The actions of a desperate woman, they were.

She slipped from his light embrace and poured her tea. "What is today's challenge, then?"

Theo helped himself to his own tea, pouring in enough milk to turn the deep-brown liquid a creamy color. "No idea. Pentshire's not here yet." He picked up a scone from a plate piled high. "Eat this."

She accepted it and nibbled around the edges.

"Good morning!" Pentshire strode into the room, arms held high and wide, his voice booming. "Are you ready for today's challenge?"

A tepid chorus greeted him.

"It appears you're not the only one lacking cheer this morning." Theo flicked her cup, and the nail dinged against the fine china.

"I'm not lacking cheer. I'm *focused*. There's a distinct difference." She narrowed her eyes. "You seem to have more than your usual fair share of cheer this morning. More than the rest of the guests combined, perhaps." She took a large bite of the scone and washed it down a long sip of tea. Inelegant, but efficient. "What has you so jovial?"

"Jovial?" Theo snorted. "You know me better than that." But his eyes sparkled just a bit, and that brought his face to life. And the tip of his tongue darted out to outline his full bottom lip in a way that made her heart flutter and her cheeks heat. "I am merely ... well-sated. I might conjure up some joviality if"—his hand snuck around her waist—"you considered helping me find a quite deserted corner to ..." His words trailed off as his lips lowered toward hers.

"No, Theo." She jerked away from the all-too-public kiss. No one would mind, of course. Not these people. But now that they kissed in private, public kisses felt fake. And they must stay on task. That was the more important reason. Naturally. "We're focusing today, remember?"

He glared. "Lacking cheer, I say. *Humph*. But I can focus, too. Quite well, in fact. I'm still not convinced I've found all there is to find regarding our host and his lady love." Theo's gaze trailed the other man across the room.

Pentshire stopped to speak with each guest with an authentic friendliness, and she felt a bit bad for him. How would he feel after Theo sold his sketches to the printshops? She'd seen nothing objectionable from him so far. Except, of course, treating his mistress like the lady of the house, outside of his public demonstrations of affection for her. A bit cruel of him perhaps, though his affection for her seemed easy and true.

While there seemed to be an easy acceptance of such things from all the guests here, no one ever went terribly beyond the bounds of propriety. She'd thought they'd all be half naked all the time. She'd imagined orgies in the halls. She'd found instead a group of friendly individuals more obsessed with art than with debauchery. In fact, if asked, they might take offense at the mere mention of debauchery, as it could steal away hours they'd rather spend on their next masterpieces.

She did not believe Pentshire deserved what Theo planned to gift him with.

Unaware of his impending doom, the earl stopped near the windows and chuckled. "You'll all perk up when you hear what the next challenge is."

"Well," Armquist demanded, "don't string us along."

"We're switching muses." Pentshire crossed his arms over his chest, clearly pleased with himself.

Cordelia nuzzled her face into Theo's warm side and whispered, "Do you think there's some trouble between him and Miss Mires?"

Theo's eyes flashed. "Not that I've seen, but a lovers' quarrel is always welcome news to the ton."

She pulled away from him. Whenever the cynical glint sparked in his eye, a discomfort bloomed in her belly. He thought his work good, but to her it felt more like revealing people's weaknesses to give the ton a good laugh. And surely he saw the hypocrisy in their position. Five nights in his bed had made a hypocrite of him, made him into a man who certainly should not throw stones.

"Do we get to choose?" a man across the room—Lord Ellsby, possibly—asked.

"I'm not sure I like this," Theo grumbled.

"No," Pentshire said, "*you* do not get to choose. Our muses do."

"Choose Mr. Castle. He'll not mistreat you."

"No." She knew exactly whom she should choose. The one man she least wished to talk to but the one she must. Or lose hope of winning any more donations for her school. And she always had hope, especially with a scone and a bracing cup of tea in her belly. "I'm choosing Mr. Bradley." A brief but sincere conversation with the man would put things to rights.

The jerk of Theo's body sloshed a bit of his tea over the rim of his cup. "No."

"*I* get to choose."

"Not him. There're a dozen others you can choose from. Mr. Castle—"

"Is not a problem for me. Mr. Bradley is. He's turned over half the guests against me. They will not speak to me, and if they do not speak to me, I cannot convince them to donate to *your* school." The words tasted bitter. She hated the necessary lie that the school belonged to Theo. Even pretend reliance made her feel what his brother had called her —a leech.

Theo's hand crept into hers, and he squeezed, a minute

touch that demanded her attention. "Who is not speaking to you? I'll deal with it."

"What will you do about it?"

"Have a small chat with them. As I did with Bradley."

She threw his hand away. "You did what?" His jaw became a blade's edge. "When?"

"The second day here. I cornered the rat and let him know what would happen to him if he continued spreading rumors about you." He cracked his knuckles.

No. No, no, no. "Theo." His name a whine. She wanted to hiss at him. But really, it was rather sweet, wasn't it? Still, she must gather her anger. She was trying to save *herself*.

"I was not going to let him—"

"You've pushed him to greater heights, likely. Exacerbated the problem." She set her cup on the table and finished the rest of the scone.

"Cordelia, I—"

"No." She cupped his cheek, tried to placate him with the softness she'd learned he liked from her. "I'm going to speak with him. I'm going to model for him, and nothing you say will stop me. Yes?" He glowered. "Wonderful."

She patted his cheek, stepped around him, and, for the briefest moment, felt the brush of his fingertips against her wrist, tangling in her skirts. She yanked them from his reach and locked her gaze onto Bradley across the room. A woman had approached him, and not the woman who was his muse. Gathering her skirts in her hands, Cordelia ran, skidding to a stop between them.

"Mr. Bradley." She conquered the need to breathe in gasps from her small sprint.

His eyes narrowed. "*Lady* Cordelia." The way he'd used her honorific revealed his true feelings for her. He did not think her a lady one bit.

"I hope you are not yet taken by another muse. I would like to offer my services for the day."

The slits of his eyes widened a bit. "You? Hm."

"What about me, Mr. Bradley?" The woman he'd been speaking to had a high voice, made higher for her inquiry.

Cordelia stepped in front of her more fully.

"Do you know," Mr. Bradley said, scratching his jaw, "Simon has a painting of you. Had. He sold it. Got more for it than any of his other work." He snorted. "A bitter pill for him, that."

"I understand how it might be." She screwed her smile on tight lest frustration drop it to her toes. "But I am anxious to set things right."

"Are you? Hm. Very well." He looked over her shoulder to the woman behind her. "You may go, Miss Hoskins."

Miss Hoskins huffed, but the warmth of a body at Cordelia's back disappeared.

"Once everyone has their new model," Pentshire said, raising his voice above the chatter, "you may go where you like. See if you can produce a portrait of the lady better than her usual artist can."

"Well, Mr. Bradley"—Cordelia grinned—"where shall it be?"

He walked a slow circle around her that made her skin crawl. "Outside. Hm. On the bridge over the moat, I think. With your coloring, I envision you as a siren, luring sailors to their watery graves."

"My. How ... dramatic." The crawling across her skin became a stroke of anger, but she followed him from the gallery into the spiral staircase.

"Cordelia." Theo's voice echoed on the stone walls.

She stopped, finding him standing at the top of the stairs. It took her four steps and half a circle to stand face-to-face with him, as much as their heights and the steps allowed. "Yes?"

"Be careful." He leaned near, pressed a kiss to forehead and said low enough she almost did not hear. "I'll be watching."

"Thank you," she mouthed. No need for his concern, but still, it rippled something like joy through her chest. He worried. He cared. He wanted her safe. He would not traipse away and leave her alone, forgotten. He would be there, watching, so that when she returned to him safe and sound, she could gloat about how silly he'd been, then drag him back to his room and kiss him senseless.

Excellent plan. She only had six days remaining after all.

Once she and Mr. Bradley stood together on the old stone bridge above the moat, she asked, "Where do you want me?"

"Sitting on the wall, I think."

On either side of the bridge, low stone walls rose. She found a place not too bumpy and sat.

"Not like that," Mr. Bradley snapped. He approached, and she held tight to her muscles to keep from inching backward. Nowhere to go but into air and water. He pushed her shoulders and knees, turning her away from the house. Then he nudged her chin up, so she stared at the sky, and moved her hands to grip the weather-worn stones on either side of her. "Don't move."

"Yes. I mean no. I mean ... I'll remain still."

Bradley moved away and pulled a notebook and pencil from the pile of supplies he'd brought with him. "I'll sketch in what time we have, then paint later."

She remembered sitting for Simon, likely for the same painting that had brought him such a boon. It had been the first day they'd anticipated their wedding night. His gaze on her, heavy and full of desire, for several hours, had been a prelude to his hands. She'd admired those hands, lithe and agile, and though she'd known better, she'd done as he desired —disrobed, laid herself bare, assented. Because he would be her husband soon.

Such a little fool she'd been. At least she'd learned a little of the pleasures of loving that night. She'd enjoyed it, only regretted, really, that it had been with a man who had cared so little for her. She'd thought he'd loved her. Thought she'd loved him.

Little *fool*. She'd loved his art and mistaken that as affection for the man. The two had ended up being quite different —one beautiful and the other not. Was she falling into the same trap with Theo? The word love had tripped her up earlier, but perhaps the word described her feelings for his art, those bold strokes on stark white paper, those exaggerated shapes and heavy lines. No. His art made her uncomfortable, sparked an odd combination of admiration and wariness. But when she thought of *Theo*, she thought of him as a man, not an artist, a blunt beast with a surprisingly soft heart. She used to think she could look at Simon's paintings for hours and see something new each minute.

She thought the same about *Theo* now.

A complication she did not need. Focus remained her word today, and her goal the man scowling as he drew her, winning him over, stopping his malicious prattle.

She cleared her throat. "Shall we have some conversation, Mr. Bradley?"

"No."

"You do not like me."

He snorted, his pencil never stopping its scratch across the page.

"Why? When we have never met before this week."

His hand stilled before it began again at a more furious pace. "Simon is a good friend. You ruined him."

"Me? Ruin *him*?" She wanted to laugh, but she'd often

thought the same thing, had long felt guilty over his assertion, though until Mr. Bradley, no one had flung it at her but herself.

"You seduced Simon."

Well that snapped guilt in two. She gasped. "Mr. Bradley, I—"

"And then, when you saw a better opportunity, you seduced his patron."

"I. Did. *Not*. Is that what he told you?"

"And now you've seduced the dead man's son. But tell me, how are you enjoying the support of a *poor* man? I suppose his pockets don't matter when he's fucking you, but—"

"Mr. Bradley!" She shot to her feet, hands fists, nails cutting into her palms.

Not that he cared. He continued sketching as if he'd asked her about the weather instead of gravely insulting her. She shouldn't feel insulted. She *was* fucking Theo. She winced. The word itself insulted her—too hard and too coarse for the delight she found in Theo's arms every night, every morning. That word seemed a curse when Theo proved a ... a *miracle*.

"You should have just married Simon," Mr. Bradley said. "He's poor still. No one would offer their support once Lord Waneborough removed his. All because you fucked his attention away from a man with true talent."

Cordelia could no longer form words. The man had it all wrong, and if that was what he had been telling anyone who would listen ... well, no wonder no one would speak to her.

"You do understand," Mr. Bradley continued, "it's not the fucking I'm opposed to. It's that you stole a livelihood from a deserving man. A great talent. A *genius*."

She dropped back to sitting, her body heavy, and rocks crumbled from the edge of the bridge and plunked into the water below. Guilt sat heavy in her gut like one of those rocks now at the bottom of the moat. Simon had tossed her away like refuse beneath his boots, but he had been a genius, and—

The slap of boot against rock jerked her attention upward.

Mr. Bradley sauntered toward her, stopping right before her and leaning forward, forward, forward, so that she had to bend backward over the low rock wall to avoid his face just inches from hers. So close, he possessed good looks, classical, elegant lines of nose and jaw and lip, but those lips twisted into a hateful sneer.

He stroked a finger down the curve of her cheek, and bile rose in her throat.

She jerked away, yelped when she felt the nothing behind her, and fell forward into his chest. She scrambled out of his embrace. "I had determined to make friends with you today, but I see you are not a man worth knowing."

"And I see you are not worthy of that title you throw about, *Lady* Cordelia."

She remained trapped between him and the wall. She lunged to one side, and he followed. She tried the other, but he trapped her there, too.

"Still ... you are a beauty. I can see why Lord Theodore would take on his father's leavings. You could visit my bed if you tire of the Bromley men. Though there are, what, four more of them yet living. It may take you a while to—"

She slapped him, hard, spinning the vitriol of his speech into ringing silence.

"You will *not*," she snapped, "speak of me in such insulting ways. And you will stop spreading Simon's lies."

His elbow reared back as invectives left his lips, and his fist flew toward her.

She jerked away, avoided his fist, and fell backward into nothing, into rushing air, and then into the moat beneath the bridge.

Sixteen

༖

Theo had suffered nightmares like this—falling forever, a plunge into darkness, loss. Always vague, more feeling than reality. But forever after watching Cordelia fall from the bridge, new images would accompany those nightmares. It would always be her body falling, disappearing. It would always be losing her.

He had been rounding the house when he'd seen Bradley pin her against the wall. He'd started running, and he still ran, gaze trained to the moat. Where was she?

There! Her head popping above the water, her mouth open, gasping.

He didn't yell her name or make promises. He simply ran faster, dove into the moat, and swam toward her with straight, strong pulls until he had her in his arms.

"Theo," she gasped. "I-I c-can swim." Teeth chattering despite the sun above, the heat of the day. Bloody hell.

He towed her toward the shore and deposited her on the grass. She lay on her back for several seconds, blinking at the blue sky above.

He cupped her cheek with one hand and her shoulder

with the other. Clothing soaked. Her bones seemed so fragile beneath his touch, her skin translucent, her muscles insubstantial. Too small, too easily harmed, her chest rising and falling in a rapid, ragged rhythm. He lay beside her, angling his body into hers, pressing her into the earth, needing to feel her beneath him.

"Are you hurt?" he asked.

"No." She reached up to cup his cheek. "I'm not, Theo. I'm well."

"Good." Now he could focus elsewhere. His head whipped up to face the bridge. "You bloody bastard!"

He tried to stand, to run after the villain, but Cordelia wrapped her arms around his middle, held him tight.

She shook her head. "No."

"He tried to drown you. And who knows what else."

"What if Pentshire throws you out? No prize money. No scandal to draw."

Bradley was gathering his equipment and heading back to the house as if nothing had happened.

"I don't care." And hell if he didn't. Not with this searing rage ripping through him. "Stay here." He stood and ripped his jacket off, dropped it down to her. "Cover up with that."

Then he sprinted up the hill and toward Bradley's retreating back. Bradley must have felt the danger because he picked up the pace, darting in an almost sprint, but Theo—not weighted down by an easel and other art supplies, and brimming with the speed of retribution—reached him easily, grabbed his shoulder, swung him around, and slammed his eager fist into Bradley's shocked face.

On the periphery of his vision, he saw others arrive—faces pressed to windows above, bodies running around the side of the house. But not one of them stopped his second punch. Nor did they stop him when Bradley fell to the dusty earth and Theo knelt with him, shoving a knee into the man's gut and treating himself to a third hit.

"Theo!"

A fourth hit. Bradley gagged as Theo made a fist in the man's cravat, tugged, twisted.

"Theo!"

He pulled his fist back for another hit, and a manacle-strong hand wrapped around his wrist.

"Don't," Cordelia pleaded.

"Why not?" he growled. "I saw him pin you to the wall. He was trying to scare you. Worse, possibly. *I saw his fist.*" The last four words a growl.

"No!" Bradley cried. "Listen to the woman."

Theo tightened his grip.

"Yes." Cordelia's grip tightened, too, and even if it had been soft as a lightly-tied velvet ribbon, it still would have stayed him. "And worse no doubt. But I escaped. Rather clever of me, in fact, to tumble off that bridge."

"Do not make excuses for him."

"I'm not. I'm horribly glad you've pummeled him. But let Pentshire exile him now. That is the best punishment. Don't you think, my lord?" She wasn't talking to him. Something in the changed pitch of *my lord* told him that.

"Just so, Lady Cordelia," Pentshire said. The sound of boot steps on gravel wrested Theo's concentration from Bradley's mottled face.

Pentshire wore a grin so wide one would have thought he'd hired Theo and Bradley for his personal entertainment. "Let him go, Lord Theodore, so I can kick him out."

Theo's fists did not wish to comply, but the hand around his wrist would not let go, so Theo did, shoving Bradley into the dirt as he stood and turned to Cordelia. His jacket swallowed her, and she clutched it close to hide the muslin molded to her form. The sight of her, proud but drenched, made him want to pummel Bradley once more, but she lunged for him, wrapped herself around his arm and pulled him close.

"I'm in need of a change of clothes, my lord. Will you escort me inside?"

As they passed Pentshire while he helped Bradley to his feet, the earl put a hand on Theo's shoulder. "Don't worry. I'll see him to the gate as soon as he's packed his belongings. His muse may stay if she likes and have free passage home at the end of the party. *This man's* on his own." The earl raised his attention to the faces in the window and those gathered outdoors. "If anyone here prefers Bradley's questionable company to that of my other guests, please do feel free to accompany him off the grounds."

Theo grunted, guiding Cordelia round toward the house. Words did not come easily at the moment, with each breath a difficulty. Not words of gratitude, not words of worry. He knew one goal—get her upstairs and dry and warm.

Silence reigned within the house, a proper companion for the soft shadows, and only the sound of their footsteps on stone echoed in the staircase. At the top of the spiral stairs, he threw open the door to her bedchamber and released her arm. "I'll be here if you need me."

She nodded, then shook her head and closed the door between them. Cordelia's silence unnerved him. He missed her usual chatter, even the sort (especially the sort) she designed to tease him. What thoughts bogged down her voice? He needed to know.

But first, he needed new clothes. It did not take long to strip and dress and shake the water out of his hair with a square of linen and take up watch in the hallway once more, waiting for her to invite him in.

He shouldn't have to wait. They'd not waited for one another the past five days. They'd come to one another easily and as they wished and been welcomed with open arms. But she'd seemed too fragile when he'd pulled her out of the moat, and he'd been so enraged to see her pinned, to watch her fall. Something had snapped inside him, and he could not repair it. He'd be forever broken.

No. Nonsense, that.

He knocked on her door. "Cordelia?"

The door swung open, and she stormed through it, wagging a finger in his face. "If you are not careful, not only will you ruin your own chances to achieve your goals for coming here, but you'll ruin mine as well. If you're always growling at everyone like a rabid dog, no one will come near *me*, and if no one comes near me, how am I supposed to convince them to support my school? Hm? Beating Bradley to a bloody pulp certainly did not endear his friends to you."

Damn. She had a point. "You're right."

"Oh." She dropped her finger. "I'd not expected that. Lovely." She stepped to the side, stretching her arm toward the room. "Do come in, then."

He did, and when she closed them in together, he said, "I was frightened. I was afraid I wouldn't get to you soon enough. I had no idea whether you could swim or not. My sister Maggie can, but then, we did not have a conventional upbringing."

"I can swim."

"Your hair is wet." It hung in dark copper ropes down her back, wetting her new, dry gown, leaving murky green spots on the light-green muslin.

"Observant. I must start a fire in the grate and dry it there before I return downstairs."

"I'll help." He snatched the tinderbox from the mantel, knelt by the grate, and soon had a fire blazing there.

"Thank you."

She pulled a chair near the flames and sat, sending fleeting glances at him as if she were shy. Surely he had not made her that way?

He knelt before her and took her hands. "Did he hurt you?"

She chewed her bottom lip, not meeting his gaze. "No." A huff. "A bit. Here." She placed her fist against her heart.

And his own heart turned to ash. "What did he do?"

"Do ... do you think I hurt Simon? By accepting your father's help?"

"No."

"He's still poor. Has found no other patron, and—"

He wrapped his hands around the side of her face and forced her to look at him. "If any harm came to the man, he deserved it. For his treatment of you. And anything that happened to him is not your fault. My father acted on kind impulse to help you. I am glad he did."

Her mouth dropped open.

He used his knuckles to close it. "Don't look so shocked. For a while now I've given the old man credit for saving you. Because you deserve saving. Could there have been a better way to save you than to take everything away from one man and give it to you? Likely. I'm sorry his actions have hurt you."

"No, no they haven't." She shook her head, looking down into her lap, her hair dripping water onto her skirts.

Would she never think anything but the best of his careless father? He sighed and stood. "Do you have a brush?"

"In my valise."

He rummaged through it and returned to her side. When she reached for it, he swatted her hand away. "No," he said, "Let me." He wanted to care for her in the right way, the way she needed, in a way that wouldn't hurt her later.

Her hand hovered in the air between them before she let it fall back to her lap. His fingers on her skull, wrapped in her hair, stroking the brush through gently, gently. With each stroke, her muscles relaxed, her shoulders drooped, and her head listed in whatever way the brush pulled it.

He started with the ends of her hair, stroking the brush through the tangles, and he worked his way up, stopping to ask now and again if he'd hurt her, if he should be softer.

He could be softer. He could be as soft as she needed him to be. Yet ... touching her like this—just her hair—fanned the fire in his body higher than the flames in the grate nearby so that when his fingers finally reached her scalp, her temples, touched skin, and her head fell back into his hands as she moaned, he was hard, needy, ready to turn his soft ministrations to the rest of her body.

Head resting on the back of the chair, her heart-shaped face glowed up at him, eyes closed. His fingers explored the perimeter of that face, and she moaned again, a tiny thing that crackled like lightning across his skin and stilled his hands' journey near her ears.

Her eyes popped open. "Apologies. For the moan. *Moans*. How embarrassing. But you're rather good at this. To think, you could have been acting as my lady's maid for the last week. A missed opportunity."

She was teasing again. Good.

"I'd be better at undressing you than dressing you." He leaned down, placed a soft kiss on her forehead, then one on the very tip of her nose, then a lingering one on her lips.

When he lifted, his hands crept into movement once more, massaging her neck, her shoulders, brushing against the fine gold chain always clasped around her neck.

"Your necklace," he said. "Is there a story there?"

"My father gave it to me when my mother died. It had been hers, a gift from him on their wedding day. He always used to call me his little bird." Her voice broke.

"You don't have to—"

"I love this." She patted the chain. "Worthless though it may be to some."

"I wish your father had given you more than a necklace." He should have provided a dowry, an inheritance. Something, anything more than what she got.

"Don't, Theo. Don't be cynical about this. It may be a paltry gift to you, but it holds every memory of my former life, both good and bad. My parents loved me, though they were not careful of my circumstances. But then ... they did not think to die so soon. No one can predict the future." She outlined the bird's shape with a single finger. "It has sometimes made me sad, reminding me of what I lost—family, love, stability. But it also means hope to me. No matter how bad things are, I can soar above it."

He started to snort again, but she stopped him by placing a hand over his where it rested on her shoulder and looking up at him. "Things can have more than one meaning, even contradictory ones."

He didn't wish to argue with her, so he returned to his ministrations, massaging the hairline at her temples and dragging the brush over her scalp and down, down to the ends of her hair. She closed her eyes again, leaving him to this work, to his ministrations. A soft smile curved her lips up, and it remained until her expression slipped into the looseness of contented sleep.

"Delia." Her hair had started to fluff up with dry curls, and he gave it a gentle tug. "Delia, you've fallen asleep. Let me move you to the bed."

She made a little sound, adorable, and he lifted her in his arms and placed her on the bed, then he kicked off his boots and joined her, wrapping around her like a blanket.

"You'll stay here with me?" Her voice low and dreamy, the cadence of her words slow, as if she only *just* pieced them together. Turning in his embrace, she nuzzled against his chest.

"Yes." No other answer. Though he needed to speak with Pentshire to ensure Bradley's departure. And he needed to sniff out any of the others who might hurt her here. Hurt *her*? Who in their right mind would feel such evil for such a creature? Made him feel hard and jagged and snarling.

She yawned. "Nothing like falling into a moat to tire a lady out." A sleepy chuckle as she patted his chest. "No ideas now. A short nap. Nothing more."

No ideas?

Much too late for that. Whatever feral, possessive emotions had ridden him hard when he'd seen her fall, they would not soon dissipate. They might possibly course through him forever. Hell. What would he do when they returned to London, and he still felt wild to keep her in his arms? The same question he'd woken to the last several days. How could he stop wanting her when he didn't *want* to stop?

Perhaps he'd simply ... not stop, not give her up. Why must he? They fit so well together—their bodies perfectly matched while their souls were deliciously opposite in some ways. She moved through the world with greater comfort than he did, seeing good where he saw evil and ill intent. In other ways, they were perfectly attuned. She worked for the same causes he did, after all, desired to bring goodness to the world. As he did.

Why not keep her? As a mistress? That thought curdled the small amount of food in his belly. She could not be notorious if she planned to run a school. What then? Neither of them believed in love. But ... marriage did not require it.

Marriage then?

He peeked at her face cozied against his chest, waited for the rebellion in his gut to scream in no uncertain terms, *never*!

His gut did not speak, however. Only his heart did, increasing in a pleasant rhythm of anticipation.

Lady Theodore Bromley? A headmistress of a charitable art school as the satirist's wife?

He caught the corner of his lip lifting. Damn. He liked that. They would have little to live on, but his parents had had everything upon their marriage and lost it. Perhaps he and Cordelia could start with nothing and build up a life.

Foolish thoughts, perhaps. But damn if they didn't drift him right into a blissful sleep.

Seventeen

༄

ordelia woke first, tangled as she had been the last
many mornings with Theo's long limbs and hard
body. Unfortunately, they were clothed this time.
Another key difference—he still slept, and she was awake.
What should she do with this turn of events?

Watch him, first. Absolutely she must look her fill because
the gargoyle had brushed her hair before the fire after
pummeling a man to a bloody pulp in her defense, and
frankly, she'd never wanted a man more. Odd what that
combination of violence of caring had done to her. Each
stroke of the brush through her hair had made her damp
between the legs, had made her heart grow and grow until she
feared it would no longer fit within the confines of her ribs.

Silly little heart. Why would it do such a thing?

She suspected its reasons, but some things were better
unexamined.

So she continued examining him. Not enough of him on
display, though he did not wear a cravat. He wore only his
shirtsleeves, waistcoat, and trousers. Presumably smalls as well,
but she'd never find out. Unless she looked.

She'd get there. Eventually. She ran her fingers down his neck. Why did she like it so much? If she could draw, she'd draw him sleeping on his side, his neck curved and open above the snowy linen of his shirt.

His waistcoat was a dark gray. He always wore black and white and shades of darkest gray, as if he were his sketches. She traced the buttons of the waistcoat, and then fluttered her fingers through his hair, placed a kiss on the tip of his chin, and closed her eyes.

"What am I going to do with you?" she whispered, an echo of his morning musings.

"Keep me."

Her eyes flew open. His slack arms snaked round her, tightened, pressed her body against his. He was hard, and the knowledge made her achy. She reached between them, took him in hand and squeezed.

"Shall I?" she asked. "Keep you?" She used the tone of a tease to cover the truth. She wanted to keep him. Not just for the morning or afternoon. Not just for the length of the house party. But forever. She could not see her future clearly, but she could see him there with her, and that made the hazy fog consuming her whole not quite so terrifying.

She expected him to roll his eyes or for a teasing spark to light them up, but his gaze grew soft, softer than she'd realized it could be, and he rolled her to her back, rested his body over hers, and kissed her. He tasted of tea and cream and smelled a bit like moat water and sunshine, and his kiss made the whole world evaporate. Bradley's venom and her school's uncertainty —gone. Simon's betrayal and Lord Waneborough's possible flaws—of no matter.

For Theo kissed her and kissed her well—made an art of it, really, each stroke of his tongue better placed than some of those he put upon a slip of paper. She adored kissing him, so she joined in with a fury.

A fury he stroked calm with steady hands on her back, her hips. "Slow, Delia. Slow. Let me watch you simmer. Let me stretch out this hour."

Slow? When they'd been all frantic panting and eager limbs up until now? Hard and fast, more like a flame that rose high and hot but never lasted. Gentle? As if they had time to explore and the desire to do so?

Yes.

She undressed him slowly, as he did her, taking turns and tugging linen and wool away from skin until they were naked. Somehow, he'd stripped something else from her, too, some layer of armor always wrapped tight, and he'd shucked it off with ease as if it were the shift he'd plucked up over her head. How many times had she shared her body with him now? But this time, she felt truly naked. An unfamiliar shyness shivered across her skin, and he found it, dragged his knuckles down her arm, and ripped that shyness away, too.

"Beautiful," he breathed.

Him too. So beautiful with that thick hair and stubbled jaw, those soft gray eyes and chiseled body. A study in contrasts she would likely never tire of attempting to decipher.

She cupped the back of his neck with one hand and dragged her fingers down his chest with the other, memorizing the feel of the crisp hair, the hardness of the muscle. She discovered him with fingertips and palms. She explored her hip against his, her breasts pressed to his chest, and she agonized over his touches as well.

He took more time than she did, moving achingly slow, kissing her from head to foot in precise order, whispering words into each place too, as he did in the mornings. Though these were not words of doubt. They rang with absolute conviction. The whispers started near her ear, a single question wrapped in that gruff voice of his that made her shiver.

"What are you, Cordelia Trent?" Not *who* but *what*, and he gave her no time to answer. He moved on to her jaw and kissed one side. "I thought you were a leech." He kissed the other side. "It soon became evident you are not. And then you became a thorn. And you still retain, at times, your thorniness." He kissed down the column of her throat. "I have thought of you, in fanciful moments, as a princess, trapped in some tall tower." He kissed along her collarbone and then lingered on the round of her shoulder. "You do not stay put, though. You know where the door is, where the stairs are, and you use them." He made his way down her arm, pressing a hot kiss into the inside of her elbow before tending to her palms, sucking her thumb into his mouth. "Then I thought you an actress, my own personal one. But you were never anything other than yourself, even when you are pretending to like me. I'm convinced you *did* like me. No acting about it." He pressed a warm kiss to the inside of her wrist.

"Yes," she said, the word slipping out with a sigh. "You have"—a pause as she grasped for a breath, because he had jumped over the space between her arm and her body and found her breast—"redeemable qualities."

"You are like a Rubens painting," he said. "Such curves, such a handful. All of you beautiful. Perhaps that's just what you are."

"A painting?" she panted.

"No." He moved to the other breast, teased her nipple, grazed it gently with his teeth. "You are too alive for that, and you do not sit still enough to be a painting. I think perhaps you are my inheritance." And then he licked his way down her abdomen to her belly button and placed a kiss there, too.

Her body felt taut as a wire beneath his touch, and when his tongue slipped between the folds of her sex, she arched off the bed and clutched the sheets in her fists, cried his name. But still he moved slowly, burning the muscles of her thighs with his hands as he tasted her between her legs. Despite how slowly he moved and how gently he touched, she came harder than she ever had before, waves of pleasure crashing through her, stealing her breath, washing away the worries of her heart like sand pulled into the dark depths of the oceans. She clutched at his hair and brought him up for a kiss.

His inheritance. The word echoed in her mind. Somewhere in the pleasure-fogged corners of her brain she found a question and asked it. "Do you insist your father left me to you?" What an insinuation. And it dulled her pleasure. She did not want to be kept for any man.

"No. He would not have left me anything I actually coveted. And he did not know I would be the one of my brothers selected to find you a new patron. You are not my inheritance, after all. If you were, I would get to keep you. You would be mine. And I can still not believe that is true. Surely, I will wake up and you will be gone. Surely, you will realize I am not a man worth staying with."

Again, he returned to that word he'd woken with—*keep*. And after today, no word sounded sweeter. She rocked her hips against him, chained her arms around him and held him tight, a hug both hot and gentle. Perhaps she did not mind so much being his inheritance. If he was hers, too.

He kept saying *keep*, after all. Perhaps he meant it in jest, but now, with him inside her, caressing her everywhere, whispering everything she needed in her ear, she did want to keep him. Because she loved him.

She loved him when she'd not thought love possible. The realization rose like a sun inside her, warming her, filling her, brightening her shadows and corners.

"Impossible man," she said, pulling him to her lips for a kiss. "How did you do it?"

"Do what?" A mumbled question through the kiss.

She should tell him she loved him, but she wouldn't. Not yet. He didn't believe in love, even though he treated her like he did. She'd accept that for now. So she kissed him hard and wrapped her legs around his waist, and without asking, because he knew what she wanted most, he thrust into her.

She bit her lip hard, then he bit it for her, rocking in her as she scraped fingernails down his back. When he left her mouth to nip the line of her jaw, she bound her arms tighter around him.

"Stay with me this time," she said.

"I'm here." And he was, rocking gently and surely.

"Don't leave this time. Stay *in* me. Please."

His eyes flashed open, and the kiss stopped. Their lips grazed, and they breathed the same heated air. He understood her, but how would he answer? His hesitation bloomed doubt within her. Until he demolished the doubt with a single word.

"Yes." Then another kiss, his tongue sweeping into her mouth as his hips rocked harder against hers, faster, and she arched into each thrust, and then she was falling again, sinking into warm waters wrapped in his arms, tendrils of pleasure pulling her under, her body boneless as his own passion tore through him, the word "mine," an achy need on his tongue. A praise, a prayer, a song. Some lovely art thing spoken with gentle ferocity.

It could mean nothing. It could mean everything. He was a gentleman, after all, and if she came to be with child, he would not abandon her. And she ... she would welcome it. A child. Made by them both. Not something to be dreaded, but something to covet. And if he'd willingly spilled his seed inside her ... perhaps he coveted it, too.

Or perhaps he dared to take risks.

With a child?

She placed a kiss on his chest, pressed her ear there to hear the rhythm of Theo living.

No, he would not risk heaping misery upon any child.

One of the many reasons she loved him.

He may not love her, but he wanted her, and for now, that would be enough.

Eighteen

∽

The others were coming. Theo heard their voices bouncing around the hallway, louder and louder as Cordelia's hand swept across the paper, her mouth quirked and twisted in concentration.

"Don't move," she admonished. "I think I've finally found my proper subject." She sat at a small table with watercolors, her green gown rumpled from their recent endeavors.

He lay on a couch before her. A pink one. Quite small. And he was naked.

"If I don't put some form of clothing on," he hissed, and grabbed a nearby pillow—pink, too, and embroidered with the picture of a fluffy cat—to place over his stiff cock, "they'll all get a good look at me. All of me."

"Theo," she said, command hard in her voice. "Drop. That. Pillow. *I* need to get a good look at all of you."

He groaned but gave in. Nothing for it after she'd let him love her on the very sofa he lay across now. She'd stripped him bare, pushed him to sitting, hiked her skirts, and sat astride him, ridden him until he couldn't see and she'd clenched in ecstasy around him. He'd give her anything after that. Everything. And everyone would know what they'd been at in three ... two ...

A knock on the door preceded muffled titters from the other side.

"Er, are you two proper?" Pentshire inquired.

"Go away," Theo barked.

More chuckling, louder this time.

"I said the challenge of the day was to choose a new location to paint your muse, not to choose the best location to swive her senseless."

She'd swived him senseless. Was that a proper use of that term? Didn't matter. She'd obliterated him. "Go away," Theo repeated.

Cordelia clucked at him. "Be nice." Louder, she said, "We are on task, my lord. Only I am painting him." More laughter. "We'll join the others shortly," Cordelia called out. "Thank you for checking on us."

"Us ladies have to watch out for one another," Miss Mires said.

"I'll look out for Cordelia," Theo yelled. "And you, Miss Mires, can look out for Pentshire if you need someone to keep track of."

More cackling amusement, then the footsteps shuffled away, and Cordelia collapsed in a shaking heap across her paper. He stood and hauled her away from the table and to their pile of clothes. "As you undressed me, it's only fair you put me to rights."

She did, tried to between laughs, as he kissed the line of her neck. Damn, but he loved it when she laughed. Loved even more making her do so.

"Do you ... do you think," she said between hiccuping breaths as she twisted his cravat around his neck, "they knew exactly what we were doing?"

"Not *exactly*." He pushed a strand of hair behind her ear, kissed her forehead. "But they have very excellent guesses."

"How shall I face them?"

"As you always do. With poise and confidence."

"Heavens," she sighed, "I'm a mess."

He took her up a back staircase and to her room, helped her change, distracted her from changing. By the time they returned downstairs, everyone had gathered in the garden for tea. Some couples walked through the knot garden and others sat cozy in the bower, but Pentshire, his mistress, the Castles, the baron, and Mrs. Bexford had grouped themselves together, as usual, in the rose garden, circling a tea cart, hands filled with steaming cups. The sun shattered golden through green leaves, and the rose petals bloomed in a riot of colors around them from the palest, shyest pink to the most brazen blood red.

The rest of the guests had set up easels as well, but as usual, Theo tugged Cordelia toward the small group surrounding Pentshire, the few he trusted to treat her as she should be treated—with respect. Half the group, including Lord Ellsby, had left behind Bradley, affronted Pentshire had taken Cordelia's side. The party was safer for her now, thank God.

Pentshire, Miss Mires, the Castles, Armquist, and Mrs. Bexford hid grins behind hands and teacups as Theo and Cordelia approached, arm in arm.

"Ah," Mrs. Castle said, "young love. So passionate."

Theo grunted and sat Cordelia in the only remaining chair amongst them.

"Bah." Lord Armquist waved a hand as if smelling something unpleasant. "But at what cost? Instability, misunderstandings. I'd rather be older and wiser in love than otherwise." He picked up Mrs. Bexford's hand and kissed her knuckles.

"I must say," Mrs. Bexford said, letting her lover keep her

hand after he'd kissed it, "I've experienced no loss of passion despite my one and forty years."

Passion—a better word for what he felt. He'd witnessed no wisdom in his parents' love for one another, no matter how many years they'd gained. He shifted from foot to foot, settling his hand on Cordelia's shoulder. And love had prompted Armquist and Mrs. Bexford to give themselves outside of marriage. Love had prompted, likely, Pentshire to bring a dairy farmer's daughter into his home. Passion alone was better, determination and loyalty far superior motivations for sharing your life with another.

As he planned to share his with Cordelia.

"Where is the competition standing?" he asked Pentshire.

The earl eyed him, tapping a finger on the end of his wicker chair. "And what will you do with the money if you win?"

"I know!" Miss Mires bounced in her chair. "You'll put it all toward your school, no doubt."

Theo inclined his head. "Excellent guess, Miss Mires. I will indeed. Though ... I prefer to think of it as Lady Cordelia's school. She will manage it for me."

"An ..." Miss Mires hesitated. "Employee-employer relationship?"

Something more than that, though they'd not said it yet, and he wouldn't say it before all these people, either. So he grunted.

And Cordelia answered for him. "Of a sort. If, that is, we can get the school started."

Pentshire wagged a finger at him. "Do not think you can tempt me into giving you the prize because of your good works."

"But, Tommy"—Miss Mires tugged on his arm—"I would like you to donate *something*. And if you won't, well then, I will!"

Pentshire glanced around the group before stroking her arm. "I'll help. Don't worry, poppet." The look he gave her ... hell, Theo's own face had likely looked that way recently when staring at Cordelia, something he couldn't keep himself from doing. Was the earl's expression sincere? Did he admire the woman as Theo admired Cordelia? And if so, why keep her as he currently was—a mistress living like a countess. Not just a scandal, but a painful one to Miss Mires, surely. Because she'd have to step away from the house, the wealth, the earl himself when he took a wife from the ton. As he would do. All men of his stature did. And with his parliamentary passions, he'd likely choose a woman whose father's politics suited his own. An alliance.

"Miss Mires," Theo said, looking about the garden as if what he planned to say did not matter much, "are charitable works of great interest to you?"

The girl's face brightened, and her curls bobbed. "Oh, yes."

"And what, besides art, do you spend your time championing?"

"Orphans." Her passionate expression took on a hard edge at odds with her round cheeks and golden curls.

"Admirable," Cordelia said.

Just his thoughts. Too bad the girl would be cast away. But Pentshire would pay for his callousness. Every home in London would know of it, of her, and how he treated her.

Cordelia stirred beside him. "I am an orphan, I suppose." Why did her voice sound so empty? Was she thinking of her father's death? Of her betrothed's betrayal? Of how she'd been alone for so long?

He clasped her hand and pulled her closer, dipped to nudge the top of her head with his chin until she looked up with a huff and an irritated eye.

"Yes?" she inquired.

"Nothing." He'd just wanted to see her smile.

"Have you made any ground," Mrs. Castle asked, leaning forward to refill her teacup, "with those who previously crowded about Mr. Bradley?"

"No. And I am unlikely to," Cordelia admitted. "The ones who refused to speak with me have left. To their minds, I've ruined two genius artists now. The remaining guests have already pledged small donations, what they can. And I am grateful for all of it."

"Are you worried?" Mr. Castle asked.

"Not at all."

That was his Delia—bright and sunny and always optimistic. Thank God worry did not consume her. Because it ate him alive. He could not regret coming here. He doubted very much he'd have given into his desires for Cordelia had he not had her so close day in and day out. And he'd never regret having her in his bed, possibly getting her with child. He'd never regret finding a woman he could shake off his loneliness with.

But he'd learned the extent of her reputation here, and they seemed to have harmed it further with Bradley. Added to that, he'd not been able to find the sort of gossip, the severity of sins, that would sell on the Strand and in the printshops. He could get shillings, but nothing to set up a school, a life with a wife.

Except for the relationship between Pentshire and Miss Mires.

His hand on Cordelia's shoulder must have tightened a bit too much. Her hand lighted onto his, and she twisted to smile up at him. "Are you well? You've gone gargoyle."

He nodded, a curt thing that made him feel like stone. "Walk with me?"

She stood in answer, and the others waved them away.

"Not many dark corners in that direction," Pentshire called after them.

"Just go up to your bedchamber," Armquist yelled. "Much more comfortable."

"Ronny!" Mrs. Bexford slapped her lover's arm.

"What?" he demanded. "Do you wish to retire to *our* bedchamber?"

"Oh, Ronny." This time softer.

Then the couple left arm in arm.

Miss Mires frowned. "Would you like to go upstairs?" she asked her earl.

Pentshire patted her hand. "We'll stay right here. In case our guests need us. Yes?"

"Yes."

Theo wrapped his arm around Cordelia's shoulders and walked her through the knot garden and out of the hedge wall on the far end. They ambled down a grassy slope to the moat on the far side of the house. A light breeze ruffled the grass and swayed the meadow flowers, lifting purple and yellow petals skyward at times. The moat was a still and silver mirror, blue in places from the sky, darker where trees' reflections drew jagged lines across the blue. Birds sang in the distance, and a peace settled over Theo. A foreign feeling.

"Theo?" She looked down as they walked, and he studied her profile. Pouty lips, high brow, lovely little nose he wanted to kiss. She wore no bonnet, and her freckles glowed in the afternoon sun. He'd kiss each of those, too. Had already done so. Counted the hours till he could do so again. "Theo, perhaps we should discuss what happens when we leave here in three days' time."

"Yes." He'd been thinking the same thing. The time had come, and he was ready for it.

"I know you do not love me, but—"

"Love does not matter. I admire you, Cordelia. And I

want you, I hope you already know. In every way a man can want a woman." She bit her bottom lip, continued staring at her feet. "And," he said, pulling her closer to his side, "I want to continue helping with your school. As an instructor if you'll have it."

Her hands on his jacket tugged him to a stop. "Theodore Bromley! You're offering to teach art?"

"Only to the scholarship children. Not to the widows."

"Oh, but the widows would queue round the street to draw you." She sank her hands into his cravat. "Is an instructor all you propose to be?"

He cleared his throat. "Ah, no. Not quite."

"Then you're proposing to ...?" She opened her eyes wide as if the damn woman didn't already know.

"I'm proposing. In general." He scratched the back of his neck, looked to the sky for words to say and dropped his hand limp to his side when he found none. "Marry me, Cordelia?"

Her eyes shimmered. Were those ... tears? Hell.

He slipped his hand into his pocket and pulled out the paper carefully folded and placed there. "Here. I made it for you. Since I don't have a ring or anything suitable for such an occasion."

She wiped the corner of her eyes with the heel of her hand and took the paper, unfolded it, and for a moment, her face wore no expression, but then that blankness cracked open into laughter so all-consuming, she doubled over and rested her hands on her knees.

He stripped his coat off and laid it on the grassy bank, then guided her to sit atop it. Then he sat beside her and felt the pleasure of happiness curl through him. He could live off her laughter alone, rich and joyous as it was. And he'd caused it.

She collapsed backward into the grass, clutching the paper to her belly, and he joined her, folding his own hands over his chest and grinning up at the cloudless, blue sky. Open and wide like the skies of his childhood before everything changed. He'd gotten back there somehow. If only for one laughter-blessed moment.

Finally, she wiped real tears from her eyes and sighed. "Oh, Theo. It's perfection. Where did you get the idea?"

"From the ridiculous body of water beside us," he said, bending a knee.

The drawing depicted a fisherman sitting on the bridge over the moat, the one she'd fallen from, and at the end of his line was a mermaid, her long, curling hair caught in his hook. The mermaid had freckles and a heart-shaped face and wore a look of shock. The fisherman, whose hair was fashioned the same way Theo always styled his, had more of a scowl than a face—brows that hung ominously low over narrowed eyes, a cliff for a jawline, and he focused it all on his unexpected catch. Few words marred the picture, and they streamed from the granite fisherman's lips—"Can I keep you?"

He'd gotten the idea not only from the day she'd fallen, but from his every thought upon waking with her in his arms. Could he keep her? And how?

"And," he said, the words escaping on shallow breaths, "it's what you said to me." He turned on his side to face her and pushed his fingers through her hair, drew a line around the shape of her face, ran the pad of his thumb over her chin and down her neck. Her breath caught, and her gaze caught, too. On him. Good. He wanted it to be impossible to look away.

"Well?" His voice gruff. "Can I? Keep you?"

Her nod started small, a tiny shake of the head as she rolled her lips between her teeth, but it soon became a full-body thing as she rolled into him, wrapped her arms around him, and said into his chest, "Yes. Yes. Yes."

"Good." The word came out hoarse, gruff. The opposite of the lightness he felt inside, the brightness, as if this perfect day of a dying summer had leapt into his body. "Good." He kissed the top of her head and held her tight, and they stayed there until the sun began its descent, and her stomach rumbled, then they returned to the house and to raised brows from their friends.

Friends? When he must make enemies of them? Dangerous thought that, one that felt like boulders in his belly. But he must do whatever it took to provide a life for her, to help her start her school. He'd wield his weapons wisely for those who needed it, including her.

"Gone a long time," Pentshire said, bringing him a glass of wine.

Theo grunted and sipped the drink.

Pentshire pulled a square of paper from his pocket. "This came for you. From an address in Manchester."

A letter. From Drew. Would it contain more of what he'd discovered here—nothing much to set the London gossips aflame—or would it contain the bit of information he was missing, the one that might sell his sketches for enough money to set up Cordelia's school?

Nineteen

Cordelia bathed and dressed appropriately for meeting her lover, her future husband—in nothing but shift and wrapper. Even her toes she left unadorned and open to the hard floor. He liked her toes, the arch of her foot, her ankle. Sometimes he kissed and sometimes he tickled, and sometimes she did not know which one she preferred. She left her hair unplaited and streaming down her back as well. He liked that, too. Oh, how he liked it. And so did she, when he wound her tresses round his hand and tugged her closer. Made her a bit ... melty.

His door was unlocked, as she'd known it would be, and she slipped inside. A small fire crackled in the grate, sputtering out. Had he lit it only for his bath? A hip tub sat abandoned nearby, water droplets darkening the floor around it. She had a bigger bath in London, and hopefully they could make excellent use of it upon their return.

Theo sat at the writing desk nearby, shirtless, hunched over, scribbling fiercely. He'd disappeared after their walk to the moat and his proposal, saying with excitement shining in his eyes that he had work to do. Kissing her hard, he'd then bounding up the steps and had not even come down for dinner.

She leaned against the door and watched him. He'd said today that love did not matter, that he admired her, wanted her. A bit of a sting, that, but not a fatal wound. She'd known as much. Still, she almost could not quite believe his words. His actions said differently, so she'd promised to marry a man who treated her like he loved her, even if he could never say the words. He had love in him. She knew that. He would not do the work he did if he did not. He would not try so diligently to help his family if he did not.

His inability to put the right words to his emotions would not be their most pressing problem. Money would be. Where to live. How to fund the school. How much easier this would be if she'd fallen in love with a rich man. She tried to imagine it. Saw only Theo but with more money. Well, that answered that question.

She crept up behind him on tiptoe. What did he work on? She liked his work, his sketches. They revealed a silly side to him she quite liked best of all. That little bit of himself he kept hidden, going so far as to sign another name to his drawings. She got to see it, though. She got to know it, *him*, as few others did.

She slipped her arms around him, rested her head on his shoulder. "Good evening." She kissed the tip of his ear.

He kissed her briefly, but drinking fully, before returning to his work. His hands were splattered with ink, and he was outlining a pencil drawing.

"What is that?" she asked, studying the sketch.

"It's going to buy the house for your school, and it's going to make my career." His voice was as hard as his drawing was meticulous. He moved his hand slowly with each pen stroke, curving the ink into the exact right shapes.

"What—who—is it supposed to be of?" She didn't immediately recognize the people, only one of them fully inked in.

He placed the pen down and yanked a piece of creased paper from the very edge of the desk, handed it to her. "Read this. It's from Drew. That governess of his shared some interesting information with him that she said I could have. The reason she left."

"Oh?" She roamed closer to the fire and read by its dim light. Each sentence churned her gut sour. "Oh ... No ... They're married? Miss Mires and Pentshire ...?" Unbelievable.

He joined her by the fire, leaning an arm against the mantel and ruffling the hand of his other arm through his hair. He nodded, his lips a hard-pressed line. "Oh, yes. The Earl of Pentshire married a dairy maid."

"But ... but why are they hiding it?" She folded the letter and put it on the mantel, a curious buzzing in her fingertips. The paper, stark white in the shadows, winked at her like a snake bite. "He calls her Miss Mires, as does everyone else."

Theo shrugged. "I can't say. But I can guess."

She certainly could offer no suppositions, and the play of firelight over the muscled planes of his chest and abdomen almost distracted her entirely. He must have seen her glazed, lust-filled look, must have known what her slack mouth and lack of response meant. He led her toward the bed, wrapped her in his arms, and dragged her down with him so that he sat against the headboard, and she sat across his lap.

"I think," he said, "Pentshire means to take another bride."

"No!" She could not imagine that always jolly and joking man doing anything like that.

"What other reason could he have?"

"But ... but he does not need to marry a woman with a title. Does he need funds?"

"Not that I can tell."

"Then what possible reason could he have for hiding one wife in order to marry another?"

Theo shrugged, his gaze roving over her nearly undressed state, her unbound hair, down the length of her legs and over the curves of her feet. "Men do bad things for very little reason." His words distracted, his voice hoarse as his hands began to roam her body.

But she could not find distraction in his touch. Nothing quite made sense. "How will you find out why he married her only to hide her? No, not hide her. She's living here. Almost as his wife. Because she is his wife!" She jumped to her feet, chewed her fingernail. None of it made sense, and the implications shredded her good opinion of the man. Perhaps she should not have formed them to begin with. But both he and Miss Mires had seemed so happy living in scandal, and no one at the party seemed to mind overly much. They'd reacted with more vehemence to her past with Simon than to Miss Mires. And she'd never judge, not when she'd been judged so often herself, and falsely. She knew the weight of that, the eternal herculean effort to wear a smile and think the best despite everyone believing the worst.

Behind her, the mattress creaked, and Theo exhaled a heavy sigh. "I'm not worried about the why, Delia. Not right now at least. Come back."

She whirled, palms upright, demanding he place an answer there. "Why bring her here and put her on such public display when he has no intentions of acknowledging her position, her true relationship to him?" He sat on the edge of the mattress, legs spread wide, and she stepped between them, smoothed her palms over his shoulders. "Will you ask him tomorrow?"

He pulled her down onto his leg, kissed her neck. "No."

"But of course you will." What if ... what if Miss Mires needed help of some sort?

"Think it through, love."

The word, dropped so casually from his lips, startled her, but he barreled forward as if he'd not consciously chosen it, as if it were of no consequence.

"If I speak to him on the matter, and he tells me anything, I cannot publish any drawings about it. He'll know who drew them as good as if I published them under my own name."

Some dark doubt gnawed at her. "Then *I'll* ask him."

"We're to marry. And husband and wife"—he kissed her cheek, her jaw—"have no secrets from one another. He'll still have good cause to suspect me."

"It doesn't feel right."

"This feels very right." He nipped her ear.

"No. I don't mean *that*." She jumped to her feet. "I mean publishing private information regarding Lord Pentshire and Miss Mires without knowing the full story."

He sighed, falling back onto the bed, arms flailing out wide. "It's not ideal, but it's the best I've got. The pristine Earl of Pentshire hasn't just got a mistress in the country, living with him, he's got a wife pretending to be a mistress." He shook his head. "Damn odd, if you ask me."

"Ask *him*!" She jumped to her feet. "Ask him why. Discover the circumstances. They cannot be nefarious. I like Lord Pentshire. And I like Miss Mires, and I do not want to see them hurt."

"You don't know them," he groaned.

She marched to the table. The drawing he'd been working on when she arrived still lay in the middle of the desk, surrounded by other scattered and torn bits of paper, by inkblots and half-finished ideas. The paper felt thick between her fingers and already cool to the touch, and she brought it closer to the fire to better see it. The creak of the mattress told her he'd shifted somehow, but she did not look. The drawing in her hands, though half-penciled and half-inked, began to make sense.

"Oh, Theo," she breathed, disappointment coursing through her. "The earl's nose is not that big, truly. And Miss Mires's, ah"—she motioned around her breasts—"*they* are not so large either."

"Exaggeration is required. And ... she's a dairy maid, so—"

"Theo!"

He splayed on the bed, propped up with his elbows behind him, and her fingers itched to stroke the muscles she'd come to know so well. His lips quirked in a hesitant smirk, as if he wanted her to laugh and call him clever, but he rather suspected she would not. That hesitation told him true. The cad.

"This sketch suggests that Pentshire is a *bigamist*." She shook the paper at him, blurring Miss Mires, the earl, and the line of proper ton ladies lined up like cows in stalls at a dairy farm.

He scrambled to his feet. "No, it suggests he's attempting to become one."

"Who will this help, Theo?"

"The woman he intends to marry illegally."

"You don't know he intends to do that!"

His eyes widened.

She might have been a little too loud.

"Do you want to wake the whole house?" he whispered.

"No." She walked to the desk and snapped the drawing down. "Just one particular person." She strode for the door.

But before she could open it, he caught her arm, whirled her around. "Cordelia, please, listen to me. Let me explain."

She stopped, she waited.

"Drew's governess, Miss Carter, she's a reliable source. She lived here, teaching Pentshire's sister. She quit because of the marriage, because it was hidden, because she feared the reasons behind the subterfuge. And others left upon the marriage, as well. She says Pentshire's mother and sister left as well, refusing to live in the same house as the scandal."

"Discover his reasons, Theo. They must be pressing if he willingly alienated his family."

"I've poked into every corner of this house, of Pentshire's life. Into his closets and spare boots, into his not-well-hidden drawers and his cupboards and his wine cellar. He is as pristine as he looks. But for this house party, and even this is not much to make the ton gasp. Not much more scandalous than those my father and mother hosted each year. Perhaps more mistresses, but they are either well-known liaisons or partnerships that hurt no one, like Armquist and Mrs. Bexford. And even his own 'mistress' is his *wife*."

"You will hurt Miss Mires. *Lady Pentshire*." Cordelia pointed at the desk. "*That* will hurt her. And you are worried about a woman you do not know, that might not even exist? A hypothetical marriage prospect for a man already married?"

He ran his hands through his hair. "The cartoon may well help Miss Mires. If she is in a difficult spot, if she is not here by choice, then—"

"Have you seen how she looks at him? And him, at her?"

His chin jerked to the side as his mouth twisted. He'd seen it, too, then. He *knew*.

"Acting," he said, apparently happy to ignore what he'd seen, what he knew. "Pretending. Like—"

"Us?" She pulled her arm out of his grasp.

"Hell. No, not like us." He growled. "You cannot see the truth around you, Cordelia! You insist on believing the best of everyone and letting them continue to ruin things. Why? Why do you let them hurt you, hurt others, without rescinding your good will?"

"Because doubting people constantly is a misery, Theo! One must only look at you to see that. If I always trust, you never do. And do you think that suspicion is without a harmful edge? Ha. In the end, you will be just as careless of others as your father was, but in a different way. Being doubted is a misery, too. It sets you apart, isolates you. Promise me you will not do anything with that drawing until you know for sure. Until you have their wedding license in hand and a witness, their signatures in a registry. Until, even, Pentshire shows up in London courting other women."

"I can't promise that. I won't."

"Why?" She walked backward on numb feet until her back hit the door with a *thunk* that rattled her bones.

"Because what will *we* do then? You and I? If I wish to sell my art, I must make art that sells. And scandal sells; the unexpected sells. I live with my sister. I make a living, and my family, other than a room to keep me dry, cannot support me. I will not ask them to support a wife. I want you to have your school. And that drawing can get it for you. Cruikshanks makes quite a good living off his drawings. And Thomas Rowlandson. Think of it, Cordelia. I can give you everything you need with that." He reached for her hands, held them gently in his own, and closed his eyes. "It will be the start of a career for me and a life for us."

"You wish to buy our future with lies?"

He squeezed her hands, dropped them, his eyes flying open. "Not lies."

"You don't know that. You will not ask, will you?"

He pinched the bridge of his nose. "I cannot divulge my identity." He held his palms out flat. "You must understand that."

"Do you even *want* to know the truth?" She groped for the door handle behind her and twisted it, slipped into the hall, hoping to hear an answer. But the door closed behind her, its click the only sound in the heavy darkness.

She found her room and bed and lay on top of the covers, her muscles too numb to pull them back, to climb under.

Was she overreacting? Possibly. Her emotions were high, but ... the sketch had been so nasty, the opposite of the one he'd given her when he'd proposed marriage. That one had been light and humorous and filled with delight. With love. The one he'd drawn of Pentshire and Miss Mires burned with judgment and hate.

How many men like him, satirists, would love to draw something about the late Marquess of Waneborough's mistress? Or daughter. Or who knew what. All of it one and the same at the end of the day; it was *her*. If she looked for satirical drawings of herself, would she find them? Caricatures less friendly to her than Theo's, exaggerating her body through a cynic's eye and commenting on her soul?

There were two versions of Theo—the gargoyle without a heart and the man she'd discovered beneath, a funny ray of sunshine who seemed to adore her. God, her heart hurt. He wanted to help her fund her school. He wanted to provide a life for her, for them. And she wanted to accept those offers. But at what cost? She had no right to judge how others loved, and neither did he. What if Pentshire's love was innocent?

Innocent.

Like her? Did she trust too easily, look for the best in people when they did not deserve it? Refuse to see their faults? No fault there! How else would she have seen the true, the good Theo beneath his spiny armor?

Her brain hurt. Her gut a bit, too. She did not want to argue with him. They'd come here for this precise reason, to lie, to snoop, to *expose*. Not her. She'd come to court, to offer opportunities for others to do good in the world. And to save herself. The dilemma stemmed not from her reasons or his reason, but because they'd become a *them*. A fortnight ago, she'd not cared overly much how he wasted his time. And his actions would not have hurt her school. Well, except for the fact, he'd been trying to kick her out of it.

If she'd never fallen into his bed then fallen in love, she would not now be so ... broken.

She rolled onto her belly and hid her face in her hands, found her cheeks wet. Blast it all. Tears? On top of everything else?

A knock on the door before it creaked open.

"Cordelia?" Theo's voice, and then his body's weight pressing down the edge of the bed. "I want you to be able to sleep. Please let me stay here with you. Just so you can sleep. I ... I won't touch you."

She didn't say yes. But she did not say no, either. And in that silence, he lay himself down beside her, but as far away as he could manage. And in that positioning, she inched herself as far from him as she could until she teetered on the edge. A mere misplaced breath could send her falling.

"I'm here." His voice hoarse. "You're not alone, yes?"

She could not rightly answer that.

"I'm here."

The last words she heard before she fell asleep.

~

Cordelia woke when the sun in the window glowed pale pink on the horizon. Theo was curved around her, his chest hot against her back, his face buried in her shoulder. Now his arms were loose though heavy about her waist, but when she'd crept to him in the middle of the night, no longer able to resist his outstretched arm, his reassurance of "I'm here" still ringing in her heart, his hold had been tight as a vise.

She loved him. The first thought that entered her head upon waking, and the utter truth. But he would not listen to her. And she could not let him hurt others. Other truths that came in rapid succession. Hurting them would hurt him, too. He fought for justice, and he slipped past that into some gray territory he did not know how to manage because ... of her. He considered hurting them to provide for her.

She would not let him.

Yet she'd been unable to resist him last night, unable to hold steady and keep to her side of the bed. If she gave into him every time he showed his heart, the man would get away with murder. She must resist him. But his body against her felt like perfection, and his breath steady on the skin of her neck washed away her loneliness so entirely, she'd do anything—

No.

She'd long run from the discomfort of independence, fearing loneliness, fearing her own inability to care for herself. She was a pampered earl's daughter after all.

But now she must care for and protect someone else.

She rolled out of Theo's embrace, holding her breath. Then, on quiet feet, she slipped from bed and dressed. It took only a few moments and a few held breaths to sneak into his room, to gather his drawings and slip them into her valise, to write a note with his pen and ink and press a kiss to it. Stockinged feet were more silent on stairs than her half boots, so she waited until she spun down that spiral staircase one last time before she sat on the last step and put her boots on.

"Good morning, Lady Cordelia. Up mighty early. Going somewhere?"

She jumped, covered her mouth with both hands to muffle her yelp. "Lord Pentshire. My, you terrified me."

He bowed. "Apologies, my lady." His gaze flicked to the valise then back to her, accompanied by a single raised brow.

"Ah, yes." She stood, smoothed her skirts. "I am in need of conveyance back to London. Or perhaps to the nearest village so I may take the mail coach."

He shook his head. "No mail coach. You can have a carriage. But, ah, where is Lord Theodore?"

"I must return without him. A family emergency. The, ah, letter he received yesterday."

"Oh. Of course. Come, I'll walk you to the stables and keep you company as everything is prepared.

She almost ran, and he huffed at her side by the time they arrived. What if Theo woke and discovered her missing? What if he came looking for her? Of course he'd come looking for her. Why'd she taken his drawings? He could just sketch another after all. But perhaps the theft would prove to him how serious she was.

Pentshire's grooms, already up and moving about, worked quickly, and soon she settled inside.

"Please, Lady Cordelia," he said, leaning in through the open door. "Let me get you a basket so you can break your fast."

"No. Thank you. I'll stop in a village." If she must. "I am truly in a hurry." He nodded, closing the door. She stopped it just before it clicked, pushed it back open. "My lord ... may I ask a personal question?"

"I"—his mouth drew into a twisted bow then relaxed—"suppose so."

"Miss Mires. Do you love her?"

He rested a palm against his heart and laughed. "Mercy, Lady Cordelia, I thought you meant to ask something distressing. Such an easy question to answer."

"Well, then?"

"Yes." Said with no hesitation. "Quite horribly. Always have. Since we were children. There's never been anyone else but her."

She licked her lips, and sweat beaded on her palms beneath her gloves. "Then ... will you marry her?"

He startled, eyes wide then blinking rapidly. "Marry ... her ... Hm. Yes. Well, yes, things are complicated."

A confusing answer, that. Had he meant yes, he'd married

her or yes, he meant to marry her or ... Why could the man not speak plainly? She'd become too used to Theo and his plain speaking. She rather liked it now, especially when confronted with such ambiguity.

He closed the door. A distinct lack of invitation to ask more questions, that. "Have a safe journey, Lady Cordelia! It has been a *delight* to meet you. And do convince that man of yours to bring you back next year."

He seemed so very nice, but he'd not answered her question at all to her liking. Bother and blast and Theo's favorite *hell*. Had she done the right thing?

The coach lurched, but she threw the door open, stuck her head out, and it stopped just as jerkily.

"Is everything well?" Pentshire asked, running toward her.

"Yes. Yes. But please ... I have experienced the sting of gossip, and ... and I do not wish Miss Mires to suffer so. Please ... if you love her as you say you do, consider how you might make her suffering less when the party ends and the guests return to London."

His face blanched, and his mouth hovered open, a small slit of darkness through which no words escaped. He blinked but gave a small nod.

She slunk back into the coach and shut the door, and it rumbled forward once more. She pressed her palms to the window as it crossed the bridge and moat. She watched until the shrinking house disappeared entirely. Had he woken yet? Would he find the letter she'd left for him?

She turned from the window and wrapped her hands around the seat edge. She'd arrived opposite him and departed without him, but so much more than that changed. He'd embedded himself in her heart. He would, likely, be angry when he discovered the missing drawings. Would he consider it a betrayal?

The coach carried her farther from him, but she may have

already detonated a gunpowder keg over the bridge the last fortnight had built between them. She would not regret it, though. If any chance existed that Pentshire and Miss Mires did not deserve the storm Theo planned for them, Cordelia would do her best to ensure it didn't happen.

Even if saving their happiness shattered her own.

Twenty

E very muscle ached. Theo woke in the same damn position he'd fallen to sleep in—curved on his side, reaching through empty space for Cordelia. She'd fit herself into his embrace at some point, and he'd finally been able to sleep, but she must have rolled away. He did not dare stretch his angry limbs or seek a new position. He wanted to see her before she woke before he must face the anger in her eyes once more and try to find a way to make her understand. If he stretched, he might wake her and lose that moment. Licking his lips, he opened his eyes.

And bolted upright.

"Cordelia?" He twisted left and right, looking. In vain. No one but him in the room.

His heart raced with worry, and he breathed through it, raked his hands through his hair—another soothing gesture. Not quite working. She was fine. She'd just woken early to eat. Had she woken early to ... meddle?

Hell. She could right now be asking Pentshire outright about his *wife*.

He slammed his feet to the floor and found his room in a

few fast steps. He dressed quickly, barely tying his cravat as he flew for the door. Hand on the knob, he stopped. Something was ... odd about the room. Different.

He turned slowly, dragging his gaze over every detail until —the desk. Last night it had been covered with bits and pieces of paper—blotting paper, his sketches, abandoned drafts. Now only a pen, ink bottle, and single, folded piece of paper lay atop it. He ventured nearer and snapped up the paper. His name slashed black lines and curves on the front, and he unfolded it, read the short missive there.

Theo,

Don't rage. I know I've been impulsive, but I must do something to knock some sense into your head. I've taken your drawings. All of them. A silly thing to do considering you can so easily draw more. Don't do that, by the way. Please? I hope that you'll take the rest of the house party to actually understand the situation you are so eager to share with the world. Talk with the earl. There are other scandals for you to expose. Do not expose this one if it will do more harm than good.

And especially do not do that for me.

I'm returning to London. Because I fear if I stay with you, I'll give in as I did last night, I'll do anything for your embrace. Even now I'm tempted to crawl back into bed with you, to agree with you simply to keep you. I won't, though. Because Miss Mires deserves truth.

If you need a scandal to sell, draw mine. Earl's daughter ruins herself in artist's bed and then is kept by a man old enough to be her father. I'm sure you'll come up with something clever to depict it.

. . .

I love you,

Cordelia

The letter fluttered from Theo's fingertips to the desk, then he snatched it up and read it again. She'd left. She'd taken his drawings. She ... loved him. Legs going numb, he clutched for the chair and sat, crumpling the paper in his fist as a red haze fogged the room and rage rocked through him. Damn her. Straight to hell for interfering. She had no damn right to do so.

He dropped his head into his hands, something like grief following quick on rage's heels, consuming him. She'd left. She'd left and declared her love for him. Who did that?

Cordelia did that, and he wanted to shake her. But he wanted to hold her. No, he wanted to do both.

He would simply ... go after her. She could not have been on the road long. He didn't need the drawings. As she pointed out, he could draw more. But he needed to find her, to talk some sense into her. Ha. The same thing she'd said about him in her letter. She was trying to make him see sense. To force him to speak openly with Pentshire about his secrets. Didn't she know secrets didn't work that way? He had his own he needed to keep well-hidden. Sir George would not be welcome where Lord Theodore was, and what she asked him to do ...

She'd left him with few choices. He could speak with Pentshire and discover the truth, and if things were as bad as he expected, he could then publish. But he *couldn't* because Pentshire would know. How could he not after having a bloody conversation about the matter?

What if he published without talking to Pentshire? Would she refuse to marry him? Would she run? Would she refuse him entrance to her house? There would be no more house because someone else would buy it. Would she rather live on the streets than let him earn his money as he willed?

He left the room and slammed the door behind him. What would he do? She'd not threatened to leave him entirely, but ... she would. Her actions this morning posed an eternal ultimatum. He must choose between the caricature that could launch his career ... or her.

The woman who said she loved him and whom he ... he ...

He took the stairs, dangerously, two at a time, and hit the ground floor at a run. "Where the hell's Pentshire?" His yell echoed across the old house as he stormed into the great hall. A number of guests already sat there, including the Castles, and they all turned toward him. "Pentshire?"

Mr. Castle gestured at an empty seat next to him. An invitation.

Theo had no time to break his fast. But Castle wasn't offering information from across the room, so Theo joined him.

Mr. Castle leaned low. "There's a bit of a storm brewing today." He sipped his coffee, intent, it seemed to take his time telling the story.

"How so?" Theo demanded.

"Pentshire and his mistress have been up since early morning. Arguing." He said the last word with his lips at the rim of his cup, one eyebrow arched high.

"Oh?" Fascinating. Should be. Trouble between the lovers. No. Between husband and wife. But that worried him less than—

"Where is Lady Cordelia this morning?" Mrs. Castle asked.

Theo cleared his throat, tapped the table. "Traveling. Back to London. I must follow her soon. Today. Within the hour." Sooner.

"Ah." Mr. Castle downed the rest of his coffee. "That's why you're in search of Pentshire. To bid him farewell."

Theo nodded. He wasn't quite sure why he searched for Pentshire. Some part of him had determined to speak with him, but now ... he hesitated.

"Is everything well?" Mrs. Castle asked, peering into a book. "With you and Lady Cordelia."

No idea. "Yes."

"Excellent. Excellent. Would hate for two pairs of young lovers to enter the storm at the same time. I do hope your lady is well-equipped to travel alone."

"I—" Hell. She was alone. He'd been so angry, so baffled, he'd not yet considered that. He stood. "I must speak with Pentshire whether he's in the middle of an argument or not. Where are they?"

The Castles shrugged.

Theo left them, trudged back upstairs, and found the wing that housed the earl's chambers. He raised his arm to slam on the double doors at the end of the hall. But froze.

On the other side of the door—sniffling, crying, a voice low and pleading. "I don't care about my reputation! It's you who cares. Y-y-you're ashamed of me!" Miss Mires dissolved into sobs.

Hell. Did *not* want to smash right into that argument.

Low-voiced apologies. Must be Pentshire. "Just a little longer."

Theo should sneak away. No. He couldn't wait. Cordelia had left, and he must act quickly. He raised his arm again.

"Get out!" Miss Mires yelled. "I will not pretend any longer!"

Theo pulled his fist from the door, wincing at the volume of her voice. "Bloody hell."

He backed away. He'd *have* to wait.

The door flung open, forcing Theo back several stumbling steps, and Pentshire stormed out.

"Lord Theodore," he said when he saw him. His face was pale, his jaw set hard. "I blame *you*. So *you're* going to pay for it. Follow me." He strode down the hall and bounced down the stairs, led Theo to his study, a place Theo had never been to except in secret, snooping about to dig up dirt. "Sit."

Theo sat. Gingerly. Wary.

Pentshire threw open the doors of a cabinet, revealing a crystal decanter set likely filled with, judging by the color, Scottish whisky. He poured two glasses, and Theo welcomed it. He'd had a hell of a morning, too. And his day would not get easier. He had to chase down his betrothed. But first —Pentshire.

Pentshire threw himself into a seat across from Theo but didn't drink. His jaw worked and clicked as if trying to find words.

Theo helped him. "I'm at fault? For what?"

"Your ... woman ... has plucked the final thread of my conscience, and everything's fallen to pieces."

"You'll have to explain more than that."

Pentshire poured the whisky down his throat and slammed the glass on the table. "I'm married. To Miss Mires. Not Miss Mires. The Countess of Pentshire."

Theo schooled his features. "That's a surprise. You call her—"

"The marriage is a secret because her father is a villain." He laughed, a bitter, sharp thing.

"What does her father—"

"Maria is the Duke of Wallingham's illegitimate daughter. Her mother married the dairy farmer before she gave birth. The man knows—knew—she wasn't his. Loved her like his own, though." He pinched the bridge of his nose and let his head hang heavy. "Thank God for that."

Theo knit his hands together above his abdomen. Apparently, all he'd only had to do was listen, and Pentshire's secrets came tumbling out. But what did Cordelia have to do with it?

Pentshire groaned. "I'll not bore you with details."

"No. Details are fine." Hell. He'd sounded too eager.

"The dairy farmer died, and Maria was alone, and I'd been in love with her forever, so I married her. Special license."

"Congratulations?"

Pentshire hung his head lower, showing Theo the crown of his head, his hair mussed and sticking up. "But I've told no one. My mother knows. And does not approve."

"Why have you kept the true nature of your relationship a secret?" Theo asked. The question Cordelia most wanted answers to.

Pentshire's head shot up. "Because Maria's not ready to face the ton yet. She was raised as a farmer's daughter. And the duke will eviscerate her when he discovers who she is. I had hoped ... I had hoped a party would give her an opportunity to learn how to be a countess. And a coterie of artists would provide guests who were less morally ... uptight, who would not care so much about her seeming lack of position here. I knew it was a horrid idea."

Theo leaned into the back of the chair with a groan, knitting his hands together behind his head. "You mean this whole thing is about protecting your wife? It's a farce, man. A damn horrible idea."

"I know."

"What does Cordelia have to do with this?" Theo asked.

"I saw her off this morning."

Theo's muscles bunched, ready to throw a fist in the man's face for helping Cordelia flee, but he clenched his jaw and settled. For now. Waited.

"She said something curious and abrupt to me before she

left. She said that if I cared for Maria, I'd make sure she didn't suffer from gossip as she had."

"Good lord." Theo scratched his hands through his hair, threw back the rest of the whisky. "More?"

The earl replenished both their glasses. They downed them at the same time.

"I didn't think much of it at first. Except that it was odd, but then I thought of that arse Bradley and his cronies. Of his treatment of Lady Cordelia and how even after he assaulted her, he still had friends who condoned his actions, and I realized—"

"You mucked it up."

"Yes," he groaned. "I was trying to save her, protect her, but by hiding our marriage, I've made it even worse. Maria has *known* this, but she's not said a thing. Didn't want to upset me. And I didn't know that until this morning when I asked her about it. And I ... I don't know how to fix it." Pentshire sank so low in his seat, he almost fell out of it. His arse hung on to the chair's edge by a thread of his well-tailored trousers.

Hell. Cordelia had been right.

Theo pressed his fingers into his eyebrows, trying to press his thoughts into line. "Why are you telling me all of this?"

"Because you're in love with a woman the world finds unsuitable, too. You'll understand." The gaunt despair of Pentshire's face softened only a bit with a weak ray of hope. The man was innocent and optimistic as Cordelia. Especially if he thought to be chummy with Theo over love.

He opened his mouth to deny it. He wasn't in love.

But he was. He couldn't force a denial up his throat. He could never live that lie, never breathe the air he'd spoken the words into.

He snapped to standing, a curse on his lips.

Pentshire pushed to sit upright. "What do I do?"

"First"—Theo stabbed a finger in the other man's direction—"stop being a damn hypocrite." Pentshire shot to his feet, hands becoming indignant fists at his side. Theo stalked forward "I heard your wife yelling. She doesn't want secrecy. She's ready to face the danger, to be herself. Sure seems like you're the one worried about reputation. Hers? Or your own?"

Pentshire's face curled up in a snarl. Then dropped. "Hell. I'm an arse. What do I do?"

"You're asking the wrong man. But if I were you, and the woman I loved wanted me just as I was, I'd want her back. Without a single change to her. I'd rather face the jeers of the ton than the graveyard of her lost smile. In short, don't be a damn coward. If you love her, let her be herself." He made for the door. "I'm returning to London. Now."

Pentshire scrambled after him as he entered the hallway. "What will *you* do?"

Find Cordelia. Easier to focus on what the earl should do. "You will host a big bloody wedding." Theo couldn't. Not even his brother Raph, the marquess, had had a big wedding. He and his wife had married quietly in the chapel at Briarcliff. *Economically* at the chapel in Briarcliff. If—when—Theo married, he would as well. But the earl, the earl could afford a statement. A grand gesture. "Host the largest wedding possible with as many tonnish guests as you can muster. A good many will cut you and side with the duke. But don't show any shame. Let them pick sides." It's what Theo would do. Never show shame. "She's not something to be ashamed of. The only shame should be the duke's. And listen here." He stopped, turned, and stood nose to nose, cravat to cravat, with Pentshire. "You let everyone see how much you adore her. Never falter. Do you understand?"

Pentshire nodded, eyes wide. "Yes. Of course."

Theo strode away. "And no more damn house parties!"

He wound his way upstairs, packed his bags, and sent for a

carriage. If he didn't catch up to Cordelia on the road, he'd catch up to her in London. No reason to stay here any longer. The scandal of the year ... no scandal at all. A man who loved his wife acted the fool about it. No news there.

He should be glad he'd discovered the truth before publishing a falsehood. But the truth proved a sharp weapon, and now that it was pointed at him, he feared the damage it might do—had done—to the thing of beauty he and Cordelia had created between them. Because much like Pentshire, he'd mucked it up and had to find a way to make it right.

Twenty-One

Cordelia had fully expected Theo to stop her coach like a highwayman the entire ride to London. But either he never caught up with her, or he had never left.

She should feel victorious about that. Perhaps he'd stayed to do as she'd asked him to—speak with Pentshire. But she could muster only an achy sort of grumpiness. Part of her had wanted him to give chase, to prove he wouldn't, like all the rest, simply leave her. Forget her in the end.

She walked aimlessly through her house, tracing her fingers along the walls, righting picture frames, and slightly turning vases. The *plonk* of piano keys echoed from the second floor, and the voices of teachers echoed up from the ground floor. She was as surrounded as she'd been at the party, but lonelier than ever. She'd done it to herself.

But for a good cause.

The door to her Gallery of Shame was closed, and she pressed a palm to it until that hand fisted tight, the need to fling open the door and smash all her failures to the ground almost crushing her. But she flattened her palm again. Her lack of talent as an artist was no failure, but living life to please others was. Theo had called her an artist of life, and that felt much truer than painter, sculptor, or any other more esteemed title. She'd cling to that, bring her visions to life.

Even if Theo hated her now.

A banging below made her jump, and she rushed to the top of the stairs.

"Mrs. Barkley?" she called out.

Mrs. Barkley ran into the entryway, peeked through the slender window on one side of the door and screeched, "The gargoyle!"

He'd arrived. Her heart leapt, and she told it to shush. No matter how much she wanted to fling herself at him and kiss him, she had to stay strong.

She fled down the hall. "Whatever you do, do not let him in!"

The lock slammed home in the front door.

"Cordelia!" Though his yells were muffled by thick wooden doors and stout walls, they shook the rafters. "Cordelia!" More banging. "Open up!" he bellowed.

She swung into her bedroom at the front of the house and took a steadying breath. She'd have to face him, and she could not quite be sure of how she'd react. Leap out of the window and into his arms? Hopefully not. That's why she'd chosen the first-floor window in the house to speak to him through. Unlikely she'd ever be truly ready for this, so she faced it anyway, flinging the window open, sticking her head out, and wrapping her hands round the sill.

Oh. There he was, and where she'd expected to confront the gargoyle, he stood before her as the man, the Theo who brushed her hair and gave funny drawings to street children. The window wasn't that high. And he was a strong man. He'd catch her. Right? She should just jump right into his arms and—

No! She must remember her purpose, stay focused on her principles.

"Cordelia," he said, his voice a ragged breath, a tear in the air around them.

Ignore it. *Ignore* it. "Good afternoon, my lord. It is lovely to see you. Now, will you please scurry off? Return to whatever rooftop you swooped down from."

"Let me in." He lifted his hands, palms up and open, vulnerable.

"You've come for your sketches."

"I've come for *you*."

"Liar."

"Of course I want the sketches back, Cordelia! But I want you, too. Now stop being such a little fool, and—"

"A fool, am I?" Yes, quite. She disappeared back into the house, slipping her hands into her hair and tugging. She rather thought she might pull it all out before he understood her position.

"Will you come downstairs and let me in?" he called out.

"No!" she shouted, returning to the window.

"Very well, then." His gaze bounced around the front of the townhouse, then he removed his gloves, smashed them halfway into his pockets, and rubbed his bare palms together, inching toward the house.

"What are you doing?"

He put a foot on the window ledge and hauled himself upward, reaching high to grab the top edge of the window. "I think that should be obvious. If people can exit through your windows, Cordelia, then I can enter through them."

"Theo! This window is much higher up than the other!" The window she'd pushed her instructors out of had been at ground level. This one on the first floor.

"I can manage." He grunted, swung his leg up to the side, and found a step of some sort in the brick momentarily before his foot shot off and he hung from his fingers, cursing.

Cordelia gasped, her heart hammering, then he found his footing once more and somehow pulled himself atop the very small overhang above the door. He'd almost reached the level with her window now, and she knew exactly his intentions. If she wouldn't let him in through the front door, he'd find other means of entering. She wanted to slam the window closed and shut him out. But she couldn't because … what if he fell? She needed him safe, and the best way to achieve that was to pull his stubborn and attractively agile body into the house.

"Theo," she said, head stuck out of the window, "go back down. There's too much distance between that overhang and this window. You'll hurt yourself."

He grunted, determination clear as a blinding sun in his eyes. He bent his knees.

And leapt, throwing his body sideways. Cordelia yelped and scuttled away from the window as his arms wrapped with a clatter around the window ledge. He slipped, the weight of his body pulling him toward the hard street below, and she rushed toward him, slammed her hands down on top of his.

"I'm fine," he grunted. "Get back in."

"Foolish, horrid man. No." She leaned out the window and wrapped her hands around his elbows, but as she did, the muscles in his arms flexed, transforming his biceps—all of him really—to pure steel, and he pulled himself up and over, falling into a puddle on her bedroom floor.

Quick as a blink, he stood, brushed her off, and prowled toward her.

She backed away, not fearing him, but fearing herself. She'd locked him out, run away, for a very clear reason. Because when he looked at her as he did now, she melted, gave in, and this was too important for melting.

He came for her, though, forcing her backward across the room until her back *thunked* against the wall, pushing the air out of her lungs with a hard huff. He took her air for himself, bracing his forearms on the wall on either side of her head and pinning her, kissing her, hard and hungry.

She clutched at his shoulders, his neck, his lapels, kissing him back between admonitions. "You cannot simply climb through my window and kiss me."

"I can. I have."

"Aren't you angry with me?" A breathless question as he tore at her earlobe with his teeth.

"Incensed," he growled, kissing her neck. "But I missed you more. Was damn worried. God, Cordelia, the need to kiss you will always be stronger than any other emotion."

Her legs gave out.

His arm wrapped around her, pulled her close, and somehow, she was falling through air, hitting the mattress, and the hem of her gown was raked high, and her bodice pulled dangerously, deliciously low, and—

"No." She sat up, pushing him away and fixing her gown. "Did you speak with Pentshire?"

He rolled away from her and onto his back, his palms scraping down his face. "Yes. Though it's more that he spoke with me."

"And."

"Innocent. All of it." He rose from the bed, steady, each movement clipped and controlled. "Foolish and nonsensical, but … innocent."

"Ah." She stood, too, straightening her skirts, preparing for battle. "Here's the anger, I assume. Though you should be thanking me. Had you not found out the truth, you would have published lies."

His jaw ticked. "Had you left well enough alone, I would have been able to buy this house. The printshops would have battled one another for the opportunity to print it. Your school would be secured."

She shook her head. "Too high a cost. I'll not let Miss Mires, Lady Pentshire, pay that."

"She won't."

"Why do you grumble?" She rushed to him, placed her hands on his shoulders. "It is a good thing."

"Where are my sketches?" he asked, shrugging out of her light hold.

"I ... Here." She knelt near her bed and pulled his satchel from beneath it but hugged it to her as she stood.

He held out a hand.

She hugged it still. "You would have ruined her. You would have besmirched Miss Mires's name as Simon did mine." She hesitated, not wanting to say the truth. But she must. So she gathered her courage and closed her eyes and put it out into the world. "As ... as your father did mine. I am grateful"—she closed her eyes and swallowed the lump blocking her throat—"I am grateful ... I am grateful." She shook her head, unable to knock the words on repeat into something else, into the thing she meant to say.

His hands caught her wrists. "You do not have to say that. I know you are."

"But—" A sharp bite of a word that helped her find her forward trajectory as her hands clawed tighter into the satchel held like a wall between them. "Your father *was* thoughtless. I've always known that and did not wish to say it. Or even think it. Because it seemed to be the cost of being saved." She finally met his gaze. "His thoughtlessness hurt me. As it did you. And *your* thoughtlessness could hurt me, too."

"I would never hurt you. But I will do what I must to make a life for us. I have a career, and I could be good at it if—"

"You will *not* sell other people's sins to pay for my life,

Theo. Why do you wish to live off of other people's pain? Why can't you leave it alone?"

"It's not their pain I'm living off of, Cordelia, it's justice. I'm—"

"*Exposing injustice*. Yes, I know. But there's more you can do. Your drawings are funny and sweet, and—"

"Those are meaningless. A lark I should not waste time on. The satires are what I do." His hands became manacles on her wrists.

But she did not squirm. "It does not have to be. You do not have to dig up others' dirt to help the world, to make it better. The drawings you give to children make the world better. The beauty of the art you created at the party—that makes the world better, too. You have talked of teaching. Why must you play at ... artistic vigilante? I do not know if I wish to have those shadows in my life."

He let go of her wrists as if electrified. "What are you saying?"

"I don't know, Theo." She cupped her cheeks, and their heat seeped into her palms.

"You said you loved me." He pulled a folded bit of paper from his pocket, crushed it in his hand. The letter she'd left for him.

"I do." She laughed despite it all, hugged the satchel as if it were him. "God help me, I love you."

He lurched toward her, an infinitesimal movement as his mouth parted. For a brief, breathless moment she knew he'd grab her to him, return the words. He loved her. She saw it in his face, the lines of his body, his actions, even if he could not recognize it himself. But would he say it?

He rocked back onto his heels, snapping his mouth closed and shoving the letter back into his pocket. "My father pretended he loved me, too."

"Theo." She reached for him. "I'm not pretending. And neither was your father. You must stop living in the past."

"Living in the past? What does that mean?"

"It means every decision you make, every action you take is determined by your father, taken because you think it makes you less like him. How long has it been since you've asked yourself what you want to be instead of merely attempting to be as unlike him as possible?"

His cheeks hollowed, and his breaths lifted and dropped his chest in a steady but hard rhythm. "You think I'm stuck? You think I let my father define me?"

"Yes—"

He stormed from the room.

After a moment of shock, she followed, putting the satchel's strap around her shoulder, oddly unable to let it go. But when he threw open the door to her Gallery of Shame, she hesitated, her heart beats stopping just as the slap of his boots against the wood flooring had.

"Come look, Cordelia."

She closed her eyes, wrapped her hand around the doorframe, and took a step into the room.

"Open your eyes and see the past *you* live in."

She opened her eyes but kept her gaze trained on him. She had expected the mottled red-and-white of fury to distort his face, but he looked at her only with softness, a hint of despair.

"You let him tell you who to be for four long years. And even now, when you've taken on new dreams, you still keep these around you. What are they, Cordelia, and why do you keep them? You are not the failed artist my father and your instructors thought you are. You are a promising headmistress. You are a bringer of light and laughter. You are a source of good in the world. You are not—"

"Stop." She held out a hand. "You're right." Why hang onto the artifacts, why let them define her? Why continue to see herself by others' standards for happiness and success? If she asked him to step into the present, then so must she. "I have only ever been wanted for my beauty, which will fade, my connections, which I lost, or my talent, of which I have none."

She picked up a silhouette she'd drawn of Mrs. Barkley that looked more like St. Paul's Cathedral. "This? I am not good at this." She ripped it in half and let the pieces flutter to the floor. Then she picked up a ceramic ... something or other. Difficult to tell. "And this? I am not good at this either." She threw it to the floor where it shattered, a rather satisfying sound. Then she swept her arm across the entire shelf of ceramics, sending them all crashing. "Yet, you are right, I've long defined myself by them, refusing to do what I ask you to do—to see what you could be, to try to be what you most want to be, what brings you most joy."

She tugged a painting off the wall and snapped its frame across her knee.

Theo winced.

"You are right. I can inspire in other ways. I have other talents. And I will choose to define myself. My past does not have that power any longer, and *you* do not have that power. No one does anymore. I take it for myself. Now, Theodore Bromley. What will you do?"

The pile of her broken past spread between them, and he seemed broken, too, his brows drawn low, and his shoulders hunched. Then, slowly, he nodded. But still, he did not speak.

Each second that ticked by without a word boiled her anger to a pitch.

She pointed toward the door. "Leave."

Finally, he looked at her. "In a few weeks' time, this house will no longer be yours. What will you do then?"

"I will figure it out." She ripped his satchel over her head and shoved it toward him. "Leave!"

He stepped over the detritus, placing the bag's strap

around his shoulders like armor or a burden he must always carry, and she wrapped her arms around her waist. He paused in the doorway. "Cordelia, I—"

"Leave. And when you figure out what it is you want, Lord Theodore Bromley, then let me know, and I'll see if I still want you." A surprise the words did not tremble on her tongue and break into a thousand pieces once they hit the air.

He entered the hall, and she followed him.

"Your father protected me, Theo. *You* have protected me." She spoke to his retreating back. "But I will protect others from you. If I must."

He didn't turn around, and soon, even the thick wave of his hair disappeared down the stairs. She walked after him, barely aware of moving, wanting only to see him a moment or two longer.

Below, the front door opened. Then closed, and she placed a palm against the wall to steady herself, support herself, then she leaned her shoulder and hips there, too.

"Lady Cordelia." Mrs. Barkley's head, then the rest of her body, appeared, bobbing up the stairs. "Has he hurt you?"

The housekeeper would have heard the raised voices of the argument, the smashing of her pitiful collection. Yes, he'd hurt her.

But Cordelia smiled, as she always did. "I am well, Mrs. Barkley."

"Let me help." Mrs. Barkley shuffled toward her.

"Yes. Please send someone to clean up this room. Have ... have everything but the furniture removed from it. Thrown away. We will not need it when we move."

Mrs. Barkley disappeared once more, and Cordelia returned to the broken room to wander aimlessly about it, flicking that needlepoint cushion with the illegible wording and running a finger down a cup that looked more like a melted bowl. She waited for the inevitable pang of failure to come.

It didn't. Lord Waneborough had held such high hopes, and she'd disappointed him by failing to be the prodigy he'd hoped for. He'd traded an actual artistic genius for her, after all. Would only have been right, a fitting repayment for his protection, to be good at art. And she had lived by that failure for too long. And she thanked Theo for releasing her from the obligation of guilt.

She would spend no more time regretting not being good at this. She could not paint a scene, but she could organize one, find the right people and put them in the right places as she had her instructors and their students. The true shame would be in continuing to wish herself otherwise instead of using her talents as they were. Her artistic endeavors had served their purpose long ago, had helped her heal.

And now she would help others. When Mrs. Barkley arrived with boxes, and they began to empty the shelves and tables and walls, she felt like a blank canvas, ready to be filled with a design of her own choosing.

She wanted that design to include Theo but could not know what design he would choose for himself.

Twenty-Two

Ink-stained papers covered the floor of Theo's bedroom at Briarcliff. They ran from wall to wall with only small pathways winding throughout so he could walk through them, discover ... nothing so far. Every single sketch he'd produced at the house party and since then.

Knock, knock. "Theo?" His brother Atlas's honeyed voice almost made him want to open the door. "Weather's fine for a swim in the lake. Join us?"

"Will a race in which I, naturally, win, entice you, brother?" Zander, of course.

"No. Go away."

A double sigh he heard even through the thick oak of his door, then footsteps retreating down the hall. Thank goodness for small miracles.

No time for a swim. So many sketches.

All of them useless. The ones of Pentshire that offered truth depicted only soft or playful moments between a man and woman Theo now knew to be husband and wife. And those he'd made of the other guests—the Castles, the baron and his mistress particularly—just the same. No scandal there. Only pure love, a bit of pain mingled in at times.

Another knock, this one lighter but more persistent. "Theodore?" Matilda, Raph's wife. "Will you be joining us for dinner tonight?"

"We'd love your company." Fiona, Zander's wife, her voice ever hopeful.

Damn. He couldn't tell them to go away. "No. Thank you."

"Very well," Matilda said. "I'll have something sent up." As she had every night since his return here.

"Thank you." The words felt weak on his tongue as he walked his beaten path through his drawings, and his room yawned into silence once more.

There were a few sketches of that arse Bradley and his lady, but they were rather boring. Theo had asked his mother to make inquiries about the lady in letters sent to London friends, and she'd discovered scandal. Bradley's mistress from the house party was married, and her husband had no idea she'd been anywhere other than their country estate the last fortnight. Theo had drawn several usable satires since finding that bit of gossip out. The problem was he no longer wished to use them.

His wardrobe, doors slightly ajar, seemed to grow larger. He'd hidden the slim box of charcoal drawings that had arrived days ago from Holloway House there. The kind Earl of Pentshire had sent them to him with an invitation to join them next year and his sympathies for having not won the competition. Despite the wardrobe's looming presence, he ignored it.

"Theodore, my darling." No knock this time. Just his mother's voice crooning to him. "Come out, please. Tell us what has happened."

"I'm fine, Mother. I'm working." He knelt and snapped

one sketch off the ground. Bradley with a rat's face, scurrying out of a moat and running beneath a lady's skirts, the uniquely distinguishable Holloway House behind them. Promising.

"You work in London. We are not in London."

"I work where it pleases me."

"I had a dream last night," his mother said. Theo groaned. "There was a woman."

A dagger to the gut, that. Yes, there was a woman.

"But her features were unclear, and she sailed in a boat farther and farther away, and—"

"Mother, I'm fine."

"Yes. Very well." Her voice unsure, though a bit hurt. "It was likely only Lady Cordelia. Since she'll be leaving our protection soon. And I only associated it with you because you're the one who's been trying to find her a new home." A pause. "You have found her a home, haven't you?"

"Everything is fine, Mother," he snapped. He'd throw Cordelia into a coach and kidnap her if he had to, bring her here to keep her safe. She'd hate him after that, of course, but she'd enjoy the female company at Briarcliff.

"You were always such a sunny little boy." His mother sighed. How many damn sighs would he collect outside his bedchamber door? "If you need us, darling boy, we are here."

Then soft footsteps. Retreating, pulling the tissue of his heart too thin.

Bah.

Good. She'd left. Now he could concentrate, choose the sketch that would sell for enough pounds to finance Cordelia's school. He held the sketch up to study it once more, winced. He saw it not as the ton would see it—with glee and no little bit of vitriol—but as Cordelia would see it, with empathy. The publication of such information would hurt not just Bradley, but his mistress. Or her children. Her husband too. But perhaps he deserved to know. Undoubtedly, he did. And Bradley would be ruined, and justice would be upheld and ...

Cordelia would never see him again.

But without it he'd never be able to provide for her. And the one thing he'd never questioned, not even when leaving her damn house, was that he'd provide for her, care for her. She didn't want his care though. It came with stipulations. Her well-being could not be funded through the ruination of others.

And he ... admired that. His head hung back on his neck and growl that became a low, persistent scream scraped out of his throat. What was he supposed to do? He had no choices!

Not true, the wardrobe said. It seemed to have grown the size of the room, bigger, big enough to hold all his mistakes, all his faults, and the box of paintings peeked out at him.

They were not an option. He was not an artist. He'd failed to win a simple country house party competition. He tore across the path through his drawings and ripped the wardrobe door open, ripped the box open, and froze.

On top of the very first drawing he'd made of Cordelia—a kiss, her closed eye—lay an unopened letter with his name scrawled across it in his father's handwriting. Had he ... dropped it at some point? Left it in his bedchamber at Holloway House? Would have been better if the servants had never found it, if Pentshire had never returned it to him.

The tear in it from the knife he'd stabbed it with, weeks ago now, seemed a jagged wound.

He wore a corresponding one in his own gut. Cordelia had put it there with her accusations. She'd smashed the artifacts that had held so much sway over her and dared him to do the same. The letter winked up at him.

Fine. If she could rip up her old art, he could face the damn letter.

Theo kicked the drawings and sat amongst them, scattering the mermaid, the breakfast romance judges, and all the other useless and silly sketches he'd produced since leaving her in London. Most of them of her. Many of them fit for no one's eyes but his. And hers. Drawings of curves and angles and hidden bits, of the mole hidden on the inside of her knee and the scar that stretched tight over his right hip.

What good would opening the letter do? What would it solve? She'd told him to be who he was, not who his father's influence had made him. She was wrong. He'd made himself. He'd made himself.

Because of his father's actions.

Hell. He'd read it and be done with it. He tore at the wax and opened it, and his father's voice poured out like a deluge of tears.

My Theodore,

You should have had a grand career, my son. I'd planned for it, hoped for it. I thought my actions would bring you closer to it. If I steeped you deep enough in art and surrounded you with artists, I would foster that seed of talent in you. I pushed you from it, though.

That, as all the rest, my fault as well.

Do not blame your mother. We are all the products of our circumstances. Me, her, your brothers, you. Some of us do better within our circumstances than others. I wilted. But you, my son, will rise. Because you have a fierceness in you I've never had. I wish I could be there to see it.

Do not hate beauty and love because of me. They are powerful when wielded in the right way. So much more powerful than anything else. I fear I wielded them without wisdom. My greatest mistake. Sell the painting. It's yours. An apology. And one day, when you are famous, sell this drawing, too. Your juve-nilia. Priceless, though once you've grown a name for yourself there will be those who name it a steep price.

I love you,
  Your father

He found a third piece of paper sandwiched between the note and paper that had folded the two inner pieces together. It distracted from a tumult of emotions he had no wish to face, so he slipped it out. Thin, worn, the paper almost see-through in places. A watercolor with his rough signature at the bottom, the words *age 10* next to it. He ran his fingers over the sixteen-year-old watercolor painting. Delicate and lively even now. He remembered when he'd painted it. A picnic by the lake—blankets spread over thick green grass, his mother's and sister's gowned forms leaning toward one another, a third woman in the corner—Matilda when she'd been governess to Maggie—and his father and Raph, darker columns nearby. A simple painting, nothing more than colored blobs, but the outlines of ink brought each form into sharp relief, into detail, into emotion. A happy family, the wind playing with bonnet strings, and Raph and his father laughing.

And Theo had been there, too. Watching, saving the memory in paint and ink. He stood and slammed the note and the watercolor down on his writing desk, his eyes burning. He found Raph's study in a blurry fury and slammed the door open, unsure why he was running and slamming and demand-ing, just knowing he had to do it.

"If I win my inheritance, will you give the money to me?"

Sitting at the desk, Raph looked up from his books, star-tled. "Pardon?"

"If I win my inheritance and sell the Rubens, will you give the money to me? Not to me. I want it to go to Cordelia. She can buy the house or buy another or whatever she wishes. It should be hers."

Raph slowly settled the pen in his hand into the crook of the notebook before him and pushed to standing. "Are you sure?"

Theo nodded. "Hell. If she uses it to buy the house from you, you'll get it right back."

"I'm not worried about that, Theo." Raph rounded the desk and leaned against the front of it. "Are you ... well?"

Of course he bloody hell wasn't well. He dashed the evidence of his tears away.

"I think I'm in love," he admitted. There it was, hanging heavy as a wool blanket in the room and three times as itchy.

"Ah." Raph shifted. "With ... whom?"

"With whom? Lady Cordelia!" Who else could there be?

"You don't have to scream, Theo."

"I'm not screaming!" But of course he was.

"Right. Yes. I take it congratulations are ... *not* in order?"

"I don't know." He raked his hands through his hair. "She agreed to be my wife, but then ... I think ... we're arguing?" Or had she sent him away for good?

Raph's lips thinned, and he hung his head. Then his shoulders began to shake.

"Are you laughing?"

He looked up, his face cracked with mirth. "I am," he gasped. "I can't help it." He grasped for a nearby seat and fell into it, his body heaving.

Theo spun and slammed the study door closed. "Shh! They'll all hear you and come running because we belong to a family of busybodies."

"True." Raph wiped a tear from his eye. "God, it's true.

But are you sure? About being in love. Ha. Damn, my belly aches now. Haven't had that good a laugh in ages."

"I'm glad to have provided you with such amusement. And yes, I'm sure. Well, not really. I didn't think love real. No." He scratched the back of his neck. "Not true. I suppose I knew it was. But I did not think myself foolish enough to fall prey to it."

"That's outright hubris, brother."

"I see that now. How do you stand it? Survive it?" Pentshire had asked him what to do to ensure the happiness of the woman he loved. And Theo had told him, thought he'd told him true, too. But the advice he'd given Pentshire would not suit Cordelia.

She wanted him to give up the jagged outlines of his very soul. He snorted as he sank into a chair across from his brother. "Not asking much, is she?"

"What is she asking for?"

"She wants to build a school. An art school. And she wants me to help. And she wants me to ... be less of a damn gargoyle."

"You *are* a gargoyle. Apt comparison, that."

"Much thanks, brother," Theo grumbled. "The thing is I don't think I am a man of stone, a monster. Not with her. And not always." The painting in his room, drawn by a child's hand, his own hand, had not been the bitter musings of a beast. He'd kept his heart a sunny day until ... until ... "Raph, what did Father write in his letter to you?"

"Ah." Raph crossed his hands over his abdomen. "You read yours?"

"I did. Zander snuck it for me."

Raph rolled his eyes. "Naturally he did."

"Father apologized. Not that an apology solves anything."

"No. But it can help you shake off the residue."

"I don't take your meaning?"

"You understand. When there is a fire, even the things that are left standing are touched. By ash, by a film, a residue that smudges over everything. I felt like that for a long time because I was living in the fire, refusing to come out of it, and admit that the flames weren't so deadly as they were before. But when I did—when Matilda yanked me out—I could finally see past the remaining smoke and begin to brush the ash off, clean off the residue of the disaster and ... move forward. I no longer had to force myself to be Raph-in-the-fire. I could just be ... Raph."

"I'm not in a fire. I swanned along for years not knowing what was happening. Oblivious to the truth while the rest of you beat back with the flames."

"You were too young."

"So I'll do the work now."

"Do you enjoy it?" Simple words laid like firecrackers at Theo's feet.

"Enjoy ... work?"

Raph nodded.

He enjoyed drawing. He enjoyed imagining the little ridiculous things he gave to the children in the streets. He enjoyed very much the sketches he'd made for Cordelia that had made her crumple into laughter. But what *good* were they? Of what use?

Raph stood and rounded his desk. "While you're sitting there like a statue, let me show you something." He rummaged in a bottom drawer of his desk and stood back up with a paper in hand.

"Not another paper." Theo had begun to dread those.

"It's something you drew ages ago."

"Does everyone keep those old things?"

"I don't know about everyone, but you gave this one to me." He handed it over and settled back into his seat. "And I liked it. Kept it about."

The paper between Theo's finger and thumb held a drawing of a pack of bears, each with its own distinct look. They weren't bears, not really. They were the brothers. And the smallest one Theo, sat right in the middle, protected on all sides by his giant furry counterparts, one with Atlas's wide shoulders, another with Raph's broken nose, one slender like Zander, and another tall and calm like Drew.

"I suppose," Raph said, "We protected you too long. And by the time we told you, we were all in our own ways embittered toward Father's favorite thing."

"Art."

"I've changed my tune about the stuff, you know. It's not so bad. I'm not about to go buy up a gallery, but ... it has its uses. Your art, in particular I've always liked. It was about us, silly and smart and—"

"Do shut up, Raph. You've gone soft."

Raph chuckled. "Not necessarily a bad thing, I think. Your art was colorful. Full of life. *Our* life."

"Cordelia thinks art can heal."

Raph shrugged. "Maybe it can."

"It destroyed us."

"No." Raph leaned forward. "And here's the hard thing to admit, but the thing Father pleaded with me to understand in the letter he wrote me. Art didn't destroy us. He did. Art was merely his weapon. Above all, he wanted to take all the responsibility so we did not misplace guilt on something ... good."

Theo slumped in his chair. Where was some of Pentshire's excellent whisky when needed? "The old man was—"

"Very ill at making decisions," Raph offered.

"More than a bit thoughtless."

"Not at all prepared for the responsibilities of a title."

Theo snorted. "Horrid at finances."

"Absolute fact, that. And ... and he loved us. Was proud of us, even when we turned on him."

"Hell."

"Quite."

They sat in silence as the clock on the mantel ticked louder and louder.

Theo stood, his ascent lighter than he thought it would be. "I can't buy the house from you."

"But you can use the funds from the sale of your Rubens to buy *a* house. Will that be good enough?"

Damn but he hoped so. "I must leave for London." He strode for the door, pivoted, returned to Raph. "No. First I must speak to Mother."

"Do you have something prepared to show her?"

An entire box of things, starting with a kiss that was a closed eye. He nodded. "Then to London. As soon as can be."

"Excellent. Perhaps you can meet the buyer of the Drury Lane house. He wishes a tour before he purchases. I thought I'd have to travel, what with you languishing here, but—"

"I wasn't languishing. I was plotting. And yes, I'll meet him."

"I'll have the details of our last correspondence sent to your room."

Theo walked to the door but faced Raph once more before leaving. "What if ... how would you feel if ... I made a career of art? Not the sort I do now but ... I don't know. I ... I'll ..." He couldn't finish. Couldn't quite say it, though the unsaid words felt right.

Raph ran his thumb back and forth over his nails as if inspecting them before dropping his hand in his lap with a shrug. "Your art is not bad, nor is it worthless. It can do good in the hands of a man with good intentions." A pointed raise of a single brow. "Now, should I tell Mother to begin planning a wedding?"

How could he know? The last time he'd seen her, she'd

been livid, determined, and—no. He'd borrow Cordelia's optimism for once.

"I think she'll understand well enough after I speak with her. But have a horse prepared so I can make a quick escape."

Raph grinned.

And Theo marched toward his room, sorted through the art he'd drawn for himself on parchment piece after parchment piece over the last fortnight, then went in search of his mother.

He found her in her private drawing room and laid before her a kiss that was an eye, a mermaid from a moat, and another he'd drawn during a lonely midnight when he'd wished Cordelia curled in his arms.

His mother did not speak, but the hand she lifted to her lips trembled. With the fingers of the other hand, she traced the images without touching them. Then she turned and wrapped her arms around him tight, a hug that felt like healing, though it hurt like years of silence, too, years of stony dark.

"You love her," she sobbed.

And he could not deny it. Would not. To deny his love for Cordelia would be to deny air for breathing. A simple revelation he'd made too difficult in the past days and weeks. It did not have to be, though. It could be like breathing—easy and life giving and oh-so-sweet.

"Can I keep them?" she asked, her tears wetting his waistcoat.

"Yes." Then his hand slipped away from their hug to pick up the midnight drawing. "But not this one. It's for her." He'd be needing to offer it up to the woman he had to win back, a white flag of surrender, a token of his heart.

Twenty-Three

He had been two days in London without seeing Cordelia even though his feet itched to take him that direction. But standing on her doorstep, his palms sweated. His feet had what they wished, his heart, too, but he remained unsure.

Would she be glad to see him? Or had he stayed away too long? Theo had wanted to get Sir George's latest sketch into the right hands on the Strand. He'd wanted to make sure he had the right words, the right images. Besides that, he'd needed to check with the solicitor to start finding affordable houses, and he'd been busy organizing the Drury Lane house's purchase with the buyer. The man planned on taking ownership sooner than Theo would like. He had to warn Cordelia, bring her home to Briarcliff until they figured something out for the school.

He leaned on the wall beside the door and glanced up at the window he'd climbed through the last time he'd been in London. Was she up there? Winding her long silky hair into a knot on top of her head? Pulling on stockings over her curvy calves? Or did she meet below with teachers and students? Making lists of potential donors and strategizing?

His heart pounded, and his hand hesitated at the doorknob. He'd never knocked before. He'd just strolled right in, often bellowing. No barging or bellowing now, though. He was trying not to be a gargoyle. So he knocked. Then he knocked again. And waited. And the door never opened. So he tried to open it. No option now but to push through as if he owned the place.

But the door was locked against him.

"Hell," he breathed. Would he have to climb the window?

The door flew open, and Mrs. Barkley scowled at him. "Lord Theodore. It's you. *Humph.*"

"Mrs. Barkley! I'm glad to see you're home. Is Lady Cordelia about? I must speak with her."

"No, Lady Cordelia is not here," Mrs. Barkley answered. "I suppose I can't keep you from coming inside." She stepped aside.

Theo entered the cold entryway. "Where are the flowers?" They were always on the long, short table beneath the mirror on the left side of the foyer. "And what has happened to the students?" No strains of violin floated down the stairs, no chatter of eager widows echoed down the halls.

Mrs. Barkley sniffed. "Don't worry. She's left all the furniture that was here when she arrived. She's not a thief."

"Of course she's not," Theo snapped. "And what do you mean she's left the furniture? Left it to go where?" She stepped to the side to leave him. "Mrs. Barkley." Theo stepped with her, a necessary dance to stop her retreat. "Where is Cordelia?"

"Gone."

"Gone where?" He couldn't feel his feet. They'd gone entirely numb while his fingertips tingled, a freezing feeling that spread swiftly up his arms and pierced through the bones of his ribs to attack the softer parts.

"You think I'll tell you? You come here ranting and raving last time, leaving Lady Cordelia in tears and stomping off again. You've been nothing but heartless and coldhearted since you first showed your face here, and—"

"Coldhearted? Coldhearted, Mrs. Barkley? I'm more like a man without a heart, and do you want to know why? Because Lady Cordelia holds it in her clever little hands. And if you don't tell me where she's gone, Mrs. Barkley, I'll—"

"Do you promise not to hurt her?" Her mouth had softened, her shoulders sloping into a less militant shape. Her eyes darted toward the door then back to Theo.

"I'd rather hurt myself," he assured her.

She smoothed her hands down her apron. "She's at her new school."

～

Lady Balantine's townhouse was not as cozy as Cordelia's own, but it was perfect for her purposes. Formerly a private art gallery, its walls still hung with wonderful paintings, and its tables still were dotted with the most remarkable statuary. They'd removed the ones of a more illicit nature, and now the music room had practical, usable instruments instead of priceless ones, and the upper rooms were filled with easels and paint bladders, chalk and paper and canvas instead of artistic items of a questionable nature.

Lady Balantine had not had the funds to help Cordelia buy an entirely new house, but she'd had a house to rent to her for quite a reasonable price, a price more than easy enough to afford with the donations she'd acquired while at the house party. For the first year at least. And the Castles, lovely human beings they were, had already delivered crates of paint bladders and watercolors with the promise of more when she needed them.

She had her own little bedroom at the top of the house, a small chamber and bare but with a cheerful fireplace. She also had a study on the ground floor.

She stood there now, looking out the window and watching Mr. Spencer wish his first poetry student farewell. She allowed herself a smile, tried to stretch it wider. But it butted up against the sad bits of her soul and remained only a small thing.

"You look desolate, dear one."

Cordelia left the window to welcome Lady Balantine into her study. "How can you tell? I was not even facing you."

The dowager flicked her hand toward the window. "Beware of reflective surfaces, darling. They do not keep secrets well. Though it is no secret your heart is crying."

"It is *not.*"

"Bah." Lady Balantine dropped into a chair by the fireplace, and when Cordelia joined her, she leaned forward and dropped a pit of printed paper in her lap. "Here. I found this while browsing through *Ackermann's* this morning."

"Thank you, but I'm too tired for fashion plates."

"Look at it, dear girl. It's not a fashion plate." Lady Balantine grinned.

Cordelia held it up and froze. A woman with long curly hair—the same wild hair Theo drew on every depiction of her —and her companion, a gargoyle. A true gargoyle with wings and fangs and a little tail and made of stone that looked more than a little like the caricature she'd drawn of him in anger the first day they'd made love. But it also had Theo's hair and his broken nose, and it held in its clawed hand a stick of charcoal. The two figures stood in a room that looked very like the parlor in her old home, the same room where they'd first met. The gargoyle reached for the woman's hand, which was open and palm up and not at all empty. For he'd drawn a heart on a bit of paper, and he offered it to her bashfully.

The drawing was entitled *The Gargoyle Grows a Heart*, and the artist had signed the right-hand corner—T. Bromley.

She gasped, dropping the print as her hands flew up to cover her mouth. "I-I."

"It does boggle the mind, my dear."

"Has he really ..." She peeked at the drawing again, yelped as if it had bit her, and sat on her hands.

Lady Balantine laughed. "You're in shock. Perhaps we should have that tea." She stood and bustled toward the door. "I'll go see about it myself. You'll want to be alone for a bit."

"No, no." Cordelia held out a hand, beckoning her back.

Lady Balantine nodded toward the window behind Cordelia's desk. "You'll want some time alone."

Cordelia whipped around and gasped again. It seemed to have become her major form of communication, but what else was she to do when Theo stood in the window looking less like a stone man than she'd ever seen before. She ran to the window and slammed her palms against the panes. He lifted his hands and, briefly, his palms rested against hers, only a slim layer of glass between them, but then he snapped his arms to his side and disappeared.

Where was he going?

She ran, out the door and down the hall, skidding to a stop in the entryway when the front door opened and Theo—hair windswept and cheeks pink with embarrassment, pink as a watercolor rose—swept into the foyer, swept her up in his arms.

He kissed her. A hard kiss, his arms like chains wrapping around her waist, pulling her tight against him. She clung to his shoulders, tore at the hair at his nape, nipped at his bottom lip, gasped when he dragged his teeth down her neck, giving her room to kiss that space behind his ear.

He hissed and rocked away from her, breathing hard. "Hell. Cordelia. Apologies."

"No." She rushed toward him.

But he held up flat palms, stopping her. "No. No, no, no. I've come here for business, not pleasure."

She did not care, she took his hand and flipped it palm up, as her own had been in his drawing, and she sketched a heart there.

"Cordelia," he warned. "I'm serious."

"I saw your sketch. In *Ackermann's*."

"Ah. I had wondered if you would. Had hoped you would."

"Lady Balantine just showed me."

He looked around the foyer, shaking his head. "She has decided she can fund you after all?"

"In a way. She is renting me her second townhouse. For a very good price indeed." She traced his fingers, pulled him closer.

"Ah. You have no need of donations at the moment, then? For your school? Because I've found myself in possession of a tidy sum, and I wish to do some good with it."

She wove their fingers together, then tugged him toward her study, and once she had him inside, she shut the door, locked it, and pulled him toward the fire where she retrieved the *Ackermann's* print and held it out for him to see.

"Not my best," he said, taking the paper and sinking into a chair.

She sat across from him, not wanting to let him go. Much needed to be said, though, and if the words were right, and true, they would have more hours and days than she could count to touch and kiss and love.

Because that's what the drawing meant, wasn't it? Did he love her?

He tugged at his cravat and laid the paper on the table

between them. "Stay over there because I have several things to say, and I cannot say them if you tackle me."

"I will not tackle you. I promise." Not yet at least.

He took a deep breath and rested his elbows on his knees, leaned forward, and hung his head. "I showed my mother my drawings. The ones I made of you at the party. She saw in them what I'd been hiding from myself."

She held her breath.

"She rewarded me with my inheritance. A valuable Rubens that Zander has already found a buyer for. I want you to have it. For your school."

"Thank you. But ... what will you do if you give your money to me?"

"I sold an entire portfolio of sketches to *Ackermann's*, that one included." He nodded at the paper. "They offered quite a bit and asked for more when I have them. Not as much as I would have gotten for a scandal, but ... I've changed my mind on that pursuit. One cannot guarantee a scandal. It's a dicey business, not nearly steady enough for a man who wishes to marry. But the sort of sketches I sold this week ... they provide steady income."

"Is that all, then? Steady income?"

He shook his head, ducked it so she could no longer see his expression.

She knelt before him and cupped his face, lifted it so she could see his eyes. "What else then, Theo?"

The corner of his lip quirked up. "They make me laugh. I have recently discovered it's one of my favorite activities. Not my absolute favorite one, though." His gaze dropped to her lips then lower, stopping at the low line of her bodice. He reached across the space between them, knocking the print to the floor, and gathered her to him, pulled her onto his lap, and kissed her cheek, her temple, her neck.

Her breathing quickened. "We're done talking, then?"

"No. I've a few more things to say."

"Say them, then. So we can *do*."

"I find I'm searching for a second position. I was hoping ... do you have an opening at the Waneborough Charitable School of Art for a drawing instructor?"

"Hmm." She tapped her cheek. "I'll have to check my notes and perhaps speak to the investors."

"I am one, or I intend to be, and we're speaking right now. I say it's a wonderful idea."

She bit her lip then buried her face in his chest, a doubt heavy as a stone in her chest. "But will you be happy?"

He lifted her chin with his knuckles until their eyes met. "My mother saw in my drawings what I'd been hiding from myself, remember?"

"What does that mean?"

"It means I love you." He kissed the words to her forehead. "I love you." He burned them into her temple. "I love you." These whispered against her lips. "I don't want to live reacting to the past. I want to live in the present. With you. If you want—"

"I do, Theo. I do, I do, I do." She untied his cravat and tugged and pulled and soon she had it off along with his coat and jacket and waistcoat so that it pooled in a puddle of wool and silk on the floor beneath them.

"You've made it farther than the widows did the first time I met you." His words, his laughter, kissed into her collarbone.

"I have," she sighed, pushing the V of his shirt wide and flattening her hands on the warm muscle beneath it.

He stood, taking her with him, cradling her in his arms as he strode for the door. "Bed."

"Too far away and up too many flights of stairs."

"Damn." But he laid her down on the thick rug before the fire and locked the door and returned to her.

She expected him to throw her skirts up.

She expected him to slide into her without hesitation.

She expected him to make her come, wild and furious and screaming.

He laid himself down beside her, gently, and pulled her to him, nestled her head against his shoulder. "Have you slept? It's a new house, and—"

And she loved him, the stony man with a soft heart.

"A bit." She found his heartbeat and placed a kiss just over it, then settled in to listen to it. "I've been so busy. That helps. And knowing ... knowing I can control my own fate. That helps, too."

He ran a hand over her head. "Sleep now, then. I'll be here when you wake. Right here."

"I'd rather"—she yawned, sleep a deluge that washed over her quickly—"do other things with you, Theo." But she would sleep, for now, in the arms of the man she loved, confident in the slow beating of their hearts together that for once beauty and truth were one and the same.

Epilogue

October 1822

The Fairworth Inn and Pub had never, in Theo's experience, been louder or more crowded. The village, it seemed, had decided to make Theo's wedding a holiday. Every table was full, and every tankard on its way to being empty.

Theo sat at the long table in the middle of the room, surrounded by family and friends. He should have been grumbling and miserable. A year ago, he would have been, preferring solitude to company and wishing everyone about him to perdition. Now ... he hated to admit it ... but he glowed.

Bah. Likely the second pint of ale's fault, that. Pentshire, sitting to his right, his wife nestled close beside him, kept asking if he needed more and waving a serving girl over. Theo should never have published that print for him. It had helped smooth the countess's way into the fringes of society, revealing the love match as well as the bride's father's callousness. But it had also gained Theo a stout friend who sparred with him at Jacksons and visited to *talk* in the evenings. Theo let him. And listened. And didn't hate it too terribly much.

His art had made two people happy. Who knew such a possibility existed.

Cordelia had.

He searched the crowd for her. She'd left his side not long ago with a kiss to his cheek and nothing more by way of explanation.

"Where's Cordelia?" he demanded.

"Check the moat," Lord Armquist shouted, and the entire table burst into laughter.

Theo never should have let the man tell that story. It had become something of joke, and—

"Raph," his mother said, "we need a moat. At Briarcliff. Don't you think?"

And that. His mother had stopped with her requests to host another house party and taken up pleas to have a moat dug around the house.

Raph groaned. "Mother. No."

"But think of how safe it will keep Matilda," his mother said.

"Do not, Franny, offer me up as a point in a moat's favor." Matilda, Raph's wife, rubbed her rounded belly.

His mother turned back to Raph. "And the baby's safety, when she comes."

Raph downed half a tankard of ale. "We do not need a moat to keep them safe. We need a roof that doesn't leak."

"You've no imagination, Raph."

"Imagination, he's got," Drew said from the other end of the table, "it's talent he's lacking." He looked over his shoulder at the wall behind him. Several very poor paintings hung there, all with Raph's scrawled signature.

"I need to take those down," Raph said.

"Don't you dare." Matilda raised a brow. Raph had painted the works on the wall for her. "Everyone adores them."

Several people coughed, including the innkeeper.

"I cannot believe," Drew said, looking to Matilda, "that you agreed to marry him after seeing these."

"Mrs. Dart." Raph attempted to croon, but it came out more like a bark. "Do you have any power over my brother to make him cease his prattling?"

Mrs. Dart sat next to Drew, drinking only a small glass of wine she'd barely touched. "None at all, I'm afraid. The man does as he pleases. I merely record his schedule. Speaking of which, my lord." She turned to Drew. "You must compose and send out your response to Hatchfield tomorrow." Her gaze flicked to his empty tankard.

Drew looked her straight in the eye and called for another, and when she looked away, his gaze exploded, from steely calm to panicked ... something. "What in hell are you wearing?"

Mrs. Dart turned slowly, the force of death in her eyes. "A very beautiful gown loaned to me by your sister-in-law. A necessity, as I do not own anything frivolous. Should I have attired myself as if for a funeral?"

"No." Drew looked into the dregs of his tankard. "As always, you're perfectly correct, Mrs. Dart."

Theo rolled his eyes and pushed to standing, his chair screeching across the floor behind him. "But where is Cordelia?"

Mr. Castle raised his drink. "I believe she retired upstairs with my wife. To discuss funding for something or other."

"Thank you!" Theo bowed his gratitude and found the stairs. His wife. Working on her wedding day. He'd soon remedy that. He found the door to the Castles' room and knocked, and it flew open before he'd even finished.

"Ah, Lord Theodore," Mrs. Castle said, wiping a smear of paint from her cheek, "I was just leaving."

"Cordelia?"

"Inside, dressing." She slapped his shoulder. "Do stop

scowling, my lord. Come in and see for yourself. I'm returning downstairs." She slipped through the cracked door and down the stairs, and Theo crept inside.

A man stood farther in, framed by the window, his hat pulled low, his greatcoat and jacket too large and gaping open, revealing—

"Cordelia? Are those my clothes?"

She grinned. "They are. From the first time we met."

"And what are you doing with them?"

Her grin grew. "Making an escape. Care to come with me?"

"Yes." He'd go anywhere with her. "But why are my clothes *here*? And why are we escaping?"

She took his hands and pulled him across the room where an easel stood. So preoccupied with the sight of his wife in trousers, he'd not noticed it until now.

"Look," she said. "Mrs. Castle is painting it of me. She's doing a series. Women dressed as men. Quite the scandal, don't you think. A statement about power and—"

Theo groaned, turning her explanation into a laugh.

It *was* a scandal. The portrait was true to life in every way, including Cordelia's curves and the feminine pout of her lips. Her hair was hidden inside the hat, but there was no doubt the figure on the canvas was a woman.

"Hell. How much does she want for it?"

"A question I do not have an answer to."

He pulled her toward the door. "Let's go ask her. I can't let that painting rest in just anyone's hands."

She dug her heels into the floor. "No. No. We're escaping, remember? You can talk to Mrs. Castle about the painting later."

"I suppose," he grumbled. "Why are we escaping again?"

Her nose wrinkled and her brows slanted together.

"Because I'd like a single hour to myself, thank you very much."

"You ... you want to be alone?" He held the back of his hand to her forehead, and she pushed him away, laughing.

"An astonishing turn of events, yes. But we have had three days of festivities without stop, and the Castles are talking about staying at the inn through the harvest celebration next week."

"Do you want to return to London?" They, too, had planned to stay for the harvest celebrations, but—

"No." She went up on tiptoe and cupped his face. I love your family. I love that you invited the Castles and Armquist and Meredith and Pentshire and Maria."

"I wanted you to have family here, too. Of some sort, at least."

She kissed him. "I did not like to be alone when I had no one. The silence reminded me too much of my state. But now that I am surrounded—your mother, your brothers, their wives, our friends—I find being alone quite lovely."

"Are you sure you don't still need me to sleep?"

She nudged his nose with her own. "Oh, yes, quite. I'll always need you to sleep. I love you, Theodore Bromley. But I would very much love, as well, a moment or two alone with you. I had planned to sneak out the window after Mrs. Castle left, sneak into the pub, and catch your attention from a corner, drag you away from them, and—"

"And what, wife? What would you have done with me then?"

She whispered in his ear.

His heart raced, and his body thrummed with desire. He clutched her waist and pulled her flush up against him. "I think we can make that happen." He pulled her out of the room, kept his voice low. "The dower house is closer than Briarcliff.

Let's go there." It was a shambles, but Atlas had been cleaning it out to prepare it for renovations. At least one room would be nice and dry. It would suffice for Cordelia's desired hour.

They ran, laughing, down the stairs and into the night, and when they undressed one another in a small room of the old dower house, their laughter became whispers of love, and Theo found that the thorn he'd thought to pluck from him all those months ago was actually a seed, spreading its roots and tendrils and slowly, surely, cracking open the stony bits of him until nothing but love for this woman bloomed in his heart.

Acknowledgments

Thank you as ever to my amazing readers. Every time I think I've face-planted, you guys pick me up, dust me off, and set me back up at my computer. I have face planted many times this year, but you guys keep me going.

So, too, does my family. Every book happens because of them.

Thank you to my editors Chris Hall and Krista Dapkey for loving my stories and helping me make them better, and to all the typo-hunting geniuses on my ARC team. Marilyn, Sharon —many, many thanks.

One final but very big thank you to Anna Volkin, the artist for The Art of Love covers. You're amazing, and I'm so lucky to get to work with you.

Also by Charlie Lane

The Cavendish Family

Leave a Widow Wanting More

Teach a Rogue New Tricks

Bring a Boxer to His Knees

Love a Lady at Midnight

Scandalizing the Scoundrel

London Secrets

The Secret Seduction

A Secret Desire

Sinning in Secret

Keep No Secrets

Secrets Between Lovers

The Debutante Dares (with WOLF Press)

Daring the Duke

A Dare Too Far

Kiss or Dare

Don't You Dare, My Dear

Only Rakes Would Dare

Daring Done Right

About the Author

CHARLIE LANE traded in academic databases and scholarly journals for writing steamy Regency romcoms like the ones she's always loved to read. When she's not writing humorous conversations, dramatic confrontations, or sexy times, she's flying high in the air as a circus-obsessed acrobat.

Visit my website with the QR code and your phone!

Made in the USA
Monee, IL
04 December 2023